Praise for Wisdom's first fiction anthology

Nixon Under the Bodhi Tree
and Other Works of
Buddhist Fiction

" 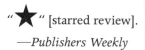 " [starred review].
—*Publishers Weekly*

D0200285

"Shows the promise of a genre that is scarcely known as such,
and also what has already been accomplished by the small but
growing band of writers melding the truth of dharma with the
invention of fiction. Marvelous!"
—*Yoga Journal*

"Surely a milestone in Western Buddhist literature—and a book that
fiction lovers, Buddhist or otherwise, will very much enjoy."
—*Tricycle*

"Some of the best Buddhist-themed fiction to come around
since the likes of Kerouac and Salinger."
—Paul W. Morris, editor of *KillingTheBuddha.com*

"Whether you are a Buddhist practitioner or just a fiction lover,
you'll want to read [these stories] with pen in hand, underlining an effective phrase or flash of literary insight. A significant debut collection."
—*Shambhala Sun*

"I've waited all my life for a book like this."
—Charles Johnson, National Book
Award-winning author of *Middle Passage* and *Turning the Wheel*

You Are Not Here
and Other Works of Buddhist Fiction

Edited by

KEITH KACHTICK

Foreword by

LAMA SURYA DAS

Wisdom Publications • Boston

Wisdom Publications, Inc.
199 Elm Street
Somerville MA 02144 USA
www.wisdompubs.org

Library of Congress Cataloging-in-Publication Data
You are not here and other works of Buddhist fiction / edited by Keith
   Kachtick ; foreword by Lama Surya Das.
     p. cm.
   ISBN 0-86171-291-9 (pbk. : alk. paper)
   1. Buddhist stories, American.   I. Kachtick, Keith.
   PS648.B84Y68 2006
   813'.0108382943—dc22

                                                              2006000537

ISBN 0-86171-291-9

09 08 07 06 06
5   4   3   2   1

Cover design by Nita Ybarra
Interior by Potter Publishing Studio. Set in ApolloMT 10.5/16.5.

Wisdom Publications' books are printed on acid-free paper and meet the guidelines
for permanence and durability of the Production Guidelines for Book Longevity
set by the Council on Library Resources.

Printed in the United States of America

This book was produced with environmental mindfulness. We have elected to
print this title on 50% PCW recycled paper. As a result, we have saved the following resources: 27 trees, 1,274 lbs. of solid waste, 9,921 gallons of water, 2,390
lbs. of greenhouse gases, and 19 million BTUs of energy. For more information,
please visit our web site, www.wisdompubs.org.

Table of Contents

Foreword

Believing Is Seeing

P URE VISION is one of the unique practices of Vajrayana Buddhism, the Buddhism that comes from Tibet. Cultivating this kind of sacred outlook—termed *dak-nang* in Tibetan—helps us see the Buddha, the light, the divinity in everyone and everything, and to experience this very world we live in as a Buddha field, a Pure Land or paradise. This is not just something we superimpose upon reality, like donning rose-colored glasses; nor is it merely a form of visualization. It is more akin to seeing things as they actually are. This is something we actually practice, a way of cultivating Buddha Vision.

Before glimpsing sacred vision in reality, we may hear about it, read splendid descriptions in the sutras or in short stories like these; and perhaps we believe, wonder about its veracity, harbor doubt, and so forth. After a genuine visitation we know there is a *there* there, although we have only been there briefly.

I myself was once vouchsafed a sacred glimpse of this earth as an altar and all who walk upon it as gods and goddesses, dakas and dakinis. In fact, so strongly impressed upon my consciousness was that sacred vision twenty-eight years ago that I can still see it in some way right now. Believing is seeing. The fact is that the more real I seem to become, the more unreal everything else seems—and vice versa.

It was spring in the Catskills, 1977. My guru the Gyalwang Karmapa was giving a *phowa* (consciousness transference) empowerment and blessing of land for a new monastery to be built in Putnam County, New York. I'd come from my cabin on Woodstock's Mount Guardian for the day—and what a day it was!

There were a few dozen of us in the house. My friend Jamgon Kongtrul Rinpoche, an important reincarnate lama who was about twenty-five at that time, was sitting on a carpeted couch on His Holiness Karmapa's right-hand side. I was sitting with my friend Larry Brilliant and others on the living-room floor in front of His Holiness. I remember quipping to him that we should meditate as fast as we could. Then the ritual began.

Prayers were chanted, drums beat, incense blossomed, offerings made. His Holiness held up a luminous crystal and shouted, in Tibetan, "What is mind?" and instantly I saw all the infinite manifestations of this world and all other worlds streaming from its shimmering form. I felt as if I were holding the crystal myself; and it was perfectly clear that my heart-mind and his Buddha Mind and all beings were forever one and inseparable, and that all things arise and pass on within that vast totality, forever and always, and that somehow everything is *now*.

There I was, enjoying oneness beyond belief or concept, with the blissful energy of incandescent awareness coursing through every pore of my being, when suddenly His Holiness shouted, "*Hik!*" and I felt the crown of my head open up, and I practically levitated.

I had participated in several dozen tantric Vajrayana empowerments by then, but this was the first time that I was literally transported to another place, another plane, another reality entirely. His Holiness sat in the blazing red transrealescent form of Amitabha Buddha right before us beneath the Bodhi Tree, radiating infinite light, which both poured out of him and into me, and from me into him, at one and the same time, more powerful than a towering waterfall. I was electrified, transformed, transubstantiated—and I was no more. The page had been turned, the binding consumed. For no one can look on that burning bush and survive.

Cross-legged on the floor, my corporeal frame shook with violent spasms, and I started crying and bouncing up and down as if in the grip of a seizure; later my friend Larry said he put his hand on my knee to hold me down, but to little avail. I was unaware of anything except the Buddha of Infinite Light and the Pure Land of Great Bliss pouring in and out of me in an ecstatic cataclysm of cosmic delight.

When I returned, the chanting was winding down and everything fell back into place. Jamgon Rinpoche smiled knowingly, and all was well. I heard a voice in my head whisper: *The Buddha of Infinite Light is not in the Western Pure Land; he is right here in the world.* I knew my guru was that Buddha, and forever with me and within me.

Soon afterwards, I was on the New York State Thruway speeding south, happy as a clam. It was almost an hour before I realized that we should turn around and drive *north* to return home to Woodstock. Infinite light was before my eyes for several days before I drifted back to my normal state of semi-consciousness. I realized what Buddha meant when he said, in the Diamond Sutra, that life is like a dream, a mirage, a sitcom—a Buddhist fiction. For things are not what they seem to be; nor are they otherwise.

It is easier to visit the Pure Lands than to live there. I wonder if this isn't what is meant by heaven.

Since then, although I can still see it right before me, I have been trying to return. Perhaps I am looking west when I should be looking inwards, seeing more deeply. What we seek, we are. It is all within.

Look within these nineteen works of Buddhist fiction and see the koanlike truth of reality. That life is a story, and our dreams are no less real than our daytime dramas. That we are *all* Buddhas at heart—we only have to recognize that fact.

Many are called, but few awaken. Before I was different; now I'm the same.

Turn the searchlight, the spotlight, inwards.

I hear a voice from the past: This land where we stand is the Pure Lotus Land, this very body the body of Buddha.

Lama Surya Das
Spring 2006
Dzogchen Center, Cambridge, Massachusetts

Keith Kachtick

Introduction

A RECENT *New Yorker* cartoon depicts a middle-aged man slumped before an office computer, his tie loosened, daydreaming about playing golf. In the cartoon's second panel, the guy is on a golf course, lining up a putt, but the thought-bubble floating over his head makes clear he would rather be having sex. In the third panel, the poor fellow is in bed with a naked woman, fantasizing about the office computer.

Sound familiar? This endless wanting and wandering epitomizes *samsara*, the Sanskrit term for the wheel of suffering into which we humans are born, a condition that led Siddhartha Gautama, the historical Buddha, to proclaim after his enlightenment 2,500 years ago, "Hey, folks, life ain't elsewhere." Because we forget this simple truth, we often make ourselves miserable by focusing on what we think we *should* be feeling or doing rather than on what we actually are, reaching for the next proverbial bite of food before chewing what's in our mouth—a phenomenon that causes suffering in our romantic relationships, our relationship with the environment, even our relationship with our body. Most of us just don't know how to be with what *is*.

Sadly, since a consumer culture by definition depends upon its citizens to crave more, our society's mainstream currents have a vested interest in maintaining our amnesia: a buddha (literally an "awakened being"—Saint Francis, Mahatma Gandhi, the Dalai Lama) rarely spends his or her money on sunless airbrush tanning or apocalypse-ready Hummers. Until just a short time ago, even American literature felt co-opted by samsara. The consensus in a 2003 roundtable discussion among national magazine and newspaper editors, all of whom assigned book-reviews for their pages, was that a spiritual or "New-Agey" novel would likely be reviewed only if the book *satirized* spirituality. (The editors of a novel I published in 2003, fearing what, I'm not sure, excised the word "Buddhist" from a blurb used on its front cover.) Doesn't this degree of secularism miss the whole point of life? After all, as *The Power of Now* author Ekhart Tolle points out, "Anything that's *not* spiritual becomes little more than a three-inch dash between the birthdate and the deathdate on our tombstones."

So, it was with a fair amount of surprise that *Nixon Under the Bodhi Tree and Other Works of Buddhist Fiction*—the world's first collection of Buddhist short stories—edited by the marvelous (dare I say spiritual?) novelist Kate Wheeler, found itself not only reviewed but *warmly* reviewed by critics upon its 2004 publication. The anthology became one of Wisdom's better-selling books of the year. What's going on? Is our culture waking up to the possibility that enlightenment is a worthwhile pursuit? That literature serving or addressing this pursuit can be curative *and* commercially viable?

That said, an editor of a book like this one must be careful about proselytizing, about giving readers a potentially dangerous "we're right and they're wrong" take on the folks living next door. Fortunately, Buddhism—and the fairly malleable notion of Buddhist fiction—embraces the belief that there are many paths to the Kingdom. From a Buddhist perspective (at least the way I understand and practice it), Rumi is a Buddhist poet, as are William Blake and Emily Dickinson. The agnostic cab driver who returns the forgotten wallet is a Buddhist citizen. The Jewish baker who volunteers at the synagogue is a Buddhist mensch. Patiently holding a downward-facing dog pose in yoga class is a Buddhist meditation. As long as you're paying attention to *now*—this moment and no other; and treat the neighbors the way *you* would like to be treated; and understand that material things—your body, your house, this book you hold—are sandcastles destined, by design, to eventually wash away with the tide to become something else, you are Buddhist. And when you do this 24/7, you are enlightened. A buddha. "Do not doubt its possibilities because of the simplicity of the method," the thirteenth-century Zen master Dogen says. "If you cannot find the truth right where you are, where else do you expect to find it?"

My hope is that all of the stories in this follow-up anthology dramatize the Dharma—the tenets of Buddhism—in some distinctive and vivid way, even if they don't do so intentionally or explicitly. At the very least, I hope the stories prove absorbing enough that you won't daydream of golf while turning the pages. And I hope, for those of you who have never encountered Buddhism before, that this collection makes clear the face of Buddhism is a strangely familiar one, and that this recognition will lead you, as Lama Surya Das says in his foreword, to make a kind of return home, to look inward and see things more deeply.

The selection process for the book proved challenging but thoroughly enjoyable; over the past few months, I was blessed to receive dozens and dozens of beautifully crafted works of fiction sent from all over the world. Some of the stories employ formal Zen or Buddhist terms and practices by authors, like Geshe Michael Roach and Dan Zigmond, who have "put on the robes," as they say, and are devoting their lives to teaching the Dharma. Others are like Andrew Foster Altschul's title story, which arrived accompanied by a note that confessed, "I have no formal Buddhist training. I cannot explain why I feel this piece is appropriate for inclusion; just a sense I have of it speaking to emptiness, impermanence, and the illusory nature of the ego." Without exception, all of these stories say with verve: Pay attention—*this* is life, right here, right now. Whether set in the jungles of

Indonesia, on a sun-blistered African veldt, in a Burmese monastery surrounded by gunfire, on a dusty mountain trail in Nepal, or in the church-
like sanctuary of a Nebraska barn, each story in this collection is a gift, a
jewel in the lotus, which I pass on with heartfelt thanks and admiration.

Robert Olen Butler

A Good Scent from a Strange Mountain

H O CHI MINH came to me again last night, his hands covered with confectioners' sugar. This was something of a surprise to me, the first time I saw him beside my bed, in the dim light from the open shade. My oldest daughter leaves my shades open, I think so that I will not forget that the sun has risen again in the morning. I am a very old man. She seems to expect that one morning I will simply forget to keep living. This is very foolish. I will one night rise up from my bed and slip into her room and open the shade there. Let *her* see the sun in the morning. She is sixty-four years old and she should worry for herself. I could never die from forgetting.

But the light from the street was enough to let me recognize Ho when I woke, and he said to me, "Dao, my old friend, I have heard it is time to visit you." Already on that first night there was a sweet smell about him, very strong in the dark, even before I could see his hands. I said nothing, but I stretched to the nightstand beside me and I turned on the light to see if he would go away. And he did not. He stood there beside the bed—I could even see him reflected in the window—and I knew it was real because he did not appear as he was when I'd known him but as he was when he'd died. This was Uncle Ho before me, the thin old man with the dewlap beard wearing the dark clothes of a peasant and the rubber sandals, just like in the news pictures I studied with such a strange feeling for all those years. Strange because when I knew him, he was not yet Ho Chi Minh. It was 1917 and he was Nguyen Ai Quoc and we were both young men with clean-shaven faces, the best of friends, and we worked at the Carlton Hotel in London, where I was a dishwasher and he was a pastry cook under the great Escoffier. We were the best of friends and saw snow for the first time together. This was before we began to work at the hotel. We shoveled snow and Ho would stop for a moment and blow his breath out before him and it would make him smile, to see what was inside him, as if it were the casting of bones to tell the future.

On that first night when he came to me in my house in New Orleans, I finally saw what it was that smelled so sweet and I said to him, "Your hands are covered in sugar."

He looked at them with a kind of sadness.

I have received that look myself in the past week. It is time now for me to see my family, and the friends I have made who are still alive. This is our custom from Vietnam. When you are very old, you put aside a week or two to receive the people of your life so that you can tell one another your feelings, or try at last to understand one another, or simply say good-bye. It is a formal leave-taking, and with good luck you can do this before you have your final illness. I have lived almost a century and perhaps I should have called them all to me sooner, but at last I felt a deep weariness and I said to my oldest daughter that it was time.

They look at me with sadness, some of them. Usually the dull-witted ones, or the insincere ones. But Ho's look was, of course, not dull-witted or insincere. He considered his hands and said, "The glaze. Maestro's glaze."

There was the soft edge of yearning in his voice and I had the thought that perhaps he had come to me for some sort of help. I said to him, "I don't remember. I only washed dishes." As soon as the words were out of my mouth, I decided it was foolish for me to think he had come to ask me about the glaze.

But Ho did not treat me as foolish. He looked at me and shook his head. "It's all right," he said. "I remember the temperature now. Two hundred and thirty degrees, when the sugar is between the large thread stage and the small orb stage. The Maestro was very clear about that and I remember." I knew from his eyes, however, that there was much more that still eluded him. His eyes did not seem to move at all from my face, but there was some little shifting of them, a restlessness that perhaps only I could see, since I was his close friend from the days when the world did not know him.

I am nearly one hundred years old, but I can still read a man's face. Perhaps better than I ever have. I sit in the overstuffed chair in my living room and I receive my visitors and I want these people, even the dull-witted and insincere ones—please excuse an old man's ill temper for calling them that—I want them all to be good with one another. A Vietnamese family is extended as far as the bloodline strings us together, like so many paper lanterns around a village square. And we all give off light together. That's the way it has always been in our culture. But these people who come to visit me have been in America for a long time and there are very strange things going on that I can see in their faces.

None stranger than this morning. I was in my overstuffed chair and with me there were four of the many members of my family: my son-in-law Thang, a former colonel in the Army of the Republic of Vietnam and one of the insincere ones, sitting on my Castro convertible couch; his youngest son, Loi, who had come in late, just a few minutes earlier, and had thrown himself down on the couch as well, youngest but a man old enough to have served as a lieutenant under his father as our country fell to the communists more than a decade ago; my daughter Lam, who is Thang's wife, hovering behind the both of them and refusing all invitations to sit down; and my oldest daughter, leaning against the door frame, having no doubt just returned from my room, where she had opened the shade that I had closed when I awoke.

It was Thang who gave me the sad look I have grown accustomed to, and I perhaps seemed to him at that moment a little weak, a little distant. I had stopped listening to the small talk of these people and I had let my eyes half close, though I could still see them clearly and I was very alert. Thang has a steady face and the quick eyes of a man who is ready to come under fire, but I have always read much more there, in spite of his efforts to show nothing. So after he thought I'd faded from the room, it was with slow eyes, not quick, that he moved to his son and began to speak of the killing.

You should understand that Mr. Nguyen Bich Le had been shot dead in our community here in New Orleans just last week. There are many of us Vietnamese living in New Orleans and one man, Mr. Le, published a little newspaper for all of us. He had recently made the fatal error—though it should not be that in America—of writing that it was time to accept the reality of the communist government in Vietnam and begin to talk with them. We had to work now with those who controlled our country. He said that he remained a patriot to the Republic of Vietnam, and I believed him. If anyone had asked an old man's opinion on this whole matter, I would not have been afraid to say that Mr. Le was right.

But he was shot dead last week. He was forty-five years old and he had a wife and three children and he was shot as he sat behind the wheel of his Chevrolet pickup truck. I find a detail like that especially moving, that this man was killed in his Chevrolet, which I understand is a strongly American thing. We knew this in Saigon. In Saigon it was very American to own a Chevrolet, just as it was French to own a Citroen.

And Mr. Le had taken one more step in his trusting embrace of this new culture. He had bought not only a Chevrolet but a Chevrolet pickup truck, which made him not only American but also a man of Louisiana, where there are many pickup trucks. He did not, however, also purchase a gun rack for the back window, another sign of this place. Perhaps it would have been well if he had, for it was through the back window that the bullet was fired. Someone had hidden in the bed of his truck and had killed him from behind. In his Chevrolet and the reason for this act was made very clear in a phone call to the newspaper office by a nameless representative of the Vietnamese Party for the Annihilation of Communism and for the National Restoration.

And Thang, my son-in-law, said to his youngest son, Loi, "There is no murder weapon." What I saw was a faint lift of his eyebrows as he said this, like inviting his son to listen beneath his words. Then he said it again, more slowly, like it was a code. "There is *no weapon.*" My grandson nodded his head once, a crisp little snap. Then my daughter Lam said in a very loud voice, with her eyes on me, "That was a terrible thing, the death of Mr. Le." She nudged her husband and son, and both men turned their faces sharply to me and they looked at me squarely and said, also in very loud voices, "Yes, it was terrible."

I am not deaf, and I closed my eyes further, having seen enough and wanting them to think that their loud talk had not only failed to awake me but had put me more completely to sleep. I did not like to deceive them, however, even though I have already spoken critically of these members of my family. I am a Hoa Hao Buddhist and I believe in harmony among all living things, especially the members of a Vietnamese family.

After Ho reassured me, on that first visit, about the temperature needed to heat Maestro Escoffier's glaze, he said, "Dao, my old friend, do you still follow the path you chose in Paris?"

He meant by this my religion. It was in Paris that I embraced the Buddha and disappointed Ho. We went to France in early 1918, with the war still on, and we lived in the poorest street of the poorest part of the Seventeenth Arrondissement. Number nine, Impasse Compoint, a blind alley with a few crumbling houses, all but ours rented out for storage. The cobblestones were littered with fallen roof tiles and Quoc and I each had a tiny single room with only an iron bedstead and a crate to sit on. I could see my friend Quoc in the light of the tallow candle and he was dressed in a dark suit and a bowler hat and he looked very foolish. I did not say so, but he knew it himself and he kept seating and reseating the hat and shaking his head very slowly, with a loudly silent anger. This was near the end of our time together, for I was visiting daily with a Buddhist monk and he was drawing me back to the religion of my father. I had run from my father, gone to sea, and that was where I had met Nguyen Ai Quoc and we had gone to London and to Paris and now my father was calling me back, through a Vietnamese monk I met in the Tuileries.

Quoc, on the other hand, was being called not from his past but from his future. He had rented the dark suit and bowler and he would spend the following weeks in Versailles, walking up and down the mirrored corridors of the Palace trying to gain an audience with Woodrow Wilson. Quoc had eight requests for the Western world concerning Indochina. Simple things. Equal rights, freedom of assembly, freedom of the press. The essential things that he knew Wilson would understand, based as they were on Wilson's own Fourteen Points. And Quoc did not even intend to ask for independence. He wanted Vietnamese representatives in the French Parliament. That was all he would ask. But his bowler made him angry. He wrenched out of the puddle of candlelight, both his hands clutching the bowler, and I heard him muttering in the darkness and I felt that this was a bad sign already, even before he had set foot in Versailles. And as it turned out, he never saw Wilson, or Lloyd George either, or even Clemenceau. But somehow his frustration with his hat was what made me sad, even now, and I reached out from my bedside and said, "Uncle Ho, it's all right."

He was still beside me. This was not an awakening, as you might expect, this was not a dream ending with the bowler in Paris and I awaking to find that Ho was never there. He was still beside my bed, though he was just beyond my outstretched hand and he did not move to me. He smiled on one side of his mouth, a smile full of irony, as if he, too, were thinking about the night he'd tried on his rented clothes. He said, "Do you remember how I worked in Paris?"

I thought about this and I did remember, with the words of his advertisement in the newspaper "La Vie Ouvriere": "If you would like a lifelong memento of your family, have your photos retouched at Nguyen Ai Quoc's." This was his work in Paris; he retouched photos with a very delicate hand, the same fine hand that Monsieur Escoffier had admired in London. I said, "Yes, I remember."

Ho nodded gravely. "I painted the blush into the cheeks of Frenchmen."

I said, "A lovely portrait in a lovely frame for forty francs," another phrase from his advertisement.

"Forty-five," Ho said.

I thought now of his question that I had not answered. I motioned to the far corner of the room where the prayer table stood. "I still follow the path."

He looked and said, "At least you became a Hoa Hao."

He could tell this from the simplicity of the table. There was only a red cloth upon it and four Chinese characters: Bao So'n Ky Hhu'o'ng. This is the saying of the Hoa Haos. We follow the teachings of a monk who broke away from the fancy rituals of the other Buddhists. We do not need elaborate pagodas or rituals. The Hoa Hao believes that the maintenance of our spirits is very simple, and the mystery of joy is simple, too. The four characters mean "A good scent from a strange mountain."

I had always admired the sense of humor of my friend Quoc, so I said, "You never did stop painting the blush into the faces of Westerners."

Ho looked back to me but he did not smile. I was surprised at this but more surprised at my little joke seeming to remind him of his hands. He raised them and studied them and said, "After the heating, what was the surface for the glaze?"

"My old friend," I said, "you worry me now."

But Ho did not seem to hear. He turned away and crossed the room and I knew he was real because he did not vanish from my sight but opened the door and went out and closed the door behind him with a loud click.

I rang for my daughter. She had given me a porcelain bell, and after allowing Ho enough time to go down the stairs and out the front door, if that was where he was headed, I rang the bell, and my daughter, who is a very light sleeper, soon appeared.

"What is it, Father?" she asked with great patience in her voice. She is a good girl. She understands about Vietnamese families and she is a smart girl.

"Please feel the doorknob," I said.

She did so without the slightest hesitation and this was a lovely gesture on her part, a thing that made me wish to rise up and embrace her, though I was very tired and did not move.

"Yes?" she asked after touching the knob.

"Is it sticky?"

She touched it again. "Ever so slightly," she said. "Would you like me to clean it?"

"In the morning," I said.

She smiled and crossed the room and kissed me on the forehead. She smelled of lavender and fresh bedclothes and there are so many who have gone on before me into the world of spirits and I yearn for them all, yearn to find them all together in a village square, my wife there smelling of lavender and our own sweat, like on a night in Saigon soon after the terrible fighting in 1968 when we finally opened the windows onto the night and there were sounds of bombs falling on the horizon and there was no breeze at all, just the heavy stillness of the time between the dry season and the wet, and Saigon smelled of tar and motorcycle exhaust and cordite but when I opened the window and turned to my wife, the room was full of a wonderful scent, a sweet smell that made her sit up, for she sensed it, too. This was a smell that had nothing to do with flowers but instead reminded us that flowers were always ready to fall into dust, while this smell was as if a gemstone had begun to give off a scent, as if a mountain of emerald had found its own scent. I crossed the room to my wife and we were already old, we had already buried children and grandchildren that we prayed waited for us in that village square at the foot of the strange mountain, but when I came near the bed, she lifted her silk gown and threw it aside and I pressed close to her and our own sweat smelled sweet on that night. I want to be with her in that square and with the rest of those we'd buried, the tiny limbs and the sullen eyes and the gray faces of the puzzled children and the surprised adults and the weary old people who have gone before us, who know the secrets now. And the sweet smell of the glaze on Ho's hands reminds me of the others that I would want in the square, the people from the ship, too, the Vietnamese boy from a village near my own who died of a fever in the Indian Ocean and the natives in Dakar who were forced by colonial officials to swim out to our ship in shark-infested waters to secure the moorings and two were killed before our eyes without a French regret. Ho was very moved by this, and I want those men in our square and I want the Frenchman, too, who called Ho "monsieur" for the first time. A man on the dock in Marseilles. Ho spoke of him twice more during our years together and I want that Frenchman there. And, of course, Ho. Was he in the village square even now, waiting? Heating his glaze fondant? My daughter was smoothing my covers around me and the smell of lavender on her was still strong.

"He was in this room," I said to her to explain the sticky doorknob.

"Who was?"

But I was very sleepy and I could say no more, though perhaps she would not have understood anyway, in spite of being the smart girl that she is.

The next night I left my light on to watch for Ho's arrival, but I dozed off and he had to wake me. He was sitting in a chair that he'd brought from across the room. He said to me, "Dao. Wake up, my old friend."

I must have awakened when he pulled the chair near to me, for I heard each of these words. "I am awake," I said. "I was thinking of the poor men who had to swim out to our ship."

"They are already among those I have served," Ho said. "Before I forgot." And he raised his hands and they were still covered with sugar.

I said, "Wasn't it a marble slab?" I had a memory, strangely clear after these many years, as strange as my memory of Ho's Paris business card.

"A marble slab," Ho repeated, puzzled.

"That you poured the heated sugar on."

"Yes." Ho's sweet-smelling hands came forward but they did not quite touch me. I thought to reach out from beneath the covers and take them in my own hands, but Ho leaped up and paced about the room. "The marble slab, moderately oiled. Of course. I am to let the sugar half cool and then use the spatula to move it about in all directions, every bit of it, so that it doesn't harden and form lumps."

I asked, "Have you seen my wife?"

Ho had wandered to the far side of the room, but he turned and crossed back to me at this. "I'm sorry, my friend. I never knew her."

I must have shown some disappointment in my face, for Ho sat down and brought his own face near mine. "I'm sorry," he said. "There are many other people that I must find here."

"Are you very disappointed in me?" I asked. "For not having traveled the road with you?"

"It's very complicated," Ho said softly. "You felt that you'd taken action. I am no longer in a position to question another soul's choice."

"Are you at peace, where you are?" I asked this knowing of his worry over the recipe for the glaze, but I hoped that this was only a minor difficulty in the afterlife, like the natural anticipation of the good cook expecting guests when everything always turns out fine in the end.

But Ho said, "I am not at peace."

"Is Monsieur Escoffier over there?"

"I have not seen him. This has nothing to do with him, directly."

"What is it about?"

"I don't know."

"You won the country. You know that, don't you?"

Ho shrugged. "There are no countries here."

I should have remembered Ho's shrug when I began to see things in the faces of my son-in-law and grandson this morning. But something quickened in me, a suspicion. I kept my eyes shut and laid my head to the side, as if I were fast asleep, encouraging them to talk more.

My daughter said, "This is not the place to speak."

But the men did not regard her. "How?" Loi asked his father, referring to the missing murder weapon.

"It's best not to know too much," Thang said.

Then there was a silence. For all the quickness I'd felt at the first suspicion, I was very slow now. In fact, I did think of Ho from that second night. Not his shrug. He had fallen silent for a long time and I had closed my eyes, for the light seemed very bright. I listened to his silence just as I listened to the silence of these two conspirators before me.

And then Ho said, "They were fools, but I can't bring myself to grow angry anymore."

I opened my eyes in the bedroom and the light was off. Ho had turned it off, knowing that it was bothering me. "Who were fools?" I asked.

"We had fought together to throw out the Japanese. I had very good friends among them. I smoked their lovely Salem cigarettes. They had been repressed by colonialists themselves. Did they not know their own history?"

"Do you mean the Americans?"

"There are a million souls here with me, the young men of our country, and they are all dressed in black suits and bowler hats. In the mirrors they are made ten million, a hundred million."

"I chose my path, my dear friend Quoc, so that there might be harmony."

And even with that yearning for harmony I could not overlook what my mind made of what my ears had heard this morning. Thang was telling Loi that the murder weapon had been disposed of. Thang and Loi both knew the killers, were in sympathy with them, perhaps were part of the killing. The father and son had been airborne rangers and I had several times heard them talk bitterly of the exile of our people. We were fools for trusting the Americans all along, they said. We should have taken matters forward and disposed of the infinitely corrupt Thieu and done what needed to be done. Whenever they spoke like this in front of me, there was soon a quick exchange of sideways glances at me and then a turn and an apology. "We're sorry, Grandfather. Old times often bring old anger. We are happy our family is living a new life."

I would wave my hand at this, glad to have the peace of the family restored. Glad to turn my face and smell the dogwood tree or even smell the coffee plant across the highway. These things had come to be the new smells of our family. But then a weakness often came upon me. The others would drift away, the men, and perhaps one of my daughters would come to me and stroke my head and not say a word and none of them ever would ask why I was weeping. I would smell the rich blood smells of the afterbirth and I would hold our first son, still slippery in my arms, and there was the smell of dust from the square and the smell of the South China Sea just over the rise of the hill and there was the smell of the blood and of the inner flesh from my wife as my son's own private sea flowed from this woman that I loved, flowed and carried him into the life that would disappear so soon. In the afterlife would he stand before me on unsteady child's legs? Would I have to bend low to greet him or would he be a man now?

My grandson said, after the silence had nearly carried me into real sleep, troubled sleep, my grandson Loi said to his father, "I would be a coward not to know."

Thang laughed and said, "You have proved yourself no coward."

And I wished then to sleep, I wished to fall asleep and let go of life somewhere in my dreams and seek my village square. I have lived too long, I thought. My daughter was saying, "Are you both mad?" and then she changed her voice, making the words very precise. "Let Grandfather sleep."

So when Ho came tonight for the third time, I wanted to ask his advice. His hands were still covered with sugar and his mind was, as it had been for the past two nights, very much distracted. "There's something still wrong with the glaze," he said to me in the dark, and I pulled back the covers and swung my legs around to get up. He did not try to stop me, but he did draw back quietly into the shadows.

"I want to pace the room with you," I said. "As we did in Paris, those tiny rooms of ours. We would talk about Marx and about Buddha and I must pace with you now."

"Very well," he said. "Perhaps it will help me remember."

I slipped on my sandals and I stood up and Ho's shadow moved past me, through the spill of streetlight and into the dark near the door. I followed him, smelling the sugar on his hands, first before me and then moving past me as I went on into the darkness he'd just left. I stopped as I turned and I could see Ho outlined before the window and I said, "I believe my son-in-law and grandson are involved in the killing of a man. A political killing."

Ho stayed where he was, a dark shape against the light, and he said nothing and I could not smell his hands from across the room and I smelled only the sourness of Loi and he laid his head on my shoulder. He was a baby and my daughter Lam retreated to our balcony window after handing him to me and the boy turned his head and I turned mine to him and I could smell his mother's milk, sour on his breath, he had a sour smell and there was incense burning in the room, jasmine, the smoke of souls, and the boy sighed on my shoulder, and I turned my face away from the smell of him. Thang was across the room and his eyes were quick to find his wife and he was waiting for her to take the child from me.

"You have never done the political thing," Ho said.

"Is this true?"

"Of course."

I asked, "Are there politics where you are now, my friend?"

I did not see him moving toward me, but the smell of the sugar on his hands grew stronger, very strong, and I felt Ho Chi Minh very close to me, though I could not see him. He was very close and the smell was strong and sweet and it was filling my lungs as if from the inside, as if Ho was passing through my very body, and I heard the door open behind me and then close softly shut.

I moved across the room to the bed. I turned to sit down but I was facing the window, the scattering of a streetlamp on the window like a nova in some far part of the universe. I stepped to the window and touched the reflected light there, wondering if there was a great smell when a star explodes, a great burning smell of gas and dust. Then I closed the shade and slipped into bed, quite gracefully, I felt, I was quite wonderfully graceful, and I lie here now waiting for sleep. Ho is right, of course. I will never say a word about my grandson. And perhaps I will be as restless as Ho when I join him. But that will be all right. He and I will be together again and perhaps we can help each other. I know now what it is that he has forgotten. He has used confectioners' sugar for his glaze fondant and he should be using granulated sugar. I was only a washer of dishes but I did listen carefully when Monsieur Escoffier spoke. I wanted to understand everything. His kitchen was full of such smells that you knew you had to understand everything or you would be incomplete forever.

Kate Wheeler

Ringworm

T'S BEEN TWO YEARS since I left Pingyan Monastery, but every time my head itches I still think it's that ringworm. It was the blind cat's fault, or mine for getting distracted and feeding her and having a special feeling about her, as if her eyes full of blank green fire could see something beyond what there was—white stucco walls stained with red mud from the monsoon, beautiful brown people walking slowly up and down, meditating. Dust, red, garbage, jasmine. Every single thing, different from here.

She first showed up at the end of the hot season, gray and black tiger, like a cat I used to have in California. I couldn't tell where she came from; she was obviously from outside the orange-and-white gene pool of the monastery cats. Maybe she wandered in from the Muslim slum next door. She was so weak she fell down the steps into the basement that was given to us foreign women as a meditation hall, down under the dorm for Burmese women over fifty. There was a special building for older women, mostly devout widows who came to meditate after their familial duties were accomplished. We six Foreigner Women, all younger than that, had to walk through their quarters to get to the toilet. In the long oven of the hallway, there was mutual inspection. I'd peek sidelong into their rooms and see the grandmothers oiling their long hair or resting after lunch, always lying on their right sides because this was the posture in which the Buddha slept. They lay very still, often with their eyes open. Were they thinking of anything? Maybe not. They frequently offered me bananas or a little dish of fermented tea leaves fried with garlic and peanuts. They felt sorry for the foreigners, I think, because we had no families to come and visit us and bring us nice things to eat.

I was a nun, with a shaven head and four layers of pink, vaguely Grecian robes. I'd gone to Burma on recommendation from travelers I met in India. They said Burma was a fragment of an older world, that in isolation it had worked out the world's strictest, most effective technique for spiritual enlightenment. I waited a year and a half for a special visa, and when it finally arrived I was ready, primed: I told Pingyan's abbot that I wanted nothing but complete freedom of the heart and mind. Because I'd meditated quite a lot in the past, he offered me the robes, a nun's ten rules of conduct, and the name Sumanā, meaning "Open Mind" or "Open Heart" (Burmese don't make a distinction), and also, "Queen of Jasmine."

The monastery covered forty acres in a suburb near the British consulate, and had enough buildings to accommodate the entire bourgeoisie of Rangoon as well as devotees from places like Mandalay, Sagaing, and the Shan and Karen states. There were usually a thousand people meditating, both ordained and lay; four thousand during the Water Festival. As in any religion, females predominated in number, but there was a good minority of monks who were the authorities, as well as a dozen foreigners. We foreign women lived and meditated by ourselves and saw the men only at meals. After a while my eyes turned Asian, and Western males began to look like the barbarians on a Chinese plate, hairy and coarse, their naked pink skin like boiled shrimp.

Breakfast was at five and lunch at ten-fifteen. There was no solid food, then, until the next breakfast. The monks said eating at night causes lust. We woke at three to the clanking of an iron pipe. Each day there were seven one-hour sittings, interspersed with six or seven hours of formal walking meditation, pacing slowly up and down. At eight p.m. the abbot discoursed to the foreigners; Burmese got sermons only on Saturday. Every other day we had an interview, a completely formalized affair in which we described our meditation and the abbot instructed us about how to proceed. Bed was at eleven.

We didn't talk, nor make eye contact with anyone. We were told to keep the mind protected like a turtle in its shell, but to notice everything occurring in that field. Thus, when not sitting with eyes shut, we moved very slowly, minutely attending to sensations and avoiding complex, rapid movements. If strong thoughts or emotions came, we noticed their presence but discarded their content. This practice was intended to lead to the famous and misunderstood Nirvana, which the Burmese call Nibbāna, Liberation, the end of suffering—*cessation* was the word the Burmese used. I believed I could experience cessation because I was in Burma where, it was said, lots of people had psychic powers and the young girls would attain their cessation during summer holidays from school.

Possibly my great faith contributed to slackness in my practice. I was fascinated with everything. My notebook was stuffed with observations that I knew the monks would disapprove of. "Toothpaste tube still hot at nine p.m.," "Burmese girls grow their toenails long and paint them." I was constantly enmeshed in situations with other Westerners, or with Burmese who wanted to get visas to the States, practice English, teach me Burmese, or donate things to me because gifts to a nun would generate good karma. It didn't matter that I intended to disrobe whenever I reached Nibbāna or the government quit extending my visa—I could have been a nun for a single day and still deserved the same respect. The merit gained by paying respect to ordained people is gauged by what they represent, rather than anything personal. Once I comprehended this, it was easier to let the young girls kneel in the dirt and bow, or simply take off their shoes as they handed me a banana or a sack of boiled cane-juice candy. Giving to a male monk would have been precisely ten times better, but my Westernness seemed to give me an extra value not included in traditional calculations. I got lots of presents; I had a fan club of twenty young girls. One medical student told me I must be a very pure being indeed, for having first merited, and then forsaken, the sensual pleasures of the "United State."

At interviews the abbot said I was progressing and that I should keep a relaxed attitude. So I had little incentive to change, except perhaps the example of my senior nun, Sīlānandā, "Bliss of Morality." She was French, and had done PR for a ritzy yacht club before firmly renouncing the world. Her posture, the result of a childhood in Parisian ballet classes, impressed the girls in my fan club as evidence of deep meditative powers.

I was taking a break, standing at the row of sinks in line with the other women, all of us mixing up glucose tea, which we drank in the afternoon to keep from getting dehydrated. My feet were bare and dirty on the hot black boards, the sinks were giving off their intense slime smell, and my four layers of robes were stuck to my skin with the heat, as usual. Now I heard a thin mew, turned, and saw this pathetic creature, all bones, tottering then falling down the steps.

Next to me, Sīlānandā slowly turned her head to look, slowly turned it back again, and resumed her tea-making with glacial care. Do not be diverted, her behavior said. I watched her hand closing around the cup, its conical fingers perfectly familiar to me. In my mind I heard the abbot, our teacher.

One moment of kindness is greater than a hundred years of ordinary life. One moment of perfect attention is greater than a hundred years of kindness.

Slowly Sīlānandā raised the cup and drank.

The perfume of mindfulness rises even to the seat of the gods.

Indeed she was perfect, but I suspected she wanted all of us to notice.

Me, I'd already grabbed a spare jar lid and mixed up in it some glucose and my powdered milk from Bangkok. The cat didn't know what it was at first, but I pushed her nose into it so that she had to lick it off, with a charming little sneeze.

Now the Swiss woman came and crouched next to me, smiling intensely. I understood that she was enraptured by this feeding of the cat and also wanted an excuse to talk. This was one of the dangers of getting involved in events. There was a snowball effect. The most microscopic loophole permitted the world to draw me back into itself.

I smiled a tiny Buddha's smile and moved my hands slowly, as Sīlānandā would, to show that I was meditating diligently in spite of what might appear. In other words, Scram.

But the Swiss woman's need was great. "I am afraid," she muttered. "Office give my money back to me when I go to visa extension. My money was smelling very bad, I think."

"No, no," it was my role to say. Except that she was fed and taken care of, I thought the Swiss woman shouldn't be here. In the silence her mind created labyrinths of paranoia. "The price of visas was just reduced so we all got fifty kyaks back. Everybody's money stinks here. The bills are old. Don't worry."

"Ah."

Suddenly my pretended concentration caught, and I stopped seeing or thinking about the unbalanced Swiss woman. I was just noticing the little cat, the softness of her fur and the pain of her starvation. I felt it through me like a fire.

Her eyes were unusually glowing, like florist's green glass marbles, but I didn't realize then that she was blind and this was why they were so luminous. She didn't understand the milk; she just stood over it, weakly bobbing her head. Maybe, I think now, she couldn't find it again.

I turned to go back into the meditation hall, but the kitten tried to follow. I took her up the steps and deposited her under a jasmine bush, together with the jar lid. Ten ants already had drowned in white. As I wet the cat's nose one last time, a passing crone cried out her disapproval.

Animals are incapable of refined mental states. A gift to an animal is of little merit.

I scurried back to the meditation hall.

After that I didn't see the kitten for a long time. If I'd thought about it, I'd have guessed she died, but I didn't think of her.

THE PLACE WAS FULL OF CATS. The so-called Warden of the older women's dorm had two toms, horrid orange things with heavy heads and balls the size of grapes. They ran around pissing on everything, ate pork pasties and white rice, even slept with their mistress on her hard Burmese cot like a narrow Ping-Pong table. The rest of the cats had to compete for garbage with dogs, rats, crows, and pigeons. Kittens were loose-boweled and scrawny, but nonetheless retained an infant grace. Their mothers were pathetic. Swaybacked, degraded by constant pregnancy, at puberty they lost some core of self-respect essential to a creature. They didn't wash; they couldn't look you in the eye. One calico in particular—I'd come out from lunch and find her making obscene love to the sandals outside the dining hall. Caught, she'd cringe and slink away, as if some faint memory had stirred of a time before base drives had ruined her life. It was enough to make anyone into a feminist, or depending on your turn of mind, you might begin to agree with the pious Burmese, who say celibacy is a virtue and look down on married people.

Yesterday, sir, I sat seven hours and walked seven hours. I slept five. In sitting, the rising and falling of the abdomen was the primary object. At three o'clock, in the rising I noticed movement and tightness, in falling softness and heaviness. Burning arose in the lower back. I focused on the burning, and it became unbearable.

Did you twist and turn to find relief?

Yes.

The sufferings of life should be known. Do not move to conceal the truth from yourself. Grit your teeth. You can keep pain dancing in your hand.

EVERY SATURDAY I SHAVED MY HEAD. At a stale hour of the afternoon I would retire from the meditation hall to the green-tiled bathing room with its dark, cool tank of water. My equipment was a mirror, a thermos of hot water, a bar of blue Chinese soap, and a Gillette Trac II cartridge razor I'd brought in from Bangkok. Shaving took an hour, and except for the bliss of leaving behind the hall and my companions, suddenly comical in their diligence, I hated it. The textures put my teeth on edge—cheap lather like saliva, sandpapery stubble, sticky smoothness of my scalp. Next day, the back of my head always erupted in a thousand tiny pimples. Irritation, I suppose. Eventually I learned that a hot washrag cured this.

One shaving day I found a small, red patch on my right temple. By then I was used to various grossnesses of my flesh and found this one interesting. When I pulled my skin a little, it jumped into a perfect circle. There were few perfectly made things in that environment, and this roundness pleased me. But now it itched.

A few nights later, after the abbot's discourse, I went to ask the monastery nurse about it. She was Warden of the Foreigner Women's Dorm, and so lived downstairs from us.

Saya-ma Aye Shwe, Nurse Cool Garden, was sitting under her mosquito net. As she was deaf, I had to walk into her room and touch her shoulder.

"It 'tis a sunburn," she breathed, in English. "Leave it." Her voice was deceptive, as soft as a baby's sigh.

Though she'd trained as a nurse in East Germany and in Australia, Nurse Aye Shwe ascribed most physical ailments to faulty concentration, heat, or cold. She'd cured herself of stomach cancer by meditating alone in a forest hut, vowing not to come out until she died or attained enlightenment. Now it was her right to despise infirmity; one visited the clinic only in a mood of boldness. Westerners were too soft, always sick, always wanting pills. The body is good only for practice, we must learn that it is full of sufferings! To Sīlānandā, who had severe edema in her arms and legs, Nurse Aye Shwe refused any medicament. "It is very good to die in meditation," she reminded.

I retired from her presence that night without a murmur, even though I knew I had no sunburn. It wasn't bothering me much, yet.

A week later the spot was the size of the rubber ring on a Mason jar and itched so much I couldn't sleep. I returned to the nurse's quarters, tilted my head to the light from her barred window.

"Is it ringworm?" I asked, but she didn't have her hearing aid on. "*Ringworm?*"

It was often hard to tell what Nurse Aye Shwe had understood. Where deafness came to an end, there some obscurely motivated willfulness took over. "You are not used to our water," she said sadly. "Try with Go-Min."

"Go-Min!" I laughed, throwing my head back for Nurse Aye Shwe's benefit. In all fairness, it was very difficult to get Western medicines in Burma, especially for one such as a nurse who disapproved of the black market. But Go-Min was made in Burma, and very cheap, a rude little jar of pig fat mixed with aromatic oils. I had heard the nurse prescribe it for swollen gums, varicose veins, abdominal bleeding, scabies, and mosquito bites. Weeks ago, she'd given me a jar of it for hemorrhoids; the most I can say is that it burned as if it were having a radical effect.

"Sister Go-Min, they call me," Nurse Aye Shwe said with a smirk. "If your meditation is good, Go-Min will be very effective."

Later that day I was doing walking meditation next to the Hall of the Diamond, where the Burmese women meditated. It looked like a cinema and was fixed up inside like Versailles, with mirror mosaics and a giant aquarium up front, enclosing an enormous white enamel Buddha with a gold-leaf robe and red smiling lips. Foreigner Women were forbidden to meditate there, which was a disappointment to me. Our basement hall smelled of rotting mud and had no Buddha. Often it was invaded by fleas from the Warden's pissing tomcats. More importantly, the Burmese women seemed to have more fun than we did. Every morning they chanted in a haunting minor key. Young girls did their walking meditation arm in arm, and no one was terribly serious about the rule of silence. When sad thoughts or terrifying visions came, the women groaned and wept aloud. "Oiyy! Oiyy!" Sometimes their entire hall would erupt in these lugubrious sounds, like a pack of she-wolves howling, and I'd wish desperately to be there, not cooped up with the grim Calvinists in the Foreigner Women's Basement.

Suddenly I was at the center of a bunch of teenaged nuns who were giggling and rapidly speaking Burmese. They pulled me around the corner, out of sight of the women's supervisor or any passing monk. I nearly fainted with delight. I regularly got crushes on these temporary nuns who came, like me, to ordain for a few months or a year. Physically they were lovely—supple bodies in the narrow elegant pink robes, faces exquisite in concentration. I imagined them uncorrupted creatures, isolated in medieval Burma from the evils of the world.

One tall girl pointed at my ringworm, crying, "Pwe! Pwe!" It was so big now, they must have seen it from afar. A pudgy lay girl explained, "She bring med-cine fo' you." As we stood there, an old woman came up, as stout as a gnome and dressed in the brown laywomen's uniform of sash, sarong, and jacket. She had diamonds in her ears, rims of gold around all of her incisors. She pulled a tube out of a ratty vinyl purse.

"My son," she said, showing me the tube. TRIMOXTRIM, it said, USE ONLY UNDER THE DIRECTION OF A PHYSICIAN. "Put," she said, shaking the tube toward me. When in Rome, I thought. I put on a tiny dab.

"Tomorrow, fie o'clack," the fat girl said, pointing at the ground.

The next day they were waiting, the dry, brown gnome amid gardenias. To meet them I had to cross the Burmese women's walking ground, a no-man's land of hard, barren dirt. Slowly, slowly, eyes downcast—I was in sight of the elder monks' cottages. My shadow flew over dull rocks, smashed brick, eroded asphalt, struggling weeds. Two monks swished past on important business, as fast as Jaguars on a freeway.

The tall nun's name was Nandāsayee, Expert of Delight. She carried a long, flexible branch in her hand. "Lady gah-din, she *find*," the fat interpreter announced. Nandāsayee pulled off seven leaves, rolled a cylinder, tore off one end. She whispered to it quietly; then, puh, puh, she breathed into it.

"'Life, not life,'" the interpreter offered. "She tell to leaf."

Cradling my head, Nandāsayee now rubbed the leaves onto the ringworm, carefully following is outline counterclockwise. This stung a little. Later I learned that the leaves were from a hot pepper bush. Her finger pads were slightly moist and soft, like frogs' palps. I could smell the green crushed leaf, and her body, scorched where mine was sharp.

This could cure me of anything, I thought. I'd been there six months then, physically touched by no one.

Finished, Nandāsayee walked a few paces off and threw the leaves over her shoulder. She came back grinning.

"Tomorrow three time," the plump girl said. "Aftah brehfass, aftah lunch, fie o'clack." I pointed to the Foreigner Women's Hall, and the nuns giggled mischievously. Not long before, a man had come from the office and pounded a sign into the ground just at our door, three rows of Burmese curlicues. I'd gone to the office to ask what the words meant.

"Foreigner Women Are Practicing Meditation," the monastery vice president importantly said. Before assuming this duty he'd been Minister of Finance for all of Burma. "Do Not Stare, Do Not Go In, Do Not Try to Start a Conversation."

Before we all dispersed, the woman in brown anointed me again. Methophan was this cream's name. Read circular directions carefully.

NURSE AYE SHWE WAS IN A MOOD OF LAXITY. That night she beckoned me into her room.

"I have got! Burmese medicine for ringworm. When you are finish, please return me, unused portion." It was a whitish, grainy cream in a hot pink plastic tube. I made the first application right away. It stung fiercely, satisfactorily. Its job must be simply to kill infested flesh.

Nurse Aye Shwe offered me hot plum concentrate in an enamel cup. "I teach meditation now, in Rangoon Asylum," she remarked. "Soon cure." Her face was a mask of satisfaction; I was filled with nostalgia for such certainty as hers, the same feeling as when I wish to have been born in some past century.

"Today I select my patient," she went on, proudly. "One man present himself. 'Take me!' he say. But he is naked! I say, 'You, never.' Another man come. *Ol'* man. On his head, hat. Under hat, plastic bag. Under plastic bag, paper bag. Under paper bag, leaf! This one, I say, 'Please come with me.'"

"The Swiss woman has strange thoughts," I suggested. "*Swiss woman, very strange!*"

"I know," Nurse Aye Shwe said. "I am so sorry for the Western people."

That night I couldn't sleep. I lay under the mosquito net's stifling canopy, too dizzy to sit up and meditate. Everything was breaking into particles, the itching at my temple, the passionate sounds of the night. Crickets sawed away, lizards croaked like colliding billiard balls; in the Muslim slum, a woman sang endless Arab vowels, the very voice of unfulfilled desire. I knew I'd miss these serenades, whenever I went home.

BEFORE THE DAWN MISTS BURNED OFF, Sister Nandāsayee slipped into our basement and closed the door behind her. In the half dark, we Foreigner Women were making our postbreakfast cups of milk tea. Nandāsayee came at me with her leafy branch. I bent my head; she performed the little ritual of treatment. I felt like the birthday girl. Even Sīlānandā was intrigued enough to stand and frankly watch until Nandāsayee receded out the door, a finger to her lips.

The Swiss woman surged toward me, an ocean liner beaming, beaming, beaming sympathetic joy. Her eyes were two blue lamps. "So beautiful this Burmese nun," she breathed.

I tore a leaf from my notebook and posted a general notice. "I am being treated for ringworm with herbal medicine."

Next time Nandāsayee was more forward. She hovered over each of us in turn, frowned, and pointed at Sīlānandā's tea bags and milk powder. Obviously she'd never seen either. All of us stood around while Sīlānandā, with perfect art, showed how she prepared her tea in an old Milo jar. At the end she offered the jar to Nandāsayee, who made a suspicious face. She barely touched the liquid with her tongue's tip and scowled. All of us laughed. Dour Cathy from western Scotland presented her with a chewable vitamin C, which Nandāsayee tucked into her sash before rushing out the door as if chased by demons.

This was the beginning of my friendship with Sīlānandā. That day I found a note under my cushion in her spiky European hand. "Will the pink angel rub my swollen ankles too? Mmm."

Last night, sir, I felt strange. Objects appeared as streams of particles dissolving. When I observed the abdomen, I found no physical sensations. I was disoriented until I discovered a subtle sense of space. Happiness arose, then images of an event during the day.

How long did you dwell on the images?

Ten, fifteen minutes.

Too long.

Yes, sir.

When objects are subtle, be aware of their pleasantness or unpleasantness. If no objects appear, do not try to find them. Do not ponder, do not ask yourself, "What is this, how is this, why is this?" If you think a thousand ways, you will find a thousand answers. Only direct awareness will show you the nature of the world.

Thank you, sir.

Good. Try to sleep only four hours.

BIGGER NOW AND NOT SO WEAK, the kitten reappeared in the breezeway next to the Foreigner Women's Quarters. I brought back food for her from lunch in a thick white teacup. Chicken gizzards, hunks of pork fat; I barely had time to get my fingers out of the way of her teeth.

A circle gathered. The older women frowned, the girls seemed delightedly scandalized. "*Wet'tha*, pig meat. *Chet'tha*, chicken meat," they chanted. I realized this was better food than they'd had at lunch. Foreigners and monks ate the best foods—pork, eggs, mango, durian, birthday cake, ice cream—donated by the pious. Burmese nuns and laywomen ate in a separate dining room, directly beneath the monks'.

Tomorrow I'd bring only bones and scraps.

Nurse Aye Shwe flew out, a dark, screeching gryphon. "No yogi must have pet! This cup for monks, not animal! Very bad *kamma* for you."

The watching crowd laughed as it dispersed. For two days, the nurse's face was thunder. I persisted in feeding the cat but soon found occasion to donate my last bar of Thai disinfectant soap to the dispensary.

"Sumanā is capitalist," Nurse Aye Shwe said sourly, tucking the soap into her cabinet. But that afternoon she gave me half a coconut shell to use as the cat's dish. "Pussy very t'in. Blind." I wondered why I hadn't noticed. The way she picked her way across the monsoon gutters, shaking her paw, surprised me when she stepped in puddles near the outdoor bathing tank.

Soon Nurse Aye Shwe began to scrape her own rice bowl into the cat's. I still brought food from lunch, even though it was major complication in the closed and narrow circuit of my life. Choosing the scraps, wrapping the cup, finding the cat, enduring the watching, washing the cup and napkin, remembering to return them the next day—it all stood out as tedious labor. Our teachers said there were three kinds of suffering. The suffering of pain itself, the suffering of the alternation of pleasure and pain, and the suffering of the cumbersomeness of life. I reported to my teacher that I understood this now. He laughed and said to be more continuous.

BUT I WAS BAD, BAD. I began doing my walking meditation under the shaded breezeway where the cat liked to sit for hours on end, her paws hidden under her chest. "She is meditating," I told myself. When no one was looking, I would carry her the length of my twenty-pace walking track, cradled in my arms. She was developing a belly, a hard little ball; though it didn't look exactly healthy, it seemed an improvement, a justification for feeding her.

The breezeway fronted on another Burmese dorm, this one for younger girls and several women who were permanent residents. Walking there, I learned many more unnecessary things. I saw the wrist motion with which the women beat their laundry on the flat stone; learned that some of the young girls were lazy and would lock themselves in a room all afternoon, giggling and eating cookies. The woman who lived at the end was some sort of witch. I'd see her on a patch of waste ground at the end of my walking track, making strange passes with a twig broom and singing softly to the air. At first I thought her saintly, but one day it struck me that her face was as hard and primitive as an alcoholic's. I guessed her family had abandoned her, or died. In return for her keep, she swept the leaves from the broad cement walkways on the monks' side of the compound.

One day she gave me a boiled egg, the poorest egg I've ever tasted. The white was blue, translucent; the gray yolk tasted of fish. As I should not have done, I imagined the hen it must have come from.

THE SWISS WOMAN WAS DETERIORATING. Some days she would not come to the meditation hall at all but stayed inside her room with the door closed. Slowly pacing the breezeway, I watched and worried but didn't intervene. She blocked her transom with a cotton blanket. Ten times a day, with a great rattling of the latch, she raced to the bathroom and flung water over herself. Our tank was always empty. I wondered what she reported in her interviews, whether the monks were capable of understanding her condition. Maybe the heat was getting to her, I thought, or just the isolation.

MY RINGWORM WAS A PALE GHOST. Who knows which treatment was responsible? I used the Burmese ointment hourly; at ten, as I waited to join the lunch procession, the gnome in brown accosted me with frightening Western creams, halting tales of her son in L.A. And of course, Nandāsayee, my goddess, came three times each day. We were all in love with her. We gave her mint tea, sugar, and chocolates, and she reciprocated with jasmine and frangipani. Once I brought down my camera and got Scottish Cathy to document the treatment. Nandāsayee demanded formal portraits of herself holding hands with each of the foreigner women yogis. She stood very still, unsmiling, as if her image were a sacrifice she offered to the camera. I had several sets of prints made by the monastery photographer at fabulous expense and gave one to her in return for the treatment.

The next day she didn't come, nor the next. I began to see her in the company of senior nuns.

"Your friend, small nun, very successful meditation," Nurse Aye Shwe said.

NOW I WAS GALVANIZED BY SPIRITUAL URGENCY. I felt I had been wasting my time in Burma, socializing and feeding a cat, when I could have been saving myself from endless rebirths in the ocean of suffering, the eighteen vivid Buddhist hells. It was all right for Nandāsayee to giggle and laugh; she was Burmese, a fish in water. Circumstances rearranged themselves conveniently: the hot season was coming to an end, and the young nuns were disrobing one by one to go back to Rangoon University.

Even as her contemporaries vanished, Sister Nandāsayee was to be seen, still in pink, running about the nuns' quarters. Her experiences must have been especially profound, I thought. Yet, in my new mood, I was glad she came no more to our hall. The healing leaves withered, and I threw them into the monsoon gutter. In a spirit of divestiture, I gave the Burmese cream back to Nurse Aye Shwe and avoided the brown gnome of the squashed tubes. My ringworm must be dead by now, and if it wasn't, I would keep the pain dancing in my hand.

I even stopped feeding the cat.

The first Rains fell, thundering on the galvanized roofs with a heart-stopping roar. My mind settled along with the dust.

As I notice objects, sir, I feel deep stillness, like a forest early in the morning. I am not looking for any particular object. Sensations are mixed with calmness. Then I find nothingness as an object, more subtle even than space. Afterward I try to remember it. I think there was some kind of knowing, but very subtle. When walking I feel light, barely existing.

Stay with what is present. If your awareness vanishes, be with that too.

Am I close to cessation?

Ha, ha, maybe so.

WALKING ON THE BREEZEWAY, I feel sun's heat transmitted through iron roof. Ancient cracked cement. Crows dump over the garbage basket, rifling through fruit peels, cawing. Left foot, right foot. I am trying to concentrate because, in an hour, I have an interview.

A brown hand appears, waving in my field of vision: here are Nandā-sayee's wide feet in red velvet thongs.

I look into her dancing eyes, this tall, strong, young woman. "My mother," she says, indicating a vast coarse hag in brown. I smile and shake hands. Mother grins back genially. She must have come to celebrate Nandāsayee's finishing her meditation, from their home village a day's ferry ride up the Irrawaddy, that village I had tried to imagine.

"Potograh," Nandāsayee insists, miming a snapshot. I go up to my room and load my last roll of fresh film into the Japanese idiot camera for this occasion in my friend's life. I expect to take one or two pictures of the family, but she grabs the camera and I have no heart to refuse her. I am still trying to keep my mind like a turtle in its shell. I pretend nothing is happening, stalk up and down in a fury while Nandāsayee poses her mother with a book, asks bystanders to photograph the two of them. Girls come out and learn to push the button, laugh at the automatic flash. I learn a new thing from the gross, grinning mother, that Burmese women wipe themselves on their sarongs and hide the wet spot in the front pleat. I see this while she is rearranging herself for a portrait.

"Sistah!" I sit on the steps with my eyes shut, feigning meditation. Nandāsayee's pushes my chin up a little, then stands back and clicks the shutter. When all thirty-six frames are shot, she brings me the camera; I remove the film and hand it to her, wondering how she will find the cash to develop it.

Nandāsayee explains that she will be a nun for life. I am happy for her. Her family is poor and she will now have the chance to go to the Thilashin-jaun, nuns' school. Maybe she'll even become fully enlightened and die, when it will be her time, into the unnameable beyond the suffering of name and form; maybe when she is cremated, her bones will reveal tiny crystals.

"Sister, give me bow-peh," she says angrily, plucking at my notebook. "Bow-peh, bow-peh!" She wants my ballpoint pen. Her soft features gather at the center of her face.

"No," I finally say. "I need this for myself."

Time is moving slowly, sir.

For one who cannot sleep, the night seems long. For a lazy meditator one hour seems long.

I have been trying to make an effort.

Then there should be more activity in your practice.

This little nun came just now and disrupted my walking period.

You find many objects of interest in the body. Then you see that what is in the body is boring, of no interest.

"PUSSY HAS DELIVER," Nurse Aye Shwe announced.

"What?"

"Your cat, is mother now."

I had given up walking in the breezeway. When in the evenings I didn't see the cat, I restrained myself from asking the nurse where she had gone. Now I was sent to peek under the stairs, where my cat crouched in awkward defensiveness over two orange kittens nearly as big as she was. Aha. Now I understood her belly's sad, hard bulge. One of the orange toms had often visited her on the breezeway. She'd snarled at him and cowered in the rain gutter. No wonder, I thought. But now I had to admit she seemed happy and fulfilled, as she curled herself, purring, round her suckling children.

At once I resumed stealing pork fat and giblets from lunch. I gave her Thai milk powder, full-fat. My effort to be perfect had lasted two weeks. Now, I rationalized, if I couldn't make it to enlightenment acting normally, I didn't want to get there.

Sīlānandā wrote me a note, which I tore up. "I think I'm close! Subtle lights! *Epace!*" Her arms were sticks.

IN THE MIDDLE OF THE RAINS, the Swiss woman set fire to a straw mat and was asked to leave. She said she would go to a great Hindu teacher, Sattya Ma, who took your head in her lap as if you were a two-year-old child. I thought it would be good for her to go where she could talk, touch, and spend all day in rituals of devotion.

"I must remain as nun," she said with Swiss determination. "Nothing in the world is good for me."

The kittens made wobbly appearances in our rooms at night, left runny piles in the hall. Their mother left them mewling to resume her vigils in the breezeway. The ringworm came back in two places on my head and one on my left breast. I asked for more Burmese cream, which was slow in coming. In the end, I had to go to a clap clinic in Bangkok and a doctor in Australia, and even now I believe the fungus may be dormant in my skin.

"You will never attain cessation with all your pets," the nurse grumbled. "I will give them to ol' lady. She will feed them, you can forget about."

"All right," I said. Sīlānandā was writing me notes of triumphant phenomena; I was determined to resume my progress.

The nurse took the kittens away in a box and blocked the lower half of the Foreigner Women's Dormitory gate with chicken wire. My little cat was confused; she cried heartbreakingly at the barrier day and night. I hardened my heart and remembered the nurse's threat to report me to the abbot. The witchy sweeper was the new mother and would feed the cat only rice scraps. But walking at night in the breezeway, I watched the cat tease and kill a black scorpion and convinced myself that she could catch the food she needed, despite being blind.

One afternoon she dragged her children back and forth in the pouring rain trying to bring them back to the stairwell. The babies died, Nurse Aye Shwe told me days later.

I had known nothing; I was in the meditation hall.

Their mother forgot the kittens long before I did. I saw her meditating under the breezeway, paws tucked under, vacant eyes afire, as enigmatic as an idol of the East.

I was tortured by guilty thoughts: I never should have agreed to the eviction of the little family; my selfish spiritual desire had cost two infant lives. Finally I realized there was nothing to be done anymore and I tried to follow the cat's example, living on calmly with my share of pain. In a way, I thought, it was better for her not to have those mouths to feed.

It didn't matter what I thought.

I tried to remember what time I sat down. I think it was eleven. I felt as if I had been sitting for two minutes, but actually an hour had passed.

How was your posture?

Straight.

Did you have any dreams?

No dreams.

How did you know the time had passed?

Consciousness came back when the gong sounded midnight.

This is all right. Please continue.

Why is this happening?

Maybe later I will tell you.

Puzzled by this interview, I compared "experiences" with Sīlānandā, and found that she had undergone the same sudden, extended vanishing of time. I ran to the abbot's cottage and asked whether this was cessation. He smiled with the utmost pride and indulgence and asked me whether I thought it was. "Yes," I hazarded. The experience repeated itself for shorter periods over the following week; the abbot had me and Sīlānandā listen to a tape that described the progress of meditation and various subtleties of cessation. At the end of the tape it said:

You must look in the mirror of the truth and see whether your experiences conform to this description, whether your cessation is genuine.

My teacher wanted me to work with resolves to strengthen the mind, but I was enervated, jumpy—after so much effort, neither able to make further rules for myself nor, much less, follow them. I asked for something new: the meditation on loving-kindness. He agreed and instructed me to repeat four phrases, constantly, in my mind.

May you be free from danger. May you be physically happy. May you be mentally happy. May you have ease of well-being.

Sir, should I listen to the sound of the sentences? Should I think about the meaning? Shoulder I consider the welfare of all beings, the objects of my good wishes?

Just practice and don't worry. Send your loving feeling.

It was absolutely different. My mind was on rails, a locomotive. The body swung free, unconstrained by perpetual attention. But shortly after I began this blissful practice, I realized that the sounds I'd taken for taxis backfiring in the neighborhood were gunshots.

I went to the nurse and asked her to tell me what was going on outside the walls.

"They break the law," she said, both vague and fierce. "Do not disturb your practice."

No one wanted me to disturb my practice; but I went from one person to another, parlaying one tiny piece of information into the right to hear another. The day a machine gun shattered the air—the loudest sound I'd ever heard—I knew that unarmed demonstrators were being mowed down. The people of Rangoon had risen against the military government. During the time I'd sat with my eyes shut inside Pingyan's high, thick walls, the prices of rice and oil had risen four hundred percent, so that a single measure of each now cost two weeks' average salary. Yesterday, in the poor suburb of Okkalappa, men had beheaded two police, cut out their hearts and livers, roasted and eaten them.

May you be free from danger. May you be physically happy.

A column of children, placed at the head of a peaceful prodemocracy demonstration, had been mowed down.

May you be mentally happy. May you have ease of well-being.

Curfew: we were forbidden to walk in sight of the main gate after five P.M. The food got worse: gray, thin gruel of rice with a few dried shrimp. Like what most Burmese have been eating, I thought. People went home; Nandāsayee, too, vanished like some spirit, without a good-bye. Pingyan was nine-tenths empty, as lonely as the sky without the moon.

A green viper slithered in the bush next to the water tank; I sent it loving-kindness.

After sundown, bullhorns started squawking lies and threats; the nuns retreated into certain rooms, closed the shutters, and listened to the BBC World Service. I heard that Western embassy personnel were being evacuated; Air Force plans were on alert in Thailand to rescue U.S. citizens in the event of a general emergency.

In the depths of the hot season, I'd taken to waking at two a.m., when the air was cool and I could walk as fast as I liked, wherever I liked, unseen except by the servant who rang the hourly bells. Wrapped in the softness of sleepers, dreamers, my wakefulness was thunderbolt and diamond; I loved to look up at the enormous mango tree near the Western men's quarters, an ink cumulonimbus blocking clots of stars.

Nights were a toxic yellow now, marred by the sound of troop trucks grinding into position for the next day's massacre. Shooting began after lunch, politely at eleven-thirty a.m., and lasted three hours.

The air felt as full of passionate love as of disaster. People were willing to die for better lives. People were dying right next to us, even though we couldn't see them, because of the monastery walls.

Sound is only sound, impermanent, ungovernable, a source of pain. Sound is a material object, a wave that strikes the sensitive consciousness at the ear door. Sound is not a story. It is not your thought, it is not the image you may see in your mind about what produced the sound. For hearing to occur, three elements are needed...

EACH NIGHT, the abbot dryly dissected the process at one of the sense doors: eye, ear, nose, tongue, body, and mind. But his discourse was cut to half an hour; then he disappeared behind the curtain, leaning on his translator's arm. I knew he was going into his bedroom to listen to the BBC.

Then he stopped giving discourses at all. Interviews were left to a handsome, twenty-two-year-old monk whose name meant "Beautiful Uncle." He told me he was not qualified to instruct me in loving-kindness practice. I wanted to go to the abbot, but the jalousies and curtains were closed, and Nurse Aye Shwe was visiting the cottage twice a day, carrying a steel kidney pan covered with a handkerchief.

"Heart," she told me. Flicking up the handkerchief, she let me glimpse bottles of medicine, a blood pressure bulb.

"Has he had a heart attack?"

"No, but his heart is sick."

May you be free from danger. May you be physically happy. May you be mentally happy. May you have ease of well-being.

The phrases ground through my brain unlubricated; I began to wonder whether it was appropriate for me to stay in Rangoon. Who could possibly benefit from my presence? I went to the monastery's vice president, who reassured me. "Don't be afraid. Even besieged, we have rice and dried fish to keep you for a year. All Burmese respect a monastery, even the army."

I wasn't afraid for myself, but I imagined some U.S. Marine wading through a sea of blood to reach me, and dying—or the monastery officials gunned down for harboring me, like the doctors and nurses who'd rushed to the doors of Rangoon Hospital in an effort to protect their patients.

At last I went to the abbot's cottage. First I stood on his porch a long time, wavering. His Chinese clock played the first bar of *Eine Kleine Nachtmusik*. The house was dark, forbidding, thick with the smell of an unwashed body.

When I pushed open the door, I'd forgotten that a bell would jangle. *Come in,* he said in Burmese.

He was alone, staring at the inner side of the monastery's high, thick outer wall. "They kill those children," he said.

He spoke in English; I hadn't known he could.

BUT HE'D SPOKEN ENGLISH TO ME ONCE BEFORE. One morning, early in my stay at Pingyan, he'd come up quietly behind me as I was doing walking meditation.

"Sumanā?" he asked, gently prolonging the syllables. He always said my name so, as if in indulgent reproof.

I turned to look at him, a shaven old man a foot shorter than I was, leaning on his telescoping aluminum alpenstock. It had been a gift from some European student.

"Anything?" he'd said. Meaning, anything you need?

"Anything?"

"Anything?"

How will anyone believe in us now?

No one disbelieves in one person because of another person's unrelated crimes. As for me, my mind cannot be changed. It's settled now, because of meditation.

Good…

But I want to leave.

You want to give back your robes and precepts of morality?

I don't want anyone getting killed on my account.

That will never happen.

My parents are surely worrying.

I cannot stop the waterfall.

Thank you. I'm sorry.

We have not offered you a proper atmosphere.

No! You've influenced your students deeply—for life. Me, for example. I know there is no happiness to be found in outward things now. It's something deeper than mere belief. I've seen it for myself.

Then it should be easy for you to remain celibate. For life?

I don't know…maybe a year.

One year. Okay!

Wily old fisherman.

I held a meeting with the Foreigner Women and explained that I would leave on the first day it was safe to do so. No one wanted to come: they were in deep, practicing without regard for body or life. They didn't want to lose their time. Sīlānandā was making resolves, finding that her mind obeyed her automatically.

As it turned out, the shooting soon stopped: the army had suppressed the uprising, with four thousand dead.

But I'd already ridden to the airport with the British vice-consul's wife and daughter. We were driven in a white Land Rover down a blockaded road, lined with gray trucks full of terrified fifteen-year-old conscripts. This was the murderous army. Its helmets slid over its eyes, its rifles trembled at the ready. Even if I'd had film, I wouldn't have dared raise my camera into view.

Soon I was fingering the thick, slick paper of the airline magazine, gazing at a color photo of two women leaning across a grand piano in identical, black, backless silken gowns, advertising the state of mind that could be induced by perfume.

I took the long way home, stopping for a rest on the beaches of South Thailand, where the world's most avant-garde sybarites go to play. There I ate well and lay in the sun, my body slowly thickening into concreteness. I didn't know whether I was ahead of the game or behind it. Milanese women played in the surf, the tops of their bathing suits rolled down.

There'd be no kamikaze operation: I'd smuggle no boxes of medicines to Rangoon Hospital.

I could not stop the whirling of this world.

Was removing myself not, truly, the best that I could do? So the Burmese taught.

The Buddha said, *Long have you wandered, and filled the graveyards full. You have shed enough tears on this long way to fill the four great oceans.*

On my last day on Koh Samui, I spotted another woman with hair as short as my ex-nun's fuzz. Blond sparks in the sunrise: she picked her way across the hummocky white sand as delicately as my cat crossing rain gutters, leaning heavily on her boyfriend's arm. She wore a baggy, faded purple dress; she looked wonderful.

I was sitting cross-legged, facing the pale coralline sea from which a cooked red ball was rising. Exquisite light. The world was as delicate as baby skin.

Sister, my mind called out.

Suddenly I realized she was mind-blown, blitzed, so high on acid or the much-advertised local mushrooms that she could hardly walk

EUROPEAN CHOCOLATE. Fresh fish. Green salads. Long before arriving in the "United State," I had confirmed Nurse Aye Shwe's prediction: "Now your virtue will go down. You will eat at night, you will eat whenever you like." Generous, she was. But I kept the promise I gave to the abbot of a year's celibacy, and I dedicated any merit that might arise to the Burmese people.

I also followed his injunction not to describe cessation. There could have been a way to talk about it, but really there was nothing to describe, for there had been no experience, nothing on which to base a statement. Afterward I felt different, but not in any way I could grasp. This bothered me, subtly, pervasively. I might say it was as if I now had a hole at the bottom of my consciousness rather than any solid foundation; but this was difficult to assess.

Difficult to build any sense of achievement, even of event, on no basis. Why had I gone to Burma? What had I done there?

For a year I embodied the qualities the tape had said would reveal themselves as signs of a true cessation. I never lied, I didn't drink a drop, I had no interest in sex or money. I lived in an apartment as small and dark as Nurse Aye Shwe's rooms on the first floor of the Foreigner Women's Quarters. I felt happy to think that I no longer was a candidate for hell or rebirth in the animal realm.

And I wrote letter to my senators, asking them to remember the plight of Burma.

One night my father came to my city and took me out to a very good restaurant. He is a Republican businessman, but he'd found a way to be proud of my exploits in Burma by comparing me to some of the grand Victorian women travelers who "dressed in burnouses and went everywhere on camels." At this dinner he proposed a toast to me and my adventures. I didn't stop him from filling my glass with French wine. After he raised his glass to me, I took an experimental sip, just to see if I was capable. The first drop told me I was capable of anything.

That drop would have brought my kittens back to life; as I drank it, the monastery gates closed behind me. The most rigorous enlightenment system in the world shut me out. Or so I felt that night, not understanding my own rigorousness.

"Here's to you, too, Dad," I said, and drank the rest of the glass. I didn't quite know how I'd go on living, but I knew that I must.

Anne Donovan

Buddha Da

T WIS DAURK when ah got there and ma heid wis wasted drivin on they wee twisty roads. Ah parked the van and went intae the hoose. It wis a huge buildin, used tae be a hotel or sumpn afore the lamas took it ower. In the hall wis this big skinny guy, blue robes an a shaved heid. Wisnae Tibetan though, sounded dead posh.

"Excuse me," he says. "Could you leave your shoes in the porch please?"

"Sure thing, pal," ah says, feelin a bit stupit when ah turnt round and seen rows a boots and shoes and a big sign: "Please leave all outer footwear in the porch. Slippers only to be worn inside the house."

Course ah'd nae slippers so ah hud tae go aboot in ma stockin soles, and did ah no huv a big hole comin in the toe ae the right yin. Just as well Liz wisnae here—she'd huv been mortified. The big guy stauns waitin while ah take aff ma boots.

"Hope yous've got air freshener in here," ah says, but he just looks at me.

"My name is Vishanadanashonta." (Well, it wis sumpn like that. Ah didnae like tae ask him tae repeat it.)

"Jimmy McKenna," ah says, puttin oot ma haund but he just bows.

"I think everyone else has arrived. We're about to eat."

"Thank God. Ah could murder a plate a mince and tatties."

Ah wis jokin, ah knew the food wis aw vegetarian, but he just looks at me as if ah'm daft.

"Only jokin, Rinpoche."

"I'm not actually called Rinpoche," he says. "I'm a trainee. I haven't taken my final vows."

"Sorty apprentice, ur ye?"

"You could say that."

He opens the door on tae the main room. At the far end was a log fire wi cushions and bean bags piled roond, and in the middle were three wooden tables. Aboot thirty folk were sittin at them. The caundles on the tables and the firelight made it look kinda welcomin, but ah wis feelin definately ooty place.

"There's a chair here," says Vishanawhitsisface.

Ah sits doon at the endy the table next tae a young guy wi a shaved heid and aboot twenty-five earrings on the wan ear. Vishana pits a bowl a soup in fronty me and the wee guy passes doon a plate wi big dods a breid cut up rough on it. Ah get wired intae the soup. It wis good, dead thick wi loads a different veggies in it. "Pass us the butter, pal," ah says tae the wee guy.

"It's soya margarine," he says. "There's a lot of vegans here."

"Aw well, it's good tae mix wi folk fae another planet, intit?"

He doesnae answer, so ah try again.

"Didnae know they hud Buddhists on Vega, but. Thought they were aw Mormons there."

The wee guy nods and cairries on eatin his soup, and the auld guy opposite just looks at me as if ah'm the wan that's come fae another planet. Ah'm beginnin tae panic a bit. Ah wis really lookin forward tae this retreat but so far it's hard gaun. Then ah catch the eye of a wumman on the other side ae the table, coupla seats doon. She's smilin at me and ah'm no sure but ah think she actually winked.

Anyway at this point Vishana comes back and asks if anybody wants mair soup, and ah says, "Thanks a lot but ah'll hang on fur the next course."

"There's fruit for the next course," he says.

The wumman across saves me.

"Have some more soup," she says. Her voice is quite posh but no English, mair Edinburgh or sumpn. "You've just arrived, haven't you? You must be hungry."

"Aye," ah says, and Vishana ladles oot mair soup.

"Thanks, pal, it's great soup."

"Thank you," says he, "I made it myself."

Efter we've finished we get a cuppa tea and sit roond the fire while Vishana tells us aboot the weekend. Meditation three times a day and teachin every mornin. Efternoons free. We've got chores as well, makin meals, washin up and that. Ma job is choppin the veggies the morra efternoon. And then there's the boy scout bit—nae bevy, nae fags, boys on wan sidey the hoose, lassies on the ither. Ah didnae expect a Buddhist retreat tae be an orgy but there wis a couple there, merriet and all, and they wouldnae even be sleepin in the same room. Ah thought that wis a bit weird.

"Any other questions?" asks Vishana. Naebdy says anythin. He smiles. "All we ask of you this weekend is that you stay mindful. Pay attention."

Surely that couldnae be too difficult, no for a weekend.

THE FIRST MEDITATION SESSION WAS AT NINE O'CLOCK THAT NIGHT. The meditation room wis separate fae the main part of the buildin, a big shed wi high windaes and cushions and blankets on the flair just like the wan in the centre. At the far end wis a statue of the Buddha, sittin in the lotus position wi his eyes shut.

We filed in, efter takin aff wer shoes in the cloakroom, and took up wer places. Ah thought ah wis gettin a loat better wi this sittin cross-legged but at the centre it was only fur twenty minutes at a time. And ah don't know if it wis bein tired efter a day's work, or the drivin or whit, but ah couldnae sit still. Vishana talked us through the mindfulness a breathin meditation but ah couldnae settle. Ah kept fidgetin, and every time ah made the slightest wee movement ah felt as if everybuddy could hear it, cos it wis dead quiet except fur some guy ower tae ma right somewhere who sounded as if he wis on a life support system.

And as fur ma mind. Mindfulness aye, but no the way Vishana meant. Ma mind wis full aw right—thoughts fleein aboot lik motors on a racin track. Vroom, vroom, wan efter anither. And the main wan that kept comin up wis whit the fuck are you daein here? Ah couldnae stop thinkin aboot the look on Liz's face when ah went oot this mornin.

"See you on Sunday night, hen."

"So you're gaun, are you?"

"Ah've said..."

"Aye, ah know. Well, have a nice time."

Ah'd went tae kiss her but she turnt her face away and that wis whit kept comin back tae me as ah tried tae focus on ma breathin. That picture ae her staundin in the kitchen, butterin toast, wi her back tae me and just the line of her neck, tense, held in. If she'd only shouted at me, chucked the toast at me, that'd have been OK; ah can haundle that, blow up blow doon, but ah hate this no sayin.

Then the next thing ah know, the meditation's ower and we're back in the big room. Ah thought we'd sit roond the fire, get tae know each ither a bit but Vishana mair or less tells us tae get tae wer beds.

"Early start tomorrow morning. Meditation at 6:00 in the prayer room. See you all there."

Turnt oot ah wis sharin wi the wee guy wi the earrings and another tall, skinny bloke wi straggly grey hair tied back in a pony tail. Ex-hippy lookin. The room had three mattresses on the flair and ah chucked ma sleepin bag and rucksack on the wan unner the windae.

"Ah'm Jimmy McKenna," ah says, stickin oot ma haund. The big guy takes it and gies it a squeeze.

"Jed," he says. "Glad to meet you." Sounded a bit American.

"Gary," says the young guy, and turns his back, takin stuff oot his rucksack.

"Have yous been here afore, then?"

"I've been a few times, yeah," says Jed. "I go to other workshops too, though, not just Buddhist ones, go round them all, get a taste of everything, you know."

"Aye, right enough," ah says. "You don't need tae just support the wan team. Whit aboot you, pal?"

Gary's footerin aboot, pittin a wee widden statue of the Buddha on tae the shelf above his mattress. He doesnae turn roond.

"Ah've been coming for the past three years."

"You must be pure brilliant at this meditation lark then. God, that wis heavy gaun the night. Ma mind wis birlin."

"Some days it's like that," says Jed. "Best to accept it."

"Suppose so. It wis hard gaun at first, never thought ah'd get the hang ae it. It's just that ah thought ah wis gettin better, know?"

Jed laughs. "That's fatal."

Ah take oot a hauf bottle a Bells fae ma rucksack. "Fancy a nip, pal?"

Jed pits his haund up. "Woah, that stuff's poison. No wonder you're having a problem with focusing."

"Ah wisnae drinkin afore the meditation, but. It's just a nightcap."

"Yeah, but you're relying on it to make you feel better. It's addictive."

"Look, ah'm no an alkie, pal. Ah just like a wee bevy, right."

Jed put baith his haunds up. "Hey, it's cool, whatever. I'm just saying, it doesn't really make for clarity. And that's why we're here, right?"

Ah climbed intae ma sleepin bag, took a few swallys oot the bottle. The whisky went doon warm and rough ower ma throat. Ma body stertit tae heat up inside the sleepin bag and the tiredness hit me. Whit wis ah here fur? Fuck knows.

AH WIS NAE CLEARER THE NEXT MORNIN when ah got woken up at quarter tae six wi a bell ringin in ma ear. At furst ah thought it wis a fire drill or sumpn then ah remembered the meditation. No way. Ah turnt ower and went back tae sleep. Next thing ah knew Jed wis shakin me and the sun wis streamin through the windae.

"Christ, whit time is it?"

"Quarter to nine. The teaching starts in fifteen minutes. Thought maybe you'd like to be there."

"Thanks, pal."

Ah scrambled up and intae ma claes, splashed ma face wi cauld watter and got doon the stair in time tae grab a plate a cornflakes and a cuppa tea afore the session. They're aw sittin in this big dinin room, some on chairs set oot in a hauf-circle, ithers sittin on the flair, cross-legged. Vishana's in the lotus position at the front and beside him is a big vase a lilies.

Ah grab a seat at the back. Ma mooth feels like the insidey a budgie's cage: no that ah'd drank much whisky last night, it's just ah need aboot three mugs a tea afore ah come to in the mornin and ah'd only hud time fur wan. Ah'd nae time tae brush ma teeth either and the cornflakes were stickin tae them. Ah kept tryin tae dislodge them wi ma tongue. Ma arse is numb wi sittin on this plastic seat and ma mind sterts tae wander ootside where the trees are swayin aboot in the wind. They're pure beautiful, so they are, leaves turnin gold an red and bronze; ah love they autumn colours. Ah wanted tae paint a room in the hoose in them, thought it'd be nice in the bedroom, but Liz didnae fancy it. That's the thing aboot bein a painter, ye spend yer time paintin folk's hooses but you never get the chance tae pick the colours. Maisty the time ah don't gie a toss; it's ma job, and there's a kind a satisfaction in watchin a wall turn fae sumpn dingy and streaky tae clean and fresh. Just watchin the paintbrush travellin doon the wall, know, takin the colour wi it, that's enough. Ah've been daein it fur twenty year and ah still think it's the goods.

Suddenly ah realised that Vishana'd stoapped talkin and everybuddy wis lookin at me.

"Jimmy?"

"Sorry, Rinpoche, ah was in a dwam. Whit were you sayin?"

"I was asking how you found the meditation. How's it been since you arrived?"

"Well, tae tell the truth, it's a bit heavy gaun."

"In what way?"

"Ma mind keeps fleein. Ah cannae concentrate. And ah thought ah wis gettin a bit better at it."

"Sometimes it's like that. You just have to sit it out. I noticed you looked a little uncomfortable last night. You know you don't have to sit on the floor. You could use a chair if it's easier."

"Ah thought it wis the right way, at the centre they tellt us tae sit on the flair so's we were grounded."

Vishana smiled. There wis sumpn smarmy aboot him ah didnae like. Mibbe it wis his English accent or the way he wis dressed in they robes when he wisnae a real Tibetan or that, but he just got right up ma nose.

"Ideally, yes, but you have to remember that in the east people are used to sitting cross-legged from childhood. They don't use chairs."

"Ah know that."

"We can't expect to learn to sit in a short space of time. Sometimes it's better to forget about sitting in the lotus position. Just be comfortable and you can focus on the actual meditation."

"OK. Ah'll try it."

"I think I might try it that way too."

It was the wumman who'd spoke up last night when we were havin wer soup. She'd been sittin in the lotus position when we were meditatin.

"I find I get a sore back if I sit too long. Maybe I've been getting hung up on getting the position right."

"It's your choice," says Vishana.

At the coffee break the wumman came ower and sat beside me. She wis tall wi her hair cut dead short and she'd these big dangly earrings jinglin fae her lugs. It wis hard tae work oot whit age she wis; could of been anythin fae thirty-five tae forty-five. She wis dressed in black wi a flowery-patterned shawl thing flung ower her shooders.

"I'm Barbara," she says.

"Jimmy McKenna."

"You're from Glasgow?"

"And me wi ma posh voice on."

"I lived in Glasgow for three years; I really liked it. Beautiful buildings."

"Where d'you stay noo?"

"Edinburgh. My home town."

"Edinburgh's nice too. Anne Marie likes the castle and we used tae go tae thon Museum a Childhood when she was wee. Gettin big fur it noo."

"Anne Marie's your daughter? "

"Aye."

"How old?"

"She's twelve. First year at secondary. Looks aulder though. Big fur her age. Huv you any weans?"

"No." She lifts her coffee cup. "Better put this back. I think we're starting again. See you later."

"Aye, right."

The next session Vishana talked aboot reincarnation. This wis sumpn ah couldnae get ma heid roond. As far as ah'm concerned, wanst yer deid, yer deid. Aw the stuff ah wis brought up wi, heaven and hell and limbo and the next life—that wis daft enough, but compared tae reincarnation it sounded dead sensible. Ah mean, at least you're the same person livin yer life here on earth, then gaun somewhere else. Simple. But if yer reincarnatin aw the time, how come you don't remember who you were in the previous life? Or are you somebuddy different each time?

Somehow it hud never mattered afore, in the centre wi the lamas. Ah knew they believed in aw that stuff but ah'd never really bothered tae find oot aboot it. It wis enough just tae go there, dae a meditation, have a cuppa tea and go hame. Ah liked bein wi them; they were that funny and the way they looked at you made you feel good. But this Vishana guy—ah knew it wisnae really his fault but it's no the same. So ah just sat, lookin oot the windaes at the trees, ma belly rumblin, waiting fur the dinner break.

Mair soup fur lunch, left ower fae last night, but this time it hudnae been heated up enough. Ah hate soup that's lukewarm, but naebuddy else seemed that bothered; they were either eatin away in silence or discussin reincarnation.

"Who do you think you were in a past life, Alice?" says a big wifie wi died jet black hair hingin roond her heid like a witch.

"Cleopatra," says her pal, shovin her hair back so it didnae dangle intae the soup. It's funny, aw the folk on this retreat either have their hair long and straggly or else dead short

"Come on," says the pal. "Everyone says they were Cleopatra. Nobody ever thinks they were ordinary."

"I can dream, can't I ? How about you?" she says, noddin at me. "Who d'you think you were in a past life?'

"Huvny a scooby, missus. Tae tell the truth, ah don't really unnerstaund this reincarnation lark."

She and her pal start laughin. "Hark at you," says Alice. "If you understood it, you wouldn't be here, would you?"

Ah couldnae figure oot if they were laughin at me or no, but ah wis saved havin tae reply by Jed, who said, in a slow, serious voice, "Surely, the point isn't where we came from, but where we're going."

Gary pipes up. "Yeah, it doesn't matter who we used to be in a past life, but who we're going to be in the next life."

"I thought we were supposed to stay in the present," says Barbara.

Alice's pal stopped eatin and held her soup spoon in the air as if she wis blessin us. "Truly being in the present encompasses both the past and the future. You have to hold them all together as one."

"Amen, oh great one," says Alice. "You hit enlightenment today, Shirley?"

"Just call me Cleopatra," she says, turnin back tae her soup.

AH D AN HOUR TAE KILL AFORE AH D TAE GO and chop the veggies fur the dinner so ah went oot fur a walk. The roads roond the centre were dead quiet and it wis beautiful there, rough fields wi sheep grazin, trees turnin autumn colours. It's no sumpn ah dae much, go fur walks. Sometimes if we've a job on ootside Glesga ah drive through the countryside but ah'm aye hash-bashin alang in the van wi the guys, music blarin, no lookin at the scenery.

The conversation at dinner time had made me feel better. Alice and her pal were a laugh, and the way everybuddy wis talkin sounded as if they wereny sure whit it wis aw aboot either. Mibbe ah wisnae that daft efter aw. And there wis sumpn, no exactly excitin, couldnae find the word fur it— ah suppose mibbe you'd say stimulatin if it didnae sound sexy—but any- way, sumpn aboot listenin tae folk talkin aboot ideas, things ye couldnae quite unnerstaund. Ah mean the guys ah work wi wid be cartin ye aff tae the funny farm if ye tried tae have a serious conversation, and wi John it's the footie and Liz and me it's Anne Marie or the hoose or that. There's nae- buddy that talks aboot anythin beyond the day tae day.

AH NEVER WANT TAE SEE ANOTHER FUCKIN CARROT IN MA LIFE. Hate the orange bastards. Mountains of them in a basket in the corner of the kitchen—ah'll be in a basket in the corner by the time ah've finished chop- pin them. No that ah mind choppin a few veggies, it's no that. It's just, why don't they gie folk chores they're good at? There's this wee skinny lassie, anither wanny the pierced brigade, and she's cartin in huge logs for the fire. Ah offered tae help but she looked at me as if ah'd pit ma haund up her skirt. She's practically cairryin them in wan at a time cos they're that big fur her, and ah could of done them in five seconds flat. Ah like choppin wood an ah know how tae dae it right, worked on the forestry wan summer years ago up north.

Carrots, on the other hand, are no ma forte. Jeez, ye huvtae manhandle them tae get them tae stay on the choppin board, they keep skitin aff every time ah pit this knife in them, and as fur the shape—well ah hope they're no expectin nouvelle cuisine. No that the knife helps. It's as blunt as buggery, which is why next minute ah'm staundin here lookin like a scene fae Reservoir Dogs.

Barbara puts a clean tea towel roond ma haund but in a few seconds the blood's soaked through.

"That's a deep cut. Press hard on to the wound—there must be a first aid kit around."

Vishana appears and leads me intae a wee room aff the kitchen where he produces a green box fulla plasters and dressins. Ah let him get on wi it, cannae bear tae look at things like that.

"This is nasty. Keep the pressure on it for a few more minutes til the blood loss slows down, then I'll clean it up and dress it. Hold tight."

"Ah'm ur haudin tight."

"How d'you do it?"

"Choppin carrots. Hope there's no a bit of finger in the stew the night. Bitty a shock fur aw they vegetarians."

"It won't be the first time." He cracked a wee smile. "You're not used to chopping carrots, I take it. Or do you prefer them with bits of flesh in them?"

"Ah'm better at choppin wood actually. How come you don't gie chores tae folk that can dae them best?"

Vishana slowly unwound the tea towel. The blood was still flowin, but no as bad.

"Getting better." He started tae dab at the wound wi a bit a cotton wool. "This may sting a bit."

He wisnae kiddin.

"So, Jimmy, you think people should get to pick which chores they're going to do?'

"Might make mair sense—ah mean, thon wee lassie that wis choppin the logs..."

"You think she should have chopped the carrots?"

"No necessarily choppin carrots, but she could of done sumpn else she'd be mair suited to."

Vishana took a dressin oot a sealed pack.

"Cleaning the toilets, perhaps."

"Aw, come on, ah never said that."

"You suggested people do the chores they're most familiar with. Most women are more used to cleaning toilets than men are."

"Aye but ah'm no meanin tae be sexist; it's just that some jobs need strength."

"And some need other things."

He wrapped the dressin roond ma haund and pressed doon on it haurd.

"Jimmy, I understand what you're saying, but we allocate jobs on a random basis, not just to be fair but because sometimes you can learn more from doing an unfamiliar job you find difficult rather than one you can do easily." He smiled. "Reflect on it. While you're chopping the rest of the carrots."

But when ah got back intae the kitchen Barbara'd practically finished them.

"Thanks," ah said. "Can ah dae sumpn?"

"It's OK, that's them," she says, scrapin the last of them aff the choppin board intae a big bowl. "Take them over to Simon; he'll put them in the stew."

"Right." They were that neat the way she'd done them, no the big dods ah'd managed. "How d'you get them that neat wi thon blunt knife?"

Barbara's wipin the choppin board and the worksurface wi a cloth. She turns roond. "I sharpened it. Didn't you see this?" She points tae a big eletric knife sharpener at the other end ae the worksurface.

"Eh, naw, never seen it." How could ah have missed it? Never dawned on me tae look fur it of course. See whit Vishana wis sayin is all very well, but that's it, in't it. A wumman thinks tae sharpen a knife that's blunt but a man just goes on choppin wi it and ends up cuttin hissel.

That night in the prayer room, ah sat listenin tae the rain. Ah'd gied up on the meditaion, couldnae concentrate again. Ah wis tired and everythin that had happened ower the weekend so far wis churnin away inside me; the new folk, the stuff ah couldnae unnerstaund, Vishana and they fuckin carrots, and ah felt weary in ma bones. Ah'd taken Vishana's advice and sat on a chair insteid ae tryin tae dae the cross-legged bit, and ah fund ma fingers drummin on ma leg in time tae its rhythm. Ah stopped and pit ma haunds on ma legs, just rested them there and listened. The prayer room had a glass roof and you could hear every drap; some plip-ploppin, some squelchin and some thumpin doon as if they were gonnae break it. And somehow ah fund masel follyin the raindraps as they landed on the roof, no really listenin, no anythin, just sittin. Sometimes it got a bit heavier and sometimes the wind would blaw it soft, makin wee skittery noises, like an animal scratchin.

And it wis like the rain wis alive, know, and everythin in the prayer room seemed tae disappear, couldnae hear anybuddy or see anythin; it wis just me and the rain.

Samantha Schoech

The Good People of Lake George

A T THE LAKE, it is all her father's friends. People from New York who dress too well for Vermont and complain about the food. Bland bread. No bagels. You have to schlep up your own wine. They are funny people with book-lined shelves and a collection of music that spans many generations. Their haircuts are relentlessly good. Celeste has always liked them, but ever since her move to San Francisco they make her feel exhausted. She has spent the three days since her arrival at the lake house draping herself over the furniture and flipping through outdated magazines.

The lake itself shimmers like a piece of aluminum foil someone has crumpled and then tried to flatten out again. It is too cold to go swimming. The boat is broken. People sit around on the deck reading the *Atlantic Monthly* and drinking cup after cup of the good coffee, imported to New York via a fair-trade company in Nicaragua, until it is cocktail hour when they switch first to gin and tonics and then to wine, whatever Harry brings up from the cellar.

Celeste can spend an amazing amount of time staring. She sits on the deck, or just inside, on the wicker chairs, with a magazine flattened in her lap, watching the subtle shift of light and wind on the surface of the lake. Sometimes, the conversation will turn to her and she will have to admit she wasn't paying attention. Her father's friends, each twenty-five years her senior, smile and nod and make little jokes about how someday she will relish time away from her husband; someday all she'll want to do is spend a holiday weekend at the lake while he stays behind working. She smiles, lips closed, because, really, what is she supposed to say?

CELESTE SLEEPS IN THE SHRINE ROOM on a fold-out couch that is more comfortable than her bed at home. At night she lies between the soft cotton sheets and studies Harry's shrine: incense, candles, Buddha, color photographs of his teacher with his wide, shining, Tibetan face. Apparently *every*one in Vermont is now a Buddhist. There are things on the altar she cannot identify, little significant trinkets. A short, knobbed piece of black wood above the door. A painting of a fierce black god with many arms. Chocolate kisses in a dish of uncooked rice. She thinks this must be an offering. She knows just enough to know she doesn't know very much. But, still, her father calls her a natural, tells her she's a Buddhist at heart. She's not so sure, but she enjoys the feeling of belonging to these people and their witty opinions and good-quality things.

She inventories the shrine because she knows it will be a long time before Harry comes. He is still up talking to her father about jazz and when they are through he will have to wait until he is sure everybody in the house is asleep before he creeps across the wide wood planks of his summer home into the shrine room where she sleeps. She doesn't like to fall asleep before he comes, so she waits up for him, letting her eyes grow accustomed to the light from the bright Vermont moon and listening to her father claim that Thelonious Monk was not only a genius but something of a bodhisattva. He has moved on to scotch. She can hear the ice clink as he sips.

HARRY IS GETTING LOAFY. His summer-tanned legs are still strong and muscular, but his torso is thickening and his shoulders are becoming soft. His chest hair is turning white and it sticks out of his collar as if he's been flocked. Still, he is handsome. Celeste studies him when she believes no one is watching and she decides he is handsome because he believes he is. This is his house and his wine cellar and his music collection. Pretty little Robin with her perfectly straight blond bob and her flat, flat stomach that long ago produced two athletic sons, is also his. Harry is charming and magnanimous. If you are at his house, he will give you anything.

Still, despite his generosity and opulence, people talk about him behind his back. He is arrogant. He is too opinionated in a group full of too-opinionated people. They do not like his book collection so well; it is pretentious and there is speculation about how much he actually reads. If he weren't such a wine snob, dinner would be so much more relaxed. Why must he act as if he is teaching everybody all the time?

Her father takes turns defending Harry and criticizing him. They pick at each other like adolescent brothers, not like men in deepening middle age, men with bad backs and sagging cheeks.

"Lighten up," Celeste can hear Harry say in the living room. And her father responds, "*You* lighten up. I'm just saying something that you don't want to hear, so you're getting aggressive."

Once, when they were driving home from the lake, Celeste's father told her, "Harry is the best friend I have ever had or ever will have. I just wish I liked him better."

THERE IS NO CLOCK IN THE SHRINE ROOM, but Celeste knows it is nearly two by the time she hears Harry's heavy footsteps tiptoeing across the house. She wonders, as she often does, how many other people know what is going on, and then feels the familiar sting of anxiety at the thought.

Harry opens the door and she can see his bulky frame in the dim light of the moon. He is naked except for his boxer shorts, which accentuate his loafyness. He slips in beside her and slides a heavy hand across her exposed stomach. Celeste thinks they will not make love. Harry is too drunk and this affair is seven years old already, almost like a marriage. Their sex life has thinned and even though she has moved 3000 miles away, there is little urgency between them anymore.

"Your father," he says to her. She can smell red wine. A Burgundy from the eighties was what they were drinking when she went to bed.

"Shhh," she says, turning towards him and cupping his jaw.

"Sorry. But, God, I thought he'd never shut up. I missed you terribly this past month."

Celeste smiles and leans in to kiss his cheek. Harry turns and presses his lips to hers, breathing heavily through his nose. She is amused by his sudden passion; she knows he is making the effort for her benefit. It is his constant fear that he is not satisfying her.

"I missed you, too," she says. "California is so far away. We better get used to it."

"California. Of all places. I can never picture you there. Aren't you a bit smart for them?"

"Not smarter, but I do have a better sense of irony."

Harry laughs and moves his head away from hers to get a better look at her in the dim, gray light. "And who is this Ian fellow, anyway? How is it that such a baby could steal you away from me?"

Celeste wished many times in the last few days that Ian had been able to come with her to the lake. Instead, he is in San Francisco, their new home, living the resident's life of no sleep, bad food, case after case of things Celeste finds disgusting: infections and boils—raw, moist things not meant to be exposed.

It is so hard to explain her father's friends to Ian out of context. She tried over the phone the night before to tell him about the spontaneous dance party they'd had in the living room. How all of them had kicked off their shoes and danced raucously to Aretha Franklin and later, after they had switched from wine to brandy, how they sang along with old protest songs, belting out "try to love one another right now" into the still Vermont night. She thinks of Ian sitting in their small apartment. In her mind's eye he is smiling, but she is sure he doesn't quite get it, that there is some essential quality about these people that he does not understand.

"He's my husband and you've met him. You might remember our wedding, or then again, you probably don't." Harry had passed out well before the dancing began.

Harry turns towards the shrine, taking it in for a few moments and then changes the subject. "If that were a crucifix instead of a Buddha, we wouldn't be able to do what I hope we're about to do in here." He drops his head back against the pillow and sighs.

Unlike most of the people in what her father refers to as "the community," Harry is not Jewish. His family is Irish, what he likes to call "the Jews of Catholicism." Eight siblings, complete with priest, dead father and drinking problems.

"If that were a crucifix, we wouldn't be here in the first place. I don't know a single practicing Catholic. They scare me."

"That's your mistake," Harry says, sliding his hand over her breasts and leaning down to kiss her again. "Catholics are safe. It's the Buddhists you have to watch out for."

ON SATURDAY, CELESTE, HER FATHER, Robin, and Mariah, an old friend of theirs who Celeste was supposed to remember from childhood but didn't, decide to go for a hike in the White Mountains. Harry, who does not have the patience for group outings, decides at the last minute to stay home. Nobody objects. He would be intolerable anyway.

The four of them ride through the crazy green hills of Vermont and New Hampshire ensconced in the plush leather seats of Robin's latest luxury car. The stereo softly plays Bach as they gossip.

"I so prefer the women," her father says again. "Women are such great conversationalists." He is driving, glancing back frequently at Robin and Mariah as they tell moderately vicious stories about their mutual friends. Celeste, who remembers some of these friends and has never met others, drifts in and out of the conversation, preferring to watch the passing thickets of green and consider her situation, how she is going to end her affair with Harry with what she hopes will be a degree of grace.

"I don't think she would mind if they were just fucking. That's the agreement from what I understand. But, Karen has become like a wife to him. It's too much, really." The conversation has turned to Karen, Celeste's father's most recent ex-wife. Celeste watches her father. His eyes flit back and forth between the road and the rearview mirror.

He says, "It will come to a bad end. It will be Karen who gets hurt because I certainly cannot see the fellow leaving his wife. He won't leave her. We never do." He smiles because this is not true. He left his third wife for Karen.

"I saw them at the Midsummer's Day party," says Mariah. "They were completely out in the open. She was like his girlfriend. I think that's just tacky."

"Love is a powerful thing," Celeste's father says. "It is what it is."

"I mean," Robin says, as if continuing a sentence. "People do what they do. This is just another *thing*. It might be full of confusion, but it's just another thing." She sits forward in her seat, the diamonds gleaming in her ears.

Celeste folds her arms and concentrates on the blurring green of the roadside. Soon, they will get out of the car and she can walk ahead of them, using her youth as an excuse to leave them behind.

"Celeste, I can tell you don't approve," Robin adds.

Celeste's father asks, "Approve of what? Are we getting rancorous now?" He looks at the back seat and explains, "Robin and Karen have remained friends."

Celeste feels the familiar heat in her cheeks as her throat constricts. She cries too easily. She takes a deep, wavering breath that gives her away and says, "What do you mean 'it is what it is?' Jesus, Dad, I'm not trying to be moralistic, but what about being nice? Aren't Buddhists supposed to be nice?" Her eyes blur and she looks up at the padded roof while tears roll down her face and catch in her ears. No one is looking at her.

"You're right," Mariah says. "We should be nicer. God! I'm such a gossip."

"I don't mean *that*," Celeste says. "I mean, shouldn't we disapprove more of things like affairs? Shouldn't we say that they are a bad thing? That people are being hurt?"

In the front seat, Robin exhales through her nose and throws up her hands. "Affairs happen all the time. They are as much a part of life as marriage. People do get hurt—you're right. But there's no point in getting all prissy about it."

"I'm not talking about getting prissy." Celeste's voice is stronger now. "I'm just trying to figure out how you are supposed to love someone. How are you supposed to be good if nothing is bad?"

"Your problem is vocabulary," her father says. "Good and bad are not particularly helpful words."

THE TRAIL UP THE MOUNTAIN IS MORE LIKE AN AVALANCHE of rocks than an actual trail. Harry told them where to go, and when they reach the parking lot at the trailhead, it becomes apparent that this is not going to be an easy hike.

Celeste climbs ahead, watching her own strong thighs as she walks. The others stay together, looking at each other and talking. Occasionally, Celeste loosens a rock with her foot and sends it jumping down the trail behind her. "Rock," she yells, without turning around.

The day is hazy and thick with heat. Above her on the mountain the tanned backs of college girls wearing bikini tops disappear around a bend. Sweat trickles from beneath her hair and her breath is fast and heavy. When she stops and looks back, her father and his friends are gone, invisible behind a turn in the path.

The trail ends abruptly two miles later at the edge of a cliff. The college girls are there, standing at the edge, taking pictures of themselves on the precipice of all that green oblivion below. "Will you?" they ask, holding out a camera to Celeste as she arrives, gasping for breath.

She takes their camera and arranges the girls in the frame. All those beautiful girls and behind them, all that space. She tries to get it just right, to capture the height and danger of their position. When she is done, she too sits at the edge, dangling her feet, feeling the pull of gravity at the soles of her shoes. She is conscious of being perfectly in the moment and then wonders if that ruins it, if maybe she is trying too hard.

When her father and his friends arrive almost a half-hour later, making a big show of how old and tired they are, Celeste is glad to see them. The college girls have gone back down and it is just the four of them up there, eating handfuls of trail mix and speculating on what it would feel like to fall from such a height.

"Sometimes," Robin says, "I feel as if I have to stop myself from jumping. Not in a suicidal way, just because it could be so exuberant, you know?" They do know. They all nod. Celeste feels a surge of affection for these people she has known all her life—for her father's friends, these good people of Lake George.

WHEN THEY GET BACK TO THE HOUSE, Harry makes them all gin and tonics in big glasses. He is in fine spirits and Celeste suspects he has missed them.

"How did the Swiss Family Robinson do?" he asks.

Mariah flops into one of the wide wicker chairs and says, "Celeste is the only young one left."

"Not all that young anymore, either," says her father. "I can't believe I have a thirty-one-year-old daughter."

"Speaking of your daughter, the young doctor called. Isaac, is it?"

"It's *Ian*, Harry, Jesus!" Robin says, setting her glass down too firmly on the table. "You'd think you were jealous the way you go on about him. I suppose it's good we never had a daughter."

Celeste calls Ian from the phone in her room. She flops on her stomach like a teenager and dials their home number, still not sure she is getting it right.

"I miss you," she says when the machine picks up. "This place makes me feel like a teenager and I'm tired of sleeping alone. Four more days."

When she hangs up she stays on her stomach on the fold-out bed in Harry's shrine room. Outside, the light is fading and there is the sound of some insistent bug banging itself against the screen. The room smells of sandalwood incense and laundry detergent.

There is a knock at the door and Celeste sits up quickly, as if she has been doing something wrong. Harry opens the door.

"Oh," he says. "You're off."

"Answering machine."

"Well, I didn't want to disturb you. I'm making another round. Just came by to collect your glass."

Celeste looks to the nightstand where her half-full glass is sweating big clear drops down the side. "I'm good for now, but I'll come with you."

She gets up, grabs her glass and puts her arm through Harry's. They walk arm and arm down the hallway, and Celeste wishes they could continue like that into the living room. What she wants is for everyone to know. She is tired of this complicated secret, and sometimes she feels sure that the truth of the matter would be good for them. She imagines that Robin will not mind so very much, that she might, in fact, understand it perfectly. Seven years! Could it really have been so long? These people more than anyone else might understand her position, that she has never meant any harm.

Before they reach the threshold of the living room, Harry detaches his arm from hers and gives her bottom a light pat. They enter the room separately.

"Found her in there just mooning away. Must be some guy, this young doctor," he says to the room in general, but only Mariah turns to smile at her.

Robin is busying herself with little dishes of nuts and olives. It is the time of day in which they all sit around eating cashews and drinking cocktails. A few drops of rain patter against the boards of the deck outside. Celeste watches the tiny storm travel, like someone's personal bad day, out over the lake and then stop as if it has been sucked back up into the cloud.

"I believe Celeste used to moon for me like that," Harry says, as he twists the cap off the gin. "That was, of course, a very long time ago. When she was just a girl and I was…what was I? When I was her father's handsome older friend. Not quite a gentleman, but as close to one as she'd ever seen."

Celeste turns away from Harry and feels her lips start to stretch into a tight false grin. The room is quiet except for the jazz playing softly in the background. She doesn't have time to understand how the others are taking this.

"Harry," she says, "I never mooned over you." A dry, fake laugh escapes from her throat.

"No? If you didn't, it was only because I made myself too available to you."

Celeste hears the slop and fizz of tonic being poured over ice.

"Harry," Robin says. "What the fuck are you taking about? You're drunk."

"Yes," he says calmly, "I am."

"Poor Harry," Celeste's father says. "He loves to believe the young girls are mooning over him. I hate to break it to you, my friend, but your moonable days have come and gone."

Harry glares at him. "I know that," he says impatiently. "I know she doesn't moon over me anymore. I am talking about *before*. I am talking about before everyone got so goddamned old."

They are all looking at Harry now and no one has bothered to turn on the lights. It is dim. Soon they will light candles and Robin will put pasta on to boil. This should be their last cocktail before Harry goes to the cellar for wine.

"Even then," Celeste hears herself saying "even then I didn't long for you. It has never been like that. Being with you was like being looked at. But I didn't look back at you, Harry, not like you hoped I did."

Harry is stirring the drinks, four of them in a row, gleaming and tinkling cheerfully.

"What the fuck are you *talk*ing about?" Robin is still sitting next to Celeste's father on the couch.

"It's been a long time now—since the house on Barn Road," Harry says. It was the house he and Robin rented for years before they bought their own place. They can look out across the lake now and see it if they want.

Celeste lowers herself into one of the wicker chairs facing the water. "I don't want to do this anymore, Harry. I haven't for a while."

Her father stands up, suddenly, as if he might be about to lunge. But he is left there standing stupidly, looking old and unable to do anything, and he sits back down.

"My God," Robin says, regaining herself, "aren't we unconventional? A confession and a break-up right out in the open. Is there *noth*ing we don't share?" She opens a drawer in the coffee table, takes out a pack of cigarettes and lights one. They are her "tipsy reserve" for moments of desperation.

"Celeste," her father says, making his voice low and ominous like he used to when she misbehaved as a child, "what are you doing?"

"I am trying," Celeste says softly, looking out at the hypnotic surface of the lake, "to be good. I am trying to be a good person."

"There's no such thing as being good," Harry says, "only being human."

"Shut up, Harry," Robin says through clenched teeth.

"I'm trying to confess. But that's the wrong word because there is no one to absolve me." Celeste is taking deep breaths in an attempt to keep her voice from shaking. The room is almost dark now and they have all become dusky silhouettes. It's better that way. No one wants to look at anyone else.

"It wouldn't help," Harry says. "You're not that kind of person."

"What about Ian?" her father asks. He sounds confused and Celeste suspects he is still trying to save the situation.

"I can't tell him. He doesn't know."

"I suppose *I* can take this and he can't?" Robin asks.

"You know more about these things than he does. For him, things aren't so complicated. He thinks good people don't do bad things."

"People are people," her father says. "No good, no bad, just what is."

Celeste turns away from the lake, toward her father on the couch. "Oh Jesus Christ with that Buddhist crap! There *are* bad things. We did a bad thing, Dad."

Robin snuffs out her cigarette and lights another. Someone has finally turned on a lamp in the living room and the blue smoke swirls in its glow.

"I always loved you both," Harry says to Celeste and his wife. He is still standing at the kitchen counter behind the four gin and tonics. He starts to say something else, but then he looks down silently.

"Oh, for God's sake, give me my drink," Robin says.

Harry comes out from behind the kitchen counter holding the four drinks like a diner waitress. He offers them to Mariah, Robin, and Celeste's father, who take them silently, without meeting Harry's eyes. Celeste remembers her own now-watery drink and picks it up. If someone were to look in on them, it would appear as if they were toasting. Simultaneously, they lift their glasses to their mouths and drink.

Robin says, "You should go back to your husband. This won't be the same now. You should just go back."

"I will," Celeste answers. "I'll leave tomorrow." She looks at Harry, who has retreated behind the bar. "I'm sorry," she says. And she is.

The room is silent except for the piano tinkling softly from the speakers near the ceiling. It is a beautiful night and through the glass doors they can see the almost-dark sky, the storm clouds' huge puffs of gray lined in the violet of bruises.

"I suppose we should all get terrifically drunk," her father says.

"Someone has got to make dinner," Robin says, heaving herself off the couch. "I'll put water on for pasta if Harry will start mincing garlic." She goes to the stove and her husband hands her one of the huge pots hanging from the rack above their heads. She fills it with water, puts it on the burner, and turns around. "The worst thing is," she says to them all, her eyes brimming, "I loved these weekends. I really did."

Mary Yukari Waters

Circling the Hondo

SEVERAL DAYS before her sixty-fifth birthday, Mrs. Kimura officially relinquished her position as lady of the house. She did this during a natural break in which water was coming to a boil for that evening's somen noodles. Her daughter-in-law, in anticipation of the ceremony, had already taken off her apron. The entire process—the mutual bows, the long-rehearsed gracious phrases—lasted but five minutes, with only a slight sourness on Mrs. Kimura's part.

Mrs. Kimura was past her prime. There was word on the alley that (to use a local expression) a stitch or two was coming loose. Even before her change in roles, Mrs. Kimura's eyes had taken on a vague, inward cast; when greeted by neighbors at the open-air market, it took her just a shade too long to respond. Mrs. Kimura would pay for an expensive *aji* fillet, the fish vendor reported, only to walk off without it. Her five-year old grandson Terao, who had grown two whole centimeters that summer, boasted that Grandma sometimes mistook him for his father. Maa maa, the neighbors could only imagine what went on in that household.

It had not been this hot and muggy in years. "Must be the global warming effect," was Kanayagi District's greeting of choice that summer. Cicadas shrilled up in the ginkgo trees whose leaves, sticky with dust, cast slow-stirring shadows on the pavement. Moss pushed up through cracks in the asphalt, where housewives tossed out buckets of water to cool the alley when the sun went down.

"It's all this humidity, that's what it is," Mrs. Kimura told her son Jiro at dinner. "It plays on everybody's mind! Ne, who can remember anything in all this heat!"

"Soh soh," he agreed from behind the evening paper. He turned a page. His wife, Harumi, shot her an inscrutable glance but said nothing.

"It gives me strange dreams at night, even," Mrs. Kimura said.

While she was lady of the house, Mrs. Kimura had rarely dreamed. Now she awoke each morning engulfed in some residual mood, which spread over the day like an expanse of calm and deepening water. Sometimes no details remained, but other times she could vaguely link her emotion to some throw-away instant from her past: the play of late-afternoon sunlight in the maple trees of a schoolyard, or a certain way her late husband's shadow would fall upon the wall, almost twenty years ago, when he went over finances in the evening.

Outside her second-story window this morning, a crow wheeled over the pine branches, landed, then flapped away, leaving a branch swaying. The sun was out in full force already, white and shadowless. Mrs. Kimura lay perfectly still on her futon while last night's dream dissipated. There was no rush to rise. Meals were no longer her responsibility, and Harumi preferred her upstairs, out of the way, until breakfast was called.

All her life, Mrs. Kimura had been in awe of the passage of time and its powers of annihilation. Looking back across an ever-widening gulf, she had watched her earlier selves grow as implausible as incarnations in a previous life. (Had she really possessed the new body of an infant? Been madly in love?) But lately, she sensed that the past had never really receded, but merely accumulated right beneath her waking mind. And now with this onset of dreams, some barrier was giving way. For the dead were swimming back to life, the long-forgotten becoming the very now.

Downstairs, Harumi began chopping something with a jaunty rhythm (self-satisfied! Mrs. Kimura thought). Little Terao raised his voice in query. Somewhere out in the alley a bicycle bell tinged once, tinged again. Mrs. Kimura was conscious of this day already humming with a tireless grinding force, of which she was no longer a part.

"MOTHER-SAN? Mother-san?" said Harumi. "I was wondering if I could do this test on you from my book?" Harumi, in her new role as lady of the house, had bought an enormous hardcover book called *Caring for Your Aging Parents*. It was filled with lists of symptoms as well as photographs of boils, curved spines, and clouded irises. "Stand on one foot for me, please," Harumi said, "and I'll time how long you can hold it."

"What for! My balance is fine!" Mrs. Kimura said.

"Mother, please," Jiro said wearily from behind his morning paper. It was Sunday, his only day off. "Just go along with it. Please." So Mrs. Kimura submitted to the indignity while her grandsons Saburo and Terao, ages eight and five, giggled and leaned eagerly over the low breakfast table.

Harumi was perpetually alert for suspicious developments: sniffing the air for burning smells, halting in mid-sentence at the hint of a cough or sneeze. More than once Mrs. Kimura had been reminded of those stone-cutters she had watched as a child, patiently tap-tap-tapping until the inevitable crack appeared. "You seem a little unfocused this morning, Mother-san," her daughter-in-law said now, smiling. "Were you lost in your thoughts?" Her silver filling caught the sun and glinted brightly.

"My only thought," Mrs. Kimura said, "is a wish for peace and quiet." The boys glanced up with keen animal instinct, but the grownups' faces were as bland as ever.

Jiro folded his paper and stood up, knees cracking. "I'm going out for golf now," he announced.

"Golf, again?" said his wife. "In this heat?"

"Soh." Jiro cracked a grin for the first time that day. "All right then, ladies. Remember to keep your blood pressures down."

Mrs. Kimura's feelings for Jiro were complex. There was an old saying: "In youth, obey your father; in marriage, obey your husband; in old age, obey your son." It was one thing to defer to a father or husband, who from the outset commanded respect. But the shift in power between mother and son had cost them both something. Harumi's presence, most certainly, had not helped.

It was hard to reconcile this laconic businessman with her memory of the warm sleeping infant, strapped to her back; or the little boy standing in the doorway, his face tear-stained above a broken butterfly net. Or the young man, stiff with pride, placing his very first paycheck before the family altar. One could not help but feel (with unease—for how would Harumi's book interpret this?) that age revealed reality to be a fragmented thing.

THAT EVENING, MRS. KIMURA ENTERTAINED THE BOYS with a fairy tale while their parents attended a mid-summer PTA meeting. They sat out on the garden veranda—the boys in an after-dinner stupor, their soap-scented skin already moist with perspiration. "So young Urashimataro decended to the bottom of the sea," she said, "on the tortoise's back. The water around him changed from clear to light green, then darker green, and then a deep midnight blue." She batted away a mosquito with her paper fan. The sun had just set, and strokes of pink and orange stretched across the sky as if drawn by a half-dried brush, revealing behind its gaps the milky blue of day. "Soon they reached the underwater kingdom."

Mrs. Kimura told them how, after a short visit to the Emperor of the Sea, Urashimataro came back to his village to find with horror that a hundred years had passed. Just then a bicycle passed by in the alley, flashing in and out of view among the slats of the bamboo fence. Saburo, the older one, looked up with sharp interest. "That's Shizu-kun's big brother!" he interrupted.

Mrs. Kimura, ignoring him, continued. "Urashimataro walked down the alley," she said, "but his old house was gone." Little Terao, five years old, was listening rapt, his mouth falling open a little. "His old neighbors were gone. All of them...strangers." She looked over her bifocals into Terao's eyes. Their whites were clear and unveined. Limpid irises, like shallow water—she could see almost to the bottom. Terao must be imagining Urashimataro's predicament now, the way she did as a child, with the delicious thrill of momentarily leaving the safety of his own world. She marvelled at his innocence, at his little mind's unawareness of all that lay around and above and beneath him. His older brother's mind, on the other hand, was branching out rapidly. But he too had far to go; the expanses of time, of space, of human understanding, had yet to unfold. Mrs. Kimura felt all this vaguely, in the space of a heartbeat.

"He opened the magic box," she concluded, "and smoke poured out, and suddenly he had turned into an old man with a long white beard."

The sky's familiar blue was gone now, replaced by an ominous wall of tangerine-pink. In contrast to this incandescence, the veranda below seemed suddenly darker, the boys shadowed and featureless in the twilight. Little Terao was scratching at something on his arm. One flex of her mind...and there he was, become her own son as a little boy, sitting before her on the veranda as he had done so many summers ago. It was Jiro she saw now, from a vantage point she had never known as a young mother. With a surge of emotion, she reached out and grasped Terao's damp shoulder.

"Jiro-kun," she said.

In the dusk, Saburo snickered.

By now the color had leached from the sky. The white light of morning, the wheeling crow, was a distant memory. Even the quality of air had changed along with the fading light; she recognized in this evening the quicksilver quality, the shifting groundlessness, of her dreams. And it seemed to her that here was life's essence, revealed as it never could be in the level light of day.

"Ne, is it a true story?" asked Terao.

Saburo snorted. "Of course not!" he said.

ONE AFTERNOON IN LATE SUMMER, the mailman delivered a parcel of high-grade *gyakuro* tea, compliments of one of Jiro's business contacts. To Mrs. Kimura, an avid tea lover, it was clear that the subtle bitterness of such a tea would be wasted on ordinary bean dumplings; it required a dessert with correspondingly subtle sweetness, like plum *yokan*.

"The open-air market?" Harumi said. "Must you go right *now*, in the middle of this heat? At your *age*, Mother-san?"

"I'm not helpless yet," Mrs. Kimura said, shaking out her parasol.

"You wait till evening," said the new lady of the house.

Anger tightened around Mrs. Kimura's chest like a vise. It was hard to breathe. "Allow me the freedom," she said coldly, "to come and go in my own house."

Harumi sighed, with that puckering of brow used by long-suffering women in samurai dramas.

Seething, Mrs. Kimura stalked down Ushigome Alley and onto Kinjin Alley, past houses with their sliding doors half-open in hopes of a breeze. The children had gone back to school. All was silent save for the one-note shimmering of cicadas which, in its constancy, was a silence in itself. She passed an open window, where someone was washing dishes and humming behind a flowered curtain. She felt light-headed. It was hard to breathe. That Harumi! Suddenly the alley seemed to undulate in air as dense and distorting as old glass.

Slightly dizzy, Mrs. Kimura halted. Ara, where was she? Before her was an unfamiliar temple entrance flanked by two stone lions. She stumbled inside and sank down onto a nearby bench in the shade of a ginkgo tree.

Black spots blossomed and shrank before her eyes. She lowered her head between her knees.

As she stayed bent over in this position, the roaring in her ears subsided and she became conscious of a distant clamor: the honk of a car, bicycle bells, the bellowing of vendors. The open-air market must be nearby. From somewhere a school bell tolled—*kinn konn kann konn*—and children's voices rose to a crescendo, then faded into stillness.

When Mrs. Kimura finally sat up, an aged man was sitting beside her in the shade. A leaf drifted down between them. "Another hot day," he said, placidly fanning himself with a pocket-sized folding fan as if behavior like hers happened every day. He gestured to a water-filled paper cup on the seat between them. "From the administrative office."

Mrs. Kimura bowed her thanks, then sipped with unsteady hands. "Yes, it's gotten hot," she replied. A strand of hair had fallen loose from her bun, and she tucked it behind her ear. "It must be the global warming effect."

"Is that so?" said the aged man. His voice was clear and resonant, the voice of a younger man or even—she had the fleeting impression—of a spirit speaking through a medium. "Maybe," he continued, "the globe never really changes. Maybe it's just the people."

"Or their circumstances," said Mrs. Kimura. She smiled over her paper cup, pleased with that one.

"Aaa soh, Madam, circumstances."

What a restful conversation. It was such a relief, compared to what she went through at home: scrambling after little facts and details, all of which came naturally to the young and gave them the upper hand in everything from avoiding oncoming bicycles to making fast replies.

They sat in silence.

"Do you live nearby?" she asked, hiding her feet, with their plastic household sandals, under the bench.

"No, no. Wakayama Prefecture. I came today by train."

Ah! She must have wandered, then, into Ko-ken-ji, a well-known local

temple dedicated to the Easement of Pain. It served the blue-collar neighborhood of shopkeepers and weavers who made their living in the open-
air market. This temple was said to attract visitors from as far away as
Nagasaki—cancer victims, arthritics, the broken-hearted—who found it
out, somehow, through some underground source. Throughout the years,
Mrs. Kimura had spotted them disembarking from buses, directions in
hand: pausing dazed as straight-backed housewives whizzed past on old
bicycles; as vendors bellowed for attention up and down Kanayagi Boule-
vard—"Fresh fish, horaa! Wel-cooome, madam! FRESH-FRESH-FISH!" She
had seen them wander tentatively past shop after rickety shop, searching:
past wooden barrels of yellow pickled radishes, ivory prayer beads with
purple tassels, fragrant baked eels glistening with dark sauce.

What if someone had noticed her heading toward the Temple of Pain?
People would be interested. They would talk among themselves. She is no
longer lady of the house, they would say.

Out in the street a motorscooter sputtered past, its noise gradually fading into the distant buzz of the open-air market. She should be getting
along. Which way was it to the open-air market? Never before had Mrs.
Kimura lost her way like this. She felt an onset of dread which, lately, was
becoming familiar. She glanced over at the old man who clearly could not
help her, being from Wakayama Prefecture. He was settled on the bench,
still fanning himself. This is where I belong, his posture seemed to say.
Without his marvellous voice the aged body looked smaller, dried up and
scrawny like a grasshopper—yet with something of that concealed energy
of grasshoppers, that ability to startle you with a leap bigger than their
bodies were entitled to.

Now, with a slow movement, he lifted his arm and pointed at a shabby
wooden temple about a hundred meters away. "I was circling the *hondo,*"
he told her. Lined up along the temple's veranda was evidence of a large
attendance: glass jars, dozens and dozens of them, scrubbed clean of labels
and crammed with home-grown carnations, sweet peas, dahlias. They

seemed to belong to an intimate household whose owners could return at any time.

"At the administrative office," he said, "I bought one hundred sticks blessed by a priest. Then I circled the *hondo* one hundred times, reciting the Lotus Sutra to myself. After each round, I dropped one stick in the box."

Poor man. Mrs. Kimura, distracted from her own worries, nodded with sympathy. This ritual sounded strangely familiar. There had been something in her own past—what it was, she could not recall.

"I went round and round. And the process began to remind me of all the years of my life. How they've come and gone. You go around enough times, and it all gets blurred together. Isn't that the way, Madam? Things lose their shape."

Mrs. Kimura sat up straighter, but said nothing.

"But what's the point now of clutching at all the dates and names and places? I thought, let them go! Let them go! They've served their purpose. Madam, while I was circling the *hondo* I paused to hear the cicadas. I stood and listened, and I felt an old man inside me, and a middle-aged man too, and a young man, and a boy."

Overhead in the branches, one of the cicadas stopped shrilling, then started up again. Mrs. Kimura thought back to the evening several weeks ago, when she had sat on the veranda with her grandsons and sensed the difference in their minds' respective capacities. Now, she felt her role reversed; this old man had captured something that still eluded her, although it was encroaching closer and closer from the edges of her mind.

"Imagine how cicadas would sound to Buddha," he said, "after all His incarnations."

Was he, then, a religious follower? "I don't believe in reincarnation," Mrs. Kimura said.

"Saa, I'm not sure myself," he said, "what happens after death. But I see its pattern in this life. The ancient sages said we all have in us some larger consciousness that keeps growing, widening, with time. And they said:

that is all that matters. Our bodies must evolve, and our minds must evolve, in order to accommodate it."

It WAS NOT UNTIL THE OLD MAN HAD LEFT FOR HIS TRAIN that Mrs. Kimura remembered why the *hondo* ritual had sounded familiar. The memory came back to her untried, utterly unfamiliar, as if it belonged in someone else's mind and was slipping into hers by mistake. It was strange, how certain pockets of memory disappeared early in life. A few of them were coming back through her dreams. Others remained missing; for instance, she could not recall a single moment of that period in childhood when she had been forced to learn to write with her right hand.

It had been a muggy summer day—she was about six—when she and her parents had visited a temple and her father had circled a *hondo*. It must have been his cancer, Mrs. Kimura thought now. But on that day she knew nothing of this, and had became impatient waiting for him. While cicadas shrilled *meeeeee* up in the pine trees, her mother amused her with a Water Buddha in a corner of the yard. "Ahhh, he's saying thank you, it feels very good," her mother had said as she poured water from a bamboo dipper over the Buddha's head, "the poor thing's so hot and tired out in the sun." Mrs. Kimura had watched the gentle stone face smiling through a film of cool water that flowed down the Buddha's body into the tangled green weeds at its feet. Her mother poured over and over, and her father continued his interminable rounds.

They might have come to this very temple. It was not so implausible; her childhood town of Fukuma was no more than an hour away.

Mrs. Kimura pictured her father sitting on a bench, slumped and silent, and her mother bending over him saying, "Oto-san, here's some tea... let's rest here a little before we go home..." A few elderly people had sat nearby, discussing ailments and families and times long gone, slowly fanning themselves as if they had all the time in the world. One solitary old woman sipped her tea holding the cup with both hands, smiling up eagerly at anyone passing by.

They were all gone now, and Mrs. Kimura had taken their place. That afternoon could have happened just yesterday, a heartbeat ago. Was it an illusion, or was today's weather, even the time of day, exactly the same, right down to the ominous black shafts of shadow the *hondo's* pillars threw across the sand?—as if nothing had really happened in the meantime, as if she had blinked once, like Urashimataro, and found decades gone.

For a fleeting instant her mind was vast enough, strong enough, to inhabit both afternoons at once. Maybe those ancient sages had experienced something similar, hovering between one consciousness and another. And Buddha himself, after all those lives—a tree, a worm, a bird, a dog— was now all dimensions in one, *was all*—and something of this was coming to her in these newfound dreams, and in the twilight evenings when she reclaimed young Jiro from the past. She knew her mind to be strengthening, widening, in a way neither little Terao nor Saburo nor Harumi nor Jiro could hope to understand.

She rose from her seat and walked over to the Water Buddha, which was still standing—as she had known it would be—in the far-left corner of the yard. It looked unexpectedly dilapidated, a little worn statue with features blurred by the years. She gazed at the smooth face, almost alive in the flickering shade of the sycamore tree. It was a face spent of passion after so many incarnations, suspended in some vast, unfocused awareness that radiated from its simple features. Mrs. Kimura, squatting before it as if it were a small child, recognized in its smile her own sorrow of things passing.

"There, there," she said to the Water Buddha, lifting the dipper and scooping up water from the blue plastic bucket beside it. The water slid down the warm stone, raising a sharp whiff of moss as it sank into the ground.

Andrew Foster Altschul

You Are Not Here

Photo from Alamo Square

THAT'S OAKLAND over there. I can see Berkeley, too. Last week I was there, in a car on Telegraph, I was walking on Telegraph, I bought an old Tom Waits album I've been looking for, got it on vinyl. But from there I couldn't see here. I wonder what that means.

Lower your eyes to the water—stiff, calm, gray as the sky. Then the buildings on this side: pristine skyscrapers, City Hall's gold dome, shabby apartment buildings in the middle distance. South of Market. Western Addition. North Beach. The scene reminds me of Paris, the view from the roof of the Pompidou, west toward L'Opera. Which reminded me, at the time, of Jerusalem, pictures I'd seen in a photo album, old, squat buildings and laundry flying from invisible lines. Which reminded me of Chicago.

In the foreground, at the bottom of this hill, ladies and gentlemen, is the famous Steiner Street. You know the one: pink and yellow and baby blue Victorians lean pertly on one another's shoulders as the street slopes off beneath them. As if one day they might just slide away, leaving broken foundations to collect rainwater. These are the Painted Ladies, the houses on all the postcards, "San Francisco" in white script and this exact view, these same houses, that sweep of downtown and the bridge. Postcards people in Indianapolis get from their cousins. Little notes to the folks back home: Here I am, this is what it looks like. All around the world they're looking at the same thing I am. But I'm here. You see that tiny figure in the lower right corner, sitting on the hill? That's me.

I know some people in this city. I have a map on my wall, I've drawn little circles and stars to remind me where they live. Buses are solid lines, streetcars are broken lines. Joe says I should get out more, but every time I do I end up somewhere I've never been. On my map, this hill is the heart of the city, its dead center. I spend a lot of time here.

Yoko is far across the park playing with the other dogs. She knows where I am—I always sit in the same spot. She'll come back when she's ready to go home. If, someday, I weren't here when she came back, I know exactly what she'd do: she'd run back and forth, nose to the ground, in tight rows. Down the hill, over, back up, over, down again, over, up—covering the territory until she caught my scent. She's smart like that.

It's going to rain soon. The air is getting sharper, the sky looks like a never-laundered dishrag waiting to be wrung out. There's a photo shoot setting up down the hill, a tripod on the grass and a man with a goatee and three silver studs in his eyebrow bustling around, pulling lenses from strewn cases. You see this kind of thing all the time here. The models glance between the photographer and the city behind them, the open space, waiting to pose. They make a beautiful couple—she in a sundress, he with a white sweater draped over his shoulders. The ad agency got lucky with these two. They hold hands, smile for the camera. They have it down so well: the money shot, the look that can sell anything. They almost fool me.

A bus pulls up and sits at the curb growling. The door opens with a hiss and a swarm of tourists flows out over the hillside, pointing their cameras at one another. Someone notices the photo shoot in progress and soon they're all crowded behind the tripod, waving to the models, clicking away. The models shift their pose. The woman looks up at her partner and he tilts his jaw a little higher. The space behind them feels empty, out of scale. It's like watching an IMAX screen. Bursts of Japanese chatter ride the wind. The rain will come any minute. I wish I had my camera.

Once, back in Connecticut, I went to a parade. We were there to see the governor, I think. We all stood in front of the fire station, or the barber shop, or the hardware store, and waved when his car went by. It was what we were supposed to do. Nobody stopped to think about it. Nobody said to themselves, Now I'm doing *this*.

The first cold, heavy drops start to fall. Yoko appears from behind the tennis courts, jogs over to the crowd and sniffs their shoes. She turns her face up, hoping to be petted, but no one can take their eyes from the picture. No one notices me when I stand up and whistle. I could do cartwheels across the park and no one would notice. People in postcards never notice you.

I can't really see Berkeley. Not from here. But if I close my eyes I know exactly where it is. Sometimes I close my eyes and imagine I'm somewhere else—New England, New Orleans, it doesn't matter. I imagine I'm looking west, I can see all the way across the country, to the exact spot on the grass where I am now. I'm just a speck in this vision, but I can still find myself. I tried to tell that to this girl Rosie on a blind date recently. Joe set us up. I leaned across the table and took her wrist. I wanted to ask if that ever happened to her. She smiled at me, covered my hand, and said, You must have really good eyesight.

The Phone Rang Twice

THE FIRST TIME IT'S MY MOTHER, who says I'm glad you're not working today, James, it's about time you had a day off. I don't know what kind of place you work for that makes you come in on Saturdays, she says, her small voice in my hand. I tell her the name of the place I work and she pauses and then says I know, Jimmy. I know where you work.

I ask how things are in Wilton and she says it's awful, just awful about that man, that terrible man. I say what man and she says that man, Tim Flagg, it's just awful and haven't I heard?

It's a name I haven't heard in years, the faintest rumble in my memory. The minute she says his name I understand that he must be dead.

They found him in his bathtub, she says, he'd been there a week at least, he'd put both barrels of a shotgun in his mouth. Both barrels, she sniffles. I want to ask if she's ever heard of anybody putting just one barrel of a shotgun in his mouth, but I know how she'll get really quiet and then start to cry.

When she's calm, we hang up and I take a cup of coffee to the couch and turn on the TV. All I can find is a stock-car race. The cars buzz around and around and rain runs down the windowpanes. There's no rain in Jacksonville. But here it never seems to stop.

That morning—ten years ago? fifteen?—I remember the phone ringing in our dark, silent house. Late winter, I knew, as any kid would, that it must be a snow day. I turned off the alarm. When I opened my eyes at ten, though, there was no snow. By noon we all knew the story, already legendary. You've probably heard it, too. This is The Day Tim Flagg Canceled School.

I can picture Tim Flagg, his long hair and tattered clothes, how he looms in the hallways or the parking lot. That's what Tim Flagg does: He looms. Everyone knows him, he's just one of those kids that wasn't put together right. One night, in the darkness of a backyard party, I turn, joint in hand, to find him next to me, his eyes hooded and intense. He bares his teeth, leans menacingly toward me. Then he laughs and takes the joint, punches me in the arm as if to say look, I'm just like you, I do the same things you do.

When the police broke up the party it was the back of Tim Flagg's denim jacket they chased, over fences and through the woods and cul-de-sacs.

They hate each other, Tim Flagg and the cops. But somehow they also love each other. Somehow this is fun for them.

But this day, The Day Tim Flagg Canceled School, is different. He'd gotten in through a bathroom window, they think, demolished all the rooms on one hallway before they arrived. He works fast—smashing test tubes and beakers in the chem lab, setting papers and rulers and dictionaries on fire, pissing on the floors. When the cops get there, they can't stop him because of the barriers, the metal gates between hallways, installed to prevent just this kind of incident. But no one gave the cops the keys. Only Tim Flagg has the keys.

I can remember the scene as if I were there: the metal gates, cold alarm bells, angry cops facing off with Tim Flagg, long-haired and taunting. They say cut the crap, Flagg, come on out here. Tim Flagg laughs and rattles the gate. He's carrying a knife, a long hunting knife, I don't know how I know about that knife, but the cops draw their guns and say don't move and Tim Flagg gives them the finger and runs whooping down the hall.

It all comes back: his wild eyes, the flash of the knife, flames throwing shadows behind him. When we talked about it we all wanted to know how he'd gotten the key. Someone said Tim Flagg had made the key in wood shop and we groaned at this dumb idea and then fell quiet.

They didn't catch him for days, and the whole time I was afraid I might come home from school and find him huddled in my garage, still carrying the knife, that he'd say you gotta let me stay here, Jimmy, remember that time we smoked a joint together? But they found him eventually, and then he disappeared from our town and was forgotten. Later, I left, too. We all did.

I guess Tim Flagg came back. I wonder what he'd been doing all this time, what kind of adult he'd become. Did he have a job? A girlfriend? When he walked down the street, did he feel as though he was in a ghost town, all the people he remembered having vanished, those who were still there just walk-ons in some flimsy, substitute life? I wonder if the cops who found his body were the same ones from the school that night, whether they shook their heads and said one less scumbag to worry about. I wonder if they had any idea who he was.

The checkered flag is waving above the track. Yoko sits in front of the radiator, watching rain patter and run down the windowpanes. She hates this weather. She doesn't know what real winter is, how the bare trees and steel sky trap you inside yourself, separate you from everyone else. If I took her to Wilton she wouldn't understand. She'd think she was still in San Francisco. She'd think everything had changed without warning.

The Other Time

A WEEKDAY EVENING and I'm making dinner—cutting vegetables, boiling rice, waiting for Carol. Sunlight reflects off the windows across the street. The kitchen explodes with glare like a hospital ward. Yesterday it rained but today I need sunglasses in my own kitchen. The sound of the phone comes from far off.

When I pick it up, there's no one there at first, I hear a beep and then static and I ought to hang up the phone but I don't.

Is this Mr...um...Lowery?

I say *mmm hmmm*, sticking the phone between my ear and shoulder, slicing onions. I'm too rude to tell her I don't want any, any of whatever. I let her run through the whole pitch.

She starts talking about credit cards and restaurants, about discounts and dinner dates. I stand at the window and watch the traffic crawl by on Divisadero, a block over. I can only see segments of the street between the buildings. I watch cars glide by, disappear, reemerge. I wonder what happens to the people in those cars in the time that I can't see them.

The woman on the phone has a nice voice, mellow and familiar. It's like Muzak. It makes it easy to forget she's there.

She's asked me a question, I know by the silence. I tell her I'm sorry, but I wasn't paying attention and I don't think I want any anyway. She wants to run through it again, make sure I know what I'm missing, but I say no, really, I have to go.

And then she says, wait, James Lowery, *Jimmy* Lowery, did I by any chance go to Wilton High School? In Connecticut?

I did, I tell her, I did go to Wilton High and she says I can't believe I recognized your voice—it's me, Holli Hillis, wow this is unbelievable.

And it is Holli Hillis. It absolutely is.

Holli Hillis, who lived a short bike ride away, whose father ran against my father one time for mayor and they both lost. Holli whom I wanted to take to the Junior Prom but who had some boyfriend from Bridgeport, or Westport. Holli Hillis. Whom I'd forgotten forever, until this miraculous phone call.

She's chattering now in my ear and I am responding. We are catching up, as if we were old friends, which I guess we are. I'm sitting right in the glare, her voice hypnotizing me and I am very, very sleepy.

Wait, Holli, I say, where are you? And she says Albuquerque, where are you?

But you called *me*, I say. You must know. But she doesn't know. The machine dials for her, she says.

The doorbell buzzes and Yoko starts barking. Carol is downstairs. The kitchen is a bright capsule warmed by the sunset. Holli is saying something about college, did I go off to college, she can't remember.

Holli, I have to go, I tell her. The rice timer is ringing. I buzz Carol in downstairs and we're about to hang up when I remember something. Wait, I say, Holli, did you hear about Tim Flagg?

She hasn't, but there's no time. I tell Holli to call me back and I'll tell her the story.

But I don't have your number, she reminds me. The machine again. I open the door and Carol kisses my cheek, shows off a bottle of wine. She frowns at my sunglasses. Please, I say, here's the number and Holli says okay, Jimmy, I'll call you soon and I say I have to tell you this. It's important. There's a weird tone and then Holli is gone.

Transit

HERE'S ONE OF ME ON THE BEACH. A long stretch of dark sand under a mother-of-pearl sky, wet dunes between me and the highway. High tide, bushels of kelp dot the waterline like scrub brush. If Yoko were here, she'd sniff the kelp, lick it once, trot away.

The sun was strong when I got here. Indian Summer. Now it tries to slide out like a milkdrop from the gray underbelly. Behind me the whole city crowds toward the ocean. In San Diego I remember a long fishing pier that stretched toward the horizon. I remember pelicans swooning out of the sky. But there's no fishing pier here. The beach is empty. My shadow slides over empty sand.

Why do you think he did it? Holli said. I couldn't answer her. Do you think anyone ever asked him? she said and I said, Holli, how could they ask him? But we were talking about different things. We were in different cities. I looked at the phone in my hand and I wanted to ask, how do I know it's you?

When the phone wouldn't stop ringing I flew out of the house, I took the 66 to the end of the line, I walked a couple of blocks. Past old Cape Cod houses, rickety wood stairs and Japanese gardens, no one out walking, no sounds coming from those homes. I thought I was in one of those science-fiction movies: the last man on the planet, I could see myself from above, a shadow moving through the grid.

I see someone else, a jogger, with a dog of his own. Behind him is Sutro Tower, that giant metal insect rising above the city, its two-pronged tip slicing a wake through the fog. The jogger is coming closer, a man with a beard and a yellow lab. I give him room to pass but he swerves in my direction, runs past me, turns and jogs backward to get a better look. His dog looks up at him, barks once. I want to apologize for something. I want to get out of their way. Across the dunes I can hear cars swish by, driving from one neighborhood to another neighborhood.

Do I know you? says the jogger. His breath comes out in a puff. He puts his hands on his hips, his face red and shining with sweat.

I don't think so, I tell him, but he says, Yeah, sure I know you, how've you been. His dog runs in circles, barking, looking up at me. He wants me to throw something toward the ocean. He wants to fetch. There's no break in the clouds now, when I get back to my neighborhood it will already be dark.

Sutro Tower nearly submerged, its needles and wires reach through the fog like the rigging of a sinking yacht. I should get home. I should turn on the phone, in case Holli calls again, but every time I talk to her I close my eyes and feel like I'm somewhere else. The tower is gone now, a bleary, blank sky, and for some reason I worry this means the streetcars have stopped running. I picture myself wandering back through those empty streets, a whole vacated city to navigate, no tower to reckon by as I stumble into neighborhoods I've never seen. Polk Gulch. Sea Cliff. St. Francis Wood. I don't even know where St. Francis Wood is. I picture little thatched cottages, smoke curling from stone chimneys. I think I'd like to live in St. Francis Wood. I'd like to take Holli there.

Last Call

JOE SAYS HAVE YOU TRIED THE SUSHI PLACE in the Marina? It's after six and he's got two girls who want to have dinner with us. Let me just finish this work, I tell him, but he says no, let's get the hell out of here.

The girls are called Beth and Linda. They're from upstairs, in Product Placement. By the time the fortune cookies come, Beth has her hand on Joe's knee. Linda watches me. There's heavy-metal music playing and behind the bar two chefs are juggling knives. Up in the corner, the TV flashes baseball highlights.

Linda says you really should come out more, James, Joe always says how much fun you are. She holds my eyes for a moment and looks down into her drink. I'm thinking about Yoko, who hasn't been walked since early this morning. I'm thinking about Holli Hillis, who is supposed to call later. We talk all the time now. I know where this is going, but I just nod and smile, watch the knives flash in the air.

James here is from Connecticut, says Joe. Way back east. The girls nod their heads. What's that about? says Beth, and Linda laughs. I knew this guy, I start to say, but then I drop it.

An old man comes up to the table and puts a hand on Beth's shoulder. He just kind of appears there, and we all stare at him, white hair and perfect shave, his rosy cheeks almost cherubic. He has a bandana around his neck. When he moves his lips no sound comes out. We stare at one another and then back at the old man, glassy blue eyes smiling.

Joe says I'm sorry, what was that? The old man lifts the corner of his bandana and when his lips move again there's a strange crackling, hissing sound and I lean forward.

"You kids having a good time," he says.

We're all speechless for a moment until Joe nods and says yeah, yeah thanks, how about you? The old man opens his mouth, leans his head back and laughs, but what comes out of the hole in his throat is the sound of a car trying to start.

"These are nice girls," he says, his voice clicking and whispering like a cheap walkie-talkie. I can tell by Beth's face that he's squeezing her shoulder. "Nice girls are hard to find."

Beth looks embarrassed. Linda takes my hand under the table. The old man stands there, smiling like a little kid, holding the corner of his bandana. Above his head, a weatherman points at a map. It's raining from here to Duluth.

Linda asks if I'd mind walking her home, it's just a few blocks from here. She still has my hand. Okay, I tell her, but I can't stay long, mapping the area in my head, thinking about my car, how long it will take to get home. Holli has probably called already—I imagine Yoko staring at the answering machine, tilting her head this way and that.

Do you ever feel, I don't know, like you're not real, I said to Holli. Like I'm not real or you're not real, she said. No, seriously, you're this voice on my telephone, I said, and she said I know, isn't that beautiful?

When I wake up later I don't know where I am. I start to panic, until I recognize Linda, snoring gently next to me. The window is open, a breeze and wash of cars coming through. Everything in this room feels too light, like it's barely there. Somewhere a faucet is dripping, tapping a slow message on the surface of an unseen sink.

I lie and watch the ceiling, listening, waiting for this cold dread to draw back, waiting to feel like my old self again. But this bedroom reminds me of my own bedroom—right down to the Doisneau black and white on the wall, you know the one. Everything looks like something else, every goddamn thing. Even the back of Linda's head. I can't stand it.

In the bathroom, I twist the knobs of the sink until my hands go white but I can't stop the dripping. I lean into it, give it all I've got, break a sweat but the water still drips, plopping on the fake marble with no rhythm or clear message, another thing I ought to be able to understand but can't. I take a deep breath. I stare at myself in her mirror and wonder what I used to look like. I wonder if Holli Hillis left me a message tonight, talking through her machine into my machine. I think I might be in love with Holli Hillis. I think I left my car unlocked. I let myself out.

Tomorrow

OTHER DAYS I WAKE UP BEFORE DAWN and lie still, listening to the sounds outside the window: there are none. Sometimes I imagine the outside world is gone, everything is gone, the walls of my room are the edges of the universe, thin barriers between me and nothing. This is one of those mornings.

In the dream, Tim Flagg came to my door and said you gotta help me, friend. There were lights twirling behind him and I couldn't see his eyes. Don't you know me, Jimmy? You gotta help me, I don't know where else to go. He let his knife drop and wrapped his arms around me and I wanted so badly to help him. But when I opened my mouth no sound came out. I wanted to help him but I couldn't speak, so I squeezed his body into mine and listened to his wet breathing. I thought if I just held him for long enough those twirling lights might come closer.

Sounds start to fill in now: the dog snoring in the living room, a distant siren, the click of the thermostat. Out my window a bird calls one clear note. This is going to be one of those mornings.

While it is still dark, I will walk softly down the stairs, the dog's leash jingling gently, and open the door to the street, only a little surprised that there's a street and a world still out there. Yoko's chain and my footsteps are the only sounds, the air chilled and damp, and the only way I'll know that the large darkness ahead is Alamo Square is that this is where I left it.

We'll trudge to the top of the hill and sit in the damp grass. I'll hug my arms against the chill, Yoko scratching and yawning next to me, her chain ringing in the cold morning. I'll stare at the place where the Painted Ladies ought to be but there's only dawn fog, fog all around us. The phone kept ringing all night. Where are you, Jimmy, said the voice, a ghost in my apartment.

The fog covers everything. Even Yoko looks indistinct sitting a few feet away. It's not real, the fog. You can't touch it. You only know it's there by what it hides. One time I was here for a photo shoot, I was watching a photo shoot, models on a hill overlooking San Francisco. You remember. But the fog came in so fast that day, whispering over the hill and blotting out the whole city.

Don't move, I tried to tell them. Stay where you are. It will pass. But by then I couldn't see them. I wonder what that means.

Soon the dog will turn restless, start sniffing the grass in gradually widening circles, zeroing in on something, fading away from me. I will think about what to do with the day. If it doesn't rain maybe I'll go up to Twin Peaks, park at the lookout and take in the whole city at once, map it out in my head. I could draw a big X where I'm sitting now, I could look down and see it.

Or maybe I'll call Holli, lie on the couch with her voice in my ear and think about summers in Connecticut, when we'd all gather on hot nights and drink beer in backyards, lie in the grass together, and the shadows of bodies around you were shadows you could recognize. Where are all those faces now? Maybe Holli knows. Maybe her machine can find them all. Maybe it's time to start looking.

Maybe today's the day I'll throw everything in the car and point it east, keep driving until the bridge and the hills and the windmills and the dust are behind me, until the dark rush of the next night comes charging toward me.

There's no way to know if today is that day. No matter how hard I think about it I won't know. I'll sit on the warming grass and wonder, until the gray turns to white and then pink, and familiar shapes start to come out of the fog. If all goes well, those shapes will emerge, the bridge and the skyscrapers, the houses at the bottom of this hill. It's a miracle, every day—the city gradually waking up, everyone moving in so many directions. So many people, someone's bound to come up here and find me, sitting in the grass, holding my breath, waiting for something to happen. You see that tiny figure, alone at the top of the hill? That's me. And the person climbing the hill, a little out of breath, seeing it clearly for the first time? Well, maybe that's you.

Jess Row

For You

JANUARY, THE DEPTHS OF WINTER: nights longer than the days. Rising at four, the students bow to the Buddha one hundred and eight times, and sit meditation for an hour before breakfast, heads rolling into sleep and jerking awake. At the end of the working period the sun rises, a clear, distant light over Su Dok mountain; they put aside brooms and wheelbarrows and return to the meditation hall. When it sets, at four in the afternoon, it seems only a few hours have passed. An apprentice monk climbs the drum tower and beats a steady rhythm as he falls into shadow.

Darkness. Seoul appears in the distance, a wedge of glittering lights where two ridges meet.

Sitting on the temple steps, hunched in the parka he wears over his robe, Lewis closes his eyes and repeats to himself, *my name is Lewis Morgan. My address is 354 Chater Gardens, Central, Hong Kong. My wife's name is Melinda.* He tries to see her face again, the way it appears sometimes in his dreams, and usually he can't.

ON MONDAY EVENINGS he accompanies Hae Wol Sunim down the mountain to the local outdoor market. While the monk buys the main provisions of the temple—barrels of *kim chi*, hundred-pound sacks of rice—Lewis goes to the Super Shop for the extras the international students need. Vitamin supplements. Vegetable oil. Peanut butter. Milk powder. Nescafé. When the old woman at the register sees him, bundled in his gray robe and stocking cap, she puts her hands together in *hapchang* and addresses him as *sunim,* monk, and he has to resist the urge to shake his head and try to correct her. It's all the same to her, Hae Wol reminds him. Remember, she's not bowing to *you.*

Before Hae Wol became a monk, he was Joseph Hung, an accountant at Standard Chartered Bank, and the secretary of the Hong Kong Shim Gye Zen Center. Lewis met him for the first time two years ago, when a Zen Master from Korea came to give a public talk at Hong Kong University; Joseph was the English translator, and afterwards, Lewis walked up to him and asked, *Can you help me?* For months they met every Friday for coffee at the Fringe Club in Central, and after Joseph left for Korea they kept in touch, using the temple's email account, until he finally told Lewis, *You have to try it for yourself.* He repeated the instructions for sitting Zen, and wrote, *No more letters for six months, OK?*

How are your legs? Hae Wol asks, as they load shopping bags into the back of the temple van.

Do you really have to ask? Lewis says. They hurt like hell.

Hae Wol laughs hoarsely. Good answer, he says. One hundred percent. And how does your heart feel?

Worried. Still worried.

Too much thinking. What are you worried about?

I'm afraid I'll forget why I'm here. Lewis puts his hands on his hips and bends over backwards, trying to work the kinks out of his spine. But I don't want to dwell on it, either.

So why *are* you here?

He glares at Hae Wol. The small matter of a divorce, he says. That's all.

Wrong answer. The monk folds his arms and grins at him. You're supposed to say, *to save all beings from suffering.*

I'm supposed to lie?

You're supposed to let it go. If you've already made up your mind, not even the bodhisattva of compassion herself can save you.

But I'm not supposed to want to be saved, am I?

Here, Hae Wol says. Try me. Ask me the question.

I hate these games, Lewis thinks. All right, he says. Why are you here?

The monk puts his hands together and gives him a deep, elaborate bow. Two young girls passing by burst into loud giggles, covering their mouths.

For you, he says.

THE RETREAT WAS MELINDA'S IDEA, and that was what made him take it seriously. She'd always been suspicious of Eastern religion—her father had left her family for two years, in the late seventies, to live on a commune that practiced Transcendental Meditation—and she mocked him pitilessly when he brought home *Buddhism Without Beliefs* and *Taking the Path of Zen.* Then, during their second year in Hong Kong—when the fighting never seemed to end, only ebb and flow—she bought him a cushion and refused to talk to him in the evening until he'd sat for half an hour. This is for my own good, she told him. I don't know what it does for you, and I don't really care. I just need the *quiet,* understand?

He didn't understand: that was the first and last of it. Hong Kong was supposed to be a temporary posting for her, a two-year stint at Price Water-house Cooper's Asian headquarters, with option to renew, and now it seemed that every month her staff was expanded, her division given a new contract. In Boston she had been a star analyst, famous for her uncanny ability to find errors and gaps in a quarterly report; more than once she'd spotted a looming disaster months before it emerged in the market. But the word was that the American executives were afraid of her because she wasn't enough of a *team player*. Expert exile, it was called. If she stayed in Hong Kong, and played her cards right, she finally told him, she would be a division head in five years, and then could transfer herself anywhere—

back to Boston, or New York, London, even Paris. If not, she would have a year of severance pay, and would have to start again at the bottom.

But I can't work, Lewis said, staring into a plate of *woon sen* noodles. They were sitting on plastic chairs at an outdoor Thai restaurant downstairs from her office. No one hires American photographers here. In five years my career will be over.

And if I quit now in *zero* years my career will be.

And in six months our marriage will be.

You're being stubborn, she said. She lit a cigarette—a habit she'd picked up again in Hong Kong, after quitting six years before—and stared at him, her eyes darting from his forehead to his jaw to his sweater. How many other couples like us live here? she said. Why is it so difficult for you? What's wrong with not working for a little while?

He sat back in his chair and looked up into the glowing haze that hung over the city, blotting out the sky. If I said that to you, he said, you'd call me a sexist bastard.

That's not fair, she said. Being a freelancer is different. You'll always have slow patches.

This isn't a *slow patch,* he said, more loudly than he'd intended; an old woman with a basket of hibiscus flowers, who had been approaching their table, turned and hurried away. Haven't you been listening? If I don't work, not at all, what good am I to anyone? It isn't about the money. I don't want to wake up one of these days and realize I've turned into a hobbyist.

So, she said, I guess this is what they call an impasse.

Is it Hong Kong, he wondered, *or is it what we've known all along, that we're too different, that our lives will never really match.* She had lost weight, even in the last few weeks; in the dim light, he could see the faint blue paths of veins along her wrists, and the dark half-moons under her eyes that always reappeared in the evening, no matter how much concealer she used. *Things will be all right,* he wanted to say, but he couldn't see how they possibly would be, and there wasn't any point in lying.

NO ONE COULD SAY THEY HADN'T BEEN WARNED. An office workday ran from seven until eight, and Saturdays were workdays; an *affordable apartment* meant living in a series of walk-in closets; the summers were furnace-like, the winters endlessly dreary; there was no such thing as having a social life. And listen, an Australian woman instructed them at a cocktail party, on her third glass of Chardonnay, forget this *international city* clap-trap. Hong Kong is one hundred and ten percent Chinese. They may be the richest Chinese in the world, but they still throw their garbage out the window and kill chickens in the bathroom. And you have to accommodate them, because after all, it's their home, isn't it? It belongs to them now.

We're not like her, Melinda had said to him later, in the taxi, heading back to their hotel. Are we? It's different if you come here because you *want* to. We can explore—we'll make Chinese friends, won't we? And you'll study Cantonese.

Right. Of course.

And you can do amazing work. She rested her head against the window and stared up at the Bank of China passing above them, silhouetted against the night sky like the blade of a giant X-Acto knife. I mean, my god, this is the most photogenic city in the world, isn't it?

I shot fifty rolls yesterday, he said. You should have seen it.

He had wandered the back streets of Kowloon for hours, a side of the city he'd never imagined: streets like narrow crevasses, the signs stacked one over another overhead, blotting out the sun. Old women bent almost double with age, wearing black pajamas, their fingers dripping with gold. This was what he loved about her, he thought, her absolute certainly about these things, the way she moved instinctively, always knowing that logic would follow.

Now he thinks, *I was young. I was so, so young.*

THE PAIN IS ALWAYS WITH HIM: prickling in his ankles, needles in his knees, a fiery throbbing in the muscles around the groin. In every forty-minute session he waits for the moment when sweat beads on his forehead and his teeth begin to chatter, and then rises and stands behind his cushion until the clapper strikes. Walking, climbing the stairs, squatting on the Korean toilet, a dull ache in his knees registers every effort. He sleeps in its afterglow. Make friends with pain, Hae Wol advised him, then you'll never be lonely. And he realizes now that he feels a kind of gratitude for it, late in the evening sitting, when it is the only thing that keeps him awake.

Whole days pass in reverie, in waking dreams. A camping trip when he was twelve, along the banks of the Pee Dee River in South Carolina. Clay and sand underfoot. Campfire smoke. The rancid smell of clothes soaked in river water and dried stiff in the sun. His best friend, Will Peterson, who insisted on stopping to hunt for some kind of fossil wherever the bank crumbled away. Again he feels the heat of annoyance: the sweat stinging in his eyes, the clouds of mosquitoes that surround them whenever they stop moving. *I haven't changed at all,* he thinks, *I haven't grown: it's all an illusion. Twelve or twenty-eight, it doesn't make any difference. So what hope is there for me now?*

Filling his mug with weak barley tea, he turns to the window, and his eyes become reflecting pools; the blank, paper-white sky, the warm porcelain cradled in his hands.

TWICE A WEEK, DURING AFTERNOON SITTING, he descends the stairs and joins a line of students kneeling on mats outside the teacher's room, waiting for interviews. The hallway is not heated; he draws his robe tightly about him and tries to focus on his breathing, ignoring the murmur of voices through the wall, the slap of an open palm against the floor.

When the bell rings, Lewis opens the door, bows three times, and arranges himself on a cushion in front of the teacher. He is an American monk, from New York, dark-skinned, with deep-set eyes and a boxer's nose, twisted slightly to one side. Long white hairs sprout from his ears.

According to Hae Wol he's lived in Korea for twenty years, but he still speaks with traces of a Bronx accent.

Do you have any questions? he asks.

Not exactly.

But there's something you want to say.

I think I may need to leave, Lewis says. I don't think any of this is helping me.

The teacher stares straight into his eyes for so long he stiffens his head to keep from looking away.

Your karma's got a tight hold on you, the teacher says. Like this. He makes a fist and holds it up to the light from the window. Each finger is your situation. Your parents. Your wife. Your job. Your friends. Things that happened to you, things you've done. This is how we travel through life, all of us. He punches the air. Karma is your shell.

And now?

He spreads his fingers wide.

You're sitting still, he says. The hand relaxes. It doesn't know what to do with itself. The fingers get in the way. All of your natural responses are gone.

That's a kind of insanity, isn't it?

Hold on to your center, he says. Pay attention to your breathing. Follow the situation around you. So tell me, what is Zen?

Lewis strikes the floor as hard as he can.

Only that?

Sitting here talking to you.

Keep that mind and you won't make any new karma for yourself.

It's not that easy, Lewis says. I came here to make a decision.

The teacher adjusts his robe and takes a sip of tea. I remember, he says. You're considering getting divorced.

I'm not sure this was the best choice. Coming here, I mean.

Why not?

Well, he says, I'm not supposed to be *thinking* about anything, am I?

Haven't you already tried thinking about it? Has that worked?

It hasn't. Does that mean I should stop?

Sometimes you can't solve your problems that way, the teacher says. Your thinking-mind pulls you in one direction, then the other. There are too many variables involved. The most important decisions we make are always like that, aren't they? *Should I get married? Should I move to California?* You try and try to see all the dimensions of the question, but there's always something you can't grasp.

So you're saying that there's no way to solve these problems rationally.

Not at all. Your rational mind is very important, but it also has limitations. Ultimately you have to ask yourself, *what is my true direction in life?* Logic won't help you answer that question. Any kind of concept or metaphor will fall short. The only way is to try to keep a clear mind. And be patient.

Aren't you going to tell me that I have to become a monk?

The teacher grins so widely Lewis can see the gold crowns on his molars. Why would I do that? he asks. Being a monk won't help you. Do you think we have some magic way of escaping karma? We don't. Nobody gets away from suffering in this world. All we can do is try to see it for what it is.

Lewis rubs his eyes; he feels a dull headache approaching.

I've got a new question for you, the teacher says. Are you ready?

Lewis straightens his back and takes a deep breath.

You say you love your wife, right? What's her name?

Melinda.

You say you love Melinda. But what is love? *Show* me love.

Lewis strikes the floor and waits, but no words come. His mind is full of bees, buzzing lazily in the sunlight. Don't know, he says.

Good, the teacher says. That's your homework. He rings the bell, and they bow.

THE HOUSEKEEPER'S NAME WAS CRISTINA; she was paid for by Melinda's company, part of the package that all expatriate employees received. Two days after they moved into their apartment, she arrived with three suitcases and a woven plastic carry-all, and occupied the extra bedroom that Lewis had wanted for his studio. She was polite and efficient, and cooked wonderful food, but the apartment was small even for two people; they took to arguing in whispers, and gave up making love, feeling self-conscious. It took three weeks for Melinda to convince her supervisor that she didn't want or need an *amah*, even though every other couple in the firm had one, and the contract had to be broken at extra cost, taken out of her salary. When they told Cristina she wept and begged them not to send her away, and they were at a loss to justify themselves. I'll be more quiet! she said. Not even any telephone calls! Finally Lewis threatened to call her agency and complain, and she went to the elevator crying and wailing in Tagalog. All along the hallway he heard doors opening and closing, the neighbors talking in low tones.

Afterwards Melinda couldn't sleep for days. She might have been sent back to the Philippines, she said. That's what she was afraid of. Anytime they're out of work they risk losing their visas. Maybe we could have kept her on.

What did you want me to do? Not work?

No, she said. I know. But I don't know how we can live with ourselves.

It isn't our fault, Lewis said. Who thought that an American couple would be comfortable having a live-in housekeeper in a tiny apartment? Couldn't they at least have asked?

Everybody else has one.

Well, I'm not interested in having a servant, Lewis said, impatiently. I don't want some kind of colonial fantasy life.

I want *my* life, he wanted to add, *our* life, the one we promised each other, the one we had in Boston. He remembered what she'd said to him in the airport, when they were standing in line at the gate, clutching their tickets and carry-on bags, and staring out the window at the tarmac, as if seeing America for the last time: she'd turned to him, wide-eyed, and said, *No matter what happens, we'll still be the same, right?*

That was how it began, he thinks, staring at the ceiling, on the nights when the throbbing in his knees keeps him awake. The things they couldn't have predicted, and couldn't be faulted for. In the first month he visited the offices of a dozen magazines and journals, after sending slides and a portfolio in advance, and found himself talking to assistants and deputy editors who seemed not to have heard of *Outside, Condé Nast Traveler*, or *Architectural Digest*, and who regretted to inform him that there was a glut of photographers in Hong Kong at the moment. For the first time in six years he was officially out of work. On the bus, in the subway, in restaurants, he had moments of irrational rage, hating everything and everyone around him: the women who brayed into their mobile phones, the insolent teenagers with dyed-blond hair and purple sunglasses, the old men in stained t-shirts who stared at him balefully when he paid with the wrong coins. Cantonese was an impossible language; even people who'd lived in Hong Kong twenty years couldn't speak it. He couldn't master the tones well enough to say *thank you.*

But I'm not the only one who changed.

Melinda's cello, which had cost them a thousand dollars to ship, sat in its case in the corner of their bedroom, unopened, growing a faint green tinge of mildew. Her address book hadn't moved from its slot on the shelf above her desks in months. When he called their friends on the East Coast, waking them up after eleven at night, they asked, *What the hell's happened to her?* It wasn't just the sixty-hour weeks; it wasn't the new secretaries she had to train every month, or the global trades that could happen at any hour of the day, in Tokyo, or Bombay, or Frankfurt, so that she often had to be on call overnight. She'd always worked hard, and complained about it, and fought Coopers for every bit of time off she was entitled to. Now they never discussed her schedule at all. If he asked her about vacation time, or free weekends, or made a casual remark about never seeing her enough, she would say, *That's the last thing I want to think about right now.* Her face had taken on a kind of slackness, a faint, constant unhappiness, as if no disaster could surprise her. In bed she slept with her knees tucked up to her chest; she was constantly turning off the air conditioner, even when the apartment was stifling, complaining she was cold. Despite the subtropical sun, her skin was becoming paler; she had to throw away all her makeup and start over with lighter shades. And in three months she had gone from two cigarettes to half a pack a day.

On a Sunday afternoon in March of that first year he convinced her to come shopping with him at the new underground supermarket in Causeway Bay. She wandered through the aisles like a sleepwalker, picking up items almost at random—a jar of gherkin pickles, a packet of ramen—frowning, and putting them back. Half-joking, he said, I think we've become a reverse cliché, don't you? I'm the bored housewife, and you're the workaholic businessman. Maybe my mother was right.

She stopped in front of a pyramid of Holland tomatoes and turned to look at him, her lips pressed into a tiny pink oval. Just before the wedding, his mother had said to him, wryly, *Marry a career woman and all you'll wind up with is a career,* and they'd quickly turned it into a joke: when she kissed him, or touched him, she would say, *How do you like my career now?* But the joke isn't funny anymore, he thought, and wished he could suck the words out of the air.

Is that what you really think? she asked. Do you think I arranged it all this way? So that you'd be out of work and frustrated and taking it all out on me?

Is this what you call frustrated? he said. Making a joke? Asking an innocent question every now and then?

I'm not a workaholic. She tore off a plastic bag and began filling it with broccoli rabe, inspecting each stalk carefully for flowers. A workaholic *likes* it.

No, he said. A workaholic can't stop.

She turned away from him, sorting through mounds of imported let-tuce: American iceberg, Australian romaine, all neatly labeled and shrink-wrapped.

Can't you ask them for more time off? Lewis asked. Just one Saturday? I mean, it's the same company, isn't it? You're in a more senior position than you were in Boston, and *now* you don't have any flexibility?

Do you know what happened to the Asian markets last week? she asked. Did you even read the papers?

That isn't the issue. That's never been the issue. You'd be working this hard regardless.

I don't know how to explain it, she said. Her face darkened, and she stopped in the middle of the aisle, her shoulders drooping, as if the bags of vegetables were filled with stones. It's different here. She looked as if she would cry at any moment. A young Chinese woman passing them stared at her, then twisted her head to look at him. We have to fight for everything, she said. Clients. Market share. Out here we're not the Big Five. Accounts don't just fall in our laps here the way they do at home. And anyway, the whole economy's in a goddamned meltdown. *Nobody* wants to open up a new account right now.

He should have taken the bags from her hands, and dropped them in the cart; he should have embraced her, and said, *Forget about shopping, let's get a drink*. Instead, he crossed his arms and waited for her to finish, feel-ing impatient, irritated at her for making a scene.

And you just don't care, do you? she said. It's not that you want to see me, is it? You've just given up trying, and now you want to go home. Well, it's not that easy. You made a promise to me, and we never said that there wasn't a risk. Hong Kong isn't Boston. If you can't adapt, well, I feel sorry for you.

There was a bitter taste in his mouth. I'm glad you feel sorry for me, he said. I'm glad you feel *something*. He turned around and walked toward the escalator, and though she called after him, *Lewis, wait, I don't know how to get home,* he ignored her and kept going.

At first he thought he would head straight back to the apartment, but he turned right on Queen's Road, blindly, and walked in the opposite direction, into a neighborhood he'd never visited before. It seemed to him that everyone he passed—the old man selling watches from a suitcase, the young fashionable women laden with shopping bags, even the boys throwing a volleyball back and forth—had red, puffy eyes, as if the whole city had been crying. He was walking too slowly; people veered around him, or bumped him with their elbows as they tried to get by.

It would be so easy to leave: to buy a ticket for Boston tomorrow, to rent a studio in Central Square, to make a few phone calls, get some small assignments, to start making a life for himself again. She wouldn't fight the divorce; she would give him a fair settlement, probably more than he needed. A mediator could finish the paperwork in a few weeks. And she would stay here, getting thinner, smoking more, biding her time until her bosses realized she wasn't going to be driven away. Whatever inertia it was that gripped her now would swallow her whole. *I can't do it,* he thought, *I can't abandon her, I can't shock her out of it.* He stopped in the middle of the sidewalk and stared up at the buildings overhead, looking for a landmark to orient himself. *If I were home,* he thought bitterly, *someone would stop and ask if I needed directions. They wouldn't all stare at me and think, What are you doing here in the first place?*

I HAVE A QUESTION, he says to Hae Wol, as they are walking through the market, searching for the light-bulb store. What about change?

Change? The monk furrows his eyebrows. Everything is always changing. What kind of change?

Changing yourself. Trying to do better. Not making mistakes.

Mistakes are your mirror, Hae Wol says. They reflect your mind. Don't try to slip away from them.

Enough with the Zenspeak, Lewis says. Plain English, please.

The monk shrugs, and a look of annoyance crosses his face. You have to understand cause and effect, he says. Watch yourself. When you see the patterns in how you act, you'll begin to understand your karma. Then you won't have to be afraid of your feelings, because they won't control you.

I've *been* watching myself, Lewis says. But I keep wondering: even if I understand completely, can't I still make mistakes? How do I know that when I go back to Hong Kong things will be different?

It isn't so much a question of conscious effort. You have to give up the idea that coming here is going to *get* you anything.

Lewis looks around him, at the meat vendors carving enormous slabs of beef, the shoe repairmen, the grandmothers carrying babies tied to their backs with blankets. His eyes are watering.

I keep hearing that, he says, and it just sounds like a recipe for standing still.

No one ever said it was easy, Hae Wol says sharply. It's not like a vacation for losing weight. If you come here looking for some kind of quick fix for all your problems, you're missing the point.

There's something different about him, Lewis thinks. *I'm asking too many questions.* But it's not just that; the monk is nervous, unfocused, even a little jumpy. Every few minutes he scratches the same spot behind his right ear, automatically.

I'll tell you a story, Hae Wol says. Once there was a famous Zen master who visited a temple and asked to see the strongest students there. The abbot said, we've got one young monk who does nothing but sit Zen in his room all day. He doesn't eat, doesn't sleep, and doesn't work. So the Zen Master went to see this student. What are you trying to do by sitting so much? he asked. I'm sitting to become Buddha, the student said. So the famous master picks up a brick and starts rubbing it with his walking stick. What are you doing to that brick? the student asks. I'm trying to turn it into a mirror, the master says. You fool, the student says, that brick will never turn into a mirror, no matter how hard you rub it. Yes, says the master, and neither will you ever become Buddha by sitting this way.

You lost me.

Think of a horse and cart. Your body, your actions—they're the cart. Your mind is the horse. If you want to move, which one do you whip, the horse, or the cart?

Lewis starts to laugh, shaking his head.

I don't even know why I ask you these questions. You're no use.

It's not me, Hae Wol says. The *questions* are no use. Nothing I can tell you will ever make you satisfied, because all you really want to know is, *will everything turn out all right?*

So what should I do?

The monk stops and draws his fists together in front of his stomach, his *hara,* the center of energy. Tell yourself, *don't know,* he says to Lewis. Say it to yourself, over and over. *Don't know. Don't know.* Don't speculate. Don't make plans. Just accept it: *I don't know.*

Lewis lets out a long sigh.

So we're back at the beginning.

No, Hae Wol says, giving him a playful, twisting smile. Not yet. When you're back at the beginning, *then* you'll really be getting somewhere.

THAT NIGHT HE HAS A DREAM:

They are in Melinda's apartment in Somerville, the one she had when they met, when she was in the second year of Harvard Business School. The dream begins as their third date, just as it really happened. Late spring, twilight, the sun's last rays streaming through her bedroom window. He is sitting on the bed, and she is standing; they are having an intense conversation about some painter she admired in college, and in the middle of it she begins unbuttoning her shirt, still talking, dropping it to the floor, unhooking her bra, unzipping her jeans. He forces himself to maintain eye contact, because he understands, somehow, that that is what is required, but when he blinks he glimpses the rest of her. The light makes her skin glow like liquid gold. Every movement, every gesture, is like some beautiful dance he's never seen before; he wishes he could see it again, from the beginning; he wants to say, *Stop there, start over.* He thinks he is having a religious experience. He thinks, *I have just become a photographer.*

Good for you, she says. still standing there. You just passed the first test.

What test? he asks, trying to look incredulous.

You'd be surprised how few men can hold a conversation with a naked woman.

Stay still, he tells her. Stop moving. Her face blurs; her body vibrates in the air. What's happening to you?

There's this problem with you, Lewis, she says, her voice hollow, echoing, as if they're on opposite ends of a much larger room. You trust me too much. You believe in surfaces. Think about it this way: *You could be making the biggest mistake of your life this instant and you would never know.*

But that's what love is, isn't it? he says. You have to take that risk, don't you?

Not me, she says. That's the difference between us, Lewis. I've read your papers.

What papers, he says. What are you talking about?

A bell is ringing somewhere in the distance, heavy shoes pounding on the stairs. The monk sleeping next to him reaches up and flips the light switch, and he covers his eyes, shuddering.

THE MORNING IS COLD AND OVERCAST, the mountain hidden by low-hanging clouds. In the meditation hall he sleeps, his head fallen to his chest. A monk wakes him with a jab between the shoulder blades, and he struggles to his feet, barely able to stand.

Hae Wol passes him a note scribbled on the back of an envelope. *Demons are everywhere,* it says. *Don't follow them. You're not the only one.*

So I ask you again, the teacher says. What is love?

Today it is cloudy.

The teacher watches him for a moment, lips pressed together, and shakes his head.

Not enough? Lewis asks.

Not enough.

Lewis passes a hand over his eyes.

Love is just coming and going. Like a bad dream.

The teacher picks up his stick and taps him on the shoulder.

I give you thirty blows, he says. You understand emptiness. But emptiness is only half the story.

It's the most incredible thing, Lewis says. I don't feel my legs anymore. No more pain.

You'll want it back, the teacher says. He balances his stick on the ground and leans forward, resting his chin on his hands. Don't linger in hell, he says. Wake up!

In the fall of their second year, with nothing else to do, he decided to write a book proposal, and began reprinting every picture he'd taken in the last six years: taking out hundreds of his best negatives and re-casting them with every possible shade and filter. The third bedroom was webbed with drying lines, and the whole apartment reeked of developing fluid. He spent thousands of dollars on paper and chemicals, bought a new computer for digital editing, and still all the new work fell short, somehow. In his sleep he twitched and groaned, and Melinda made him move to the couch; then he began working later and later at night, and sleeping in the afternoon. One night, in a fit of rage, he kicked the side of his desk, putting his foot through the particle board, and smashed his favorite lens, a 75mm, three-thousand-dollar Leica telephoto. He collapsed into a corner, weeping like a child, and then fell asleep there, in the dim red glow, his head between his knees. Melinda woke him in the afternoon of the next day, pulled him out into the living room, where he sat on a chair with a blanket wrapped around him, trembling.

You need to leave, she said. Sitting in their narrow window seat, her arms wrapped around her chest, as if for warmth, she looked haggard, and frail, as if she'd aged thirty years. Go back to Boston if you have to. Or go on one of those retreats you told me about. Two months, absolute minimum. After that we can try again.

Hong Kong isn't the problem anymore, he said. *I'm* the problem. I'm useless, can't you see that? Sending me away won't help.

She leaned back against the window glass, resting her weight against it, as if daring it to break. Her eyes were horribly bloodshot, *like blood in milk*, he thought, for no good reason. I don't know what to do with you, she said. You've got one more chance, Lewis. Do whatever you have to. This paralysis—whatever you want to call it—it's *temporary*, can't you see that?

I can't, he said calmly, scratching his three-day beard. That's why I'm finished. I can't *see*.

DAYS PASS. He sits quietly, following the course of shadows across the floor. At night he tumbles exhausted onto his bedroll and sleeps without dreams. At meals he eats what is given and takes nothing extra, hardly noticing the burning taste of *kimchi*, the piquant sourness of preserved spinach. He cleans his bowls with tea and drinks the dirty remains without hesitation.

On a certain bright, cloudless day, the warmest yet, the monk who sleeps next to him gives him a note. *Bathe.*

THE MEN'S WASHROOM CONSISTS OF A SHORT HALLWAY, where clothes are left on hooks; a room with spigots protruding from the wall at waist level, low plastic stools, and small mirrors, for washing and shaving; and beyond that, closed off by a door, a room with a huge bathtub that stands empty. A sign in Korean and English says, *Conserving water, no use.* It is the middle of the day, and no one else is there. Removing his robes, Lewis winces at the cold, reaches for the nearest faucet and turns it to hot.

A strange sensation, looking at his nakedness for the first time in weeks. His legs are skinnier than before, his ribs showing slightly. When the water touches his shoulders and face, tears spring to his eyes, and he remembers Melinda showering him in their tiny bathtub, pouring body wash over his head, to his protests, working his shoulders with her loofah sponge. His muscles feel rubbery; he nearly slips from the plastic stool.

A few minutes later, when he turns off the water, he hears someone breathing hard, and close by. A plastic bag rustles. No one has come in, and the door to the outside is closed. He rises from his stool.

Hello?

He stands and opens the door to the cloakroom. Hae Wol looks over his shoulder and starts, dropping a white plastic bottle. Little orange tablets scatter everywhere across the tile floor.

Hey, Lewis says, Joseph—Sunim—I didn't hear you. He moves forward and stoops, suddenly conscious of his nakedness, gathering the pills and dropping them into his palm. What are these, anyway?

Shhh. Hae Wol squats next to him and begins scooping up the pills, pulling the cotton wadding out of the bottle and dropping it on the floor in his haste. Don't say anything about this, he says, in a high, cracking whisper, his eyes locked on the floor. I ask you as a friend, OK? You never saw me here.

All right, Lewis whispers.

After Hae Wol has left, he stands there for a moment, shivering in the blast of cold air from the corridor. Then he pulls on his robes, hardly bothering to dry himself, and leaves, keeping his eyes focused on the floor.

THE NEXT MONDAY THEY DO NOT SPEAK until they are almost finished loading the van.

Tell me what you're thinking, Hae Wol says finally. Are you angry? Are you shocked?

Shocked? He smiles; he's forgotten how conservative Joseph has always been, even a little naïve, by American standards. I'm surprised, he says. I take it those pills weren't exactly given to you by prescription.

Percocet, Hae Wol says. Painkillers. There's a laywoman who gets them for me. Her husband is a doctor. I went to him when I sprained my ankle last fall, and then I couldn't stop taking them. I just tell her, *I'm still having the pain*. Because I'm a monk, he won't say anything.

That isn't your fault, Lewis says. You need to get treatment, that's all.

Hae Wol shakes his head. No, he says. The fourth precept says, *no drinking, no intoxicants*. It doesn't say, *except when you really need it*. A vow is only a vow if you keep it one hundred percent of the time. Not ninety-nine percent.

Lewis swallows hard. Like marriage, he says. And yet, here we are.

Hae Wol squints at him with a half-smile, as if it's a joke he doesn't quite understand; then he looks away and nods, and stoops down to lift another bag of rice. You're right, he says, with a sharp, surprised laugh. Whip the horse, don't whip the cart, right?

So the question is, Lewis says, folding his arms to keep them from trembling, what will you do now, Sunim?

What do you think I should do?

Oh, no, Lewis says. Don't ask me that. Who am I to give you advice?

The monk sits down heavily on the bumper, holding out his hands to steady himself. His face is soft and slack, like a piece of rotting fruit. *Who else is there,* his body seems to say. And Lewis thinks, *What am I worth, after all, as a human being, if I can't do something for him right now?*

Give the pills to me, he hears himself saying.

Hae Wol looks up, raising his eyebrows. Now? he says. I don't have them. They're in my room.

You're lying, Lewis says fiercely, his tongue scraping the dry roof of his mouth. He holds out his hand. You want my help? he says. This is the help you get. Give them to me *now*.

Guilt flashes across the monk's face, and he reaches into his pocket. Lewis reaches over and places his hand on the bottle; Hae Wol's fingers tighten, and finally he has to pry it away. Quickly he unscrews the lid, spills the pills onto the gravel, and steps on them, twisting his foot, grinding them into the dirt.

I can always get more, Hae Wol says, unhappily. That doesn't change anything.

Listen, Lewis says. Can you get into the monastery office? Can you send a letter?

Hae Wol shrugs, and nods, reluctantly.

I want you to send a letter to Melinda for me, Lewis says. Will you do that? And then you tell that woman that the pain has gone away and you don't need any more pills.

I can't do that. The monk scratches slowly behind his ear, staring at the orange-stained pebbles around his feet. I don't have the strength, he says, tonelessly. It isn't going to work.

Do it anyway, Lewis says. Remember what you told me? *Don't know.* Just do it that way.

Hae Wol begins to laugh, his shoulders trembling. You Americans, he says, you take everything so literally. You're really going to force me to go through with this, aren't you?

Yes. Lewis forces himself to smile. You're stuck with me.

And what will you say in the letter?

I'm going to tell her that it's all right to fail, he says. That's not very American, is it? I'm going to say, *you don't really want what you're chasing after.*

That sounds like good advice.

And then chances are she'll leave me.

Don't say that, Hae Wol says, a stricken look on his face. You have to have faith in her. Even if she doesn't deserve it.

Lewis sees her sitting at the tiny dining table in their apartment, opening the letter and scanning it intently, her forehead creased with fear. Her legs are curled up underneath her; she leans forward into the pool of dim light from the window, even though the switch for the lamp is right behind her. Part of her doesn't notice, and part of her wants to stay there, crouched in the gloom, as if she doesn't deserve anything better. It isn't about sacrifice, he thinks, or mortgaging the present for the future. When did she come to believe that hating her own weakness was the only way to survive? *Melinda,* he wants to tell her, *you can choose happiness, but you have to choose.* And relief floods over him like cold rain.

I'VE BEEN THINKING ABOUT YOU, the teacher says, when Lewis enters the room and bows. Something's changed. Your face looks better.

Does it?

I have a little speech I want to give you. But you don't have to hear it if you don't want to.

Of course I do.

Every day, the teacher says, we recite the four great vows: *Sentient beings are numberless. We vow to save them all. Delusions are endless. We vow to extinguish them all. The teachings are infinite. We vow to learn them all. The Buddha way is inconceivable. We vow to attain it.*

So what does this mean? What does it mean to vow to do the impossible?

It means that we're never finished.

Yes. But what else?

It means that the standard is impossibly high. Always out of reach.

Is that the way we practice?

No. I guess not.

Our great teacher says, *Try, try, try, for ten thousand years.* Do you understand what that means?

Lewis starts to speak, and shakes his head.

This isn't a game, the teacher says, leaning forward and staring at him. Lewis feels his eyes watering, and tries not to blink. You don't *figure these things out.* The great work of life and death is happening all around us all the time. When do you have the chance to sit back and consider every possible option? You have to *act*.

And what if you're wrong? What if it turns out to be a disaster?

The teacher reaches out with his stick and raps him on the knee.

It already *is* a disaster, he says. Don't cling to some dream of a perfect world. Put down your fear and you can cut a path through the darkness.

Without thinking, Lewis bows, resting his head on the floor, raising his open palms in the air. I'm trying, he says. That's all I can do.

Now you understand, the teacher says. This is love. Go home and take this mind with you.

BEFORE CLIMBING THE STAIRS TO THE DHARMA ROOM, he opens the outside door and steps out into the courtyard. It is just sunset, and the sky above the mountain is washed with orange and gold; but in the west a dark line of clouds throws the city into shadow, and the air tastes of snow. He is wearing only socks, and the cold sears his skin with every step. *Is this what hope is like*, he wonders. *How long has it been? How would I know?* He opens the door again, and climbs the stairs slowly, staring at his feet, making no sound.

Anh Chi Pham

Mandala

In Memory of Thich Quang Duc

"Light arose in me, things not heard before."
—*Dhammacakkappavattana Sutta*

East

THAT DAY, my mother and I were walking to Cho Lon, Saigon's Chinatown. I wore a white dress and Mickey Mouse sandals that squished beneath my feet. With my left hand, I held onto my mother's wrist. With my right, I carried a *banh bao*. As we walked, I nibbled on the dough, holding its sweetness in my mouth.

We passed many monks, and when we reached a large intersection, I noticed they stood silently on all four corners. There were so many that they pushed my mother and me closer together. The monk next to me brushed my face with the sleeve of his orange robe, leaving on my cheek the scent of incense and sunshine. He held a long wooden necklace. His thumb moved over its beads, counting them the way my mother counted her rosary.

Drivers and motorcyclists honked as traffic slowed. As more monks gathered in front of us, my view of the street shrank. My mother clutched my hand tighter and tried to cross into Cho Lon. To my left, I saw a white car come to a sudden stop. The doors opened, and at that moment everyone spilled onto the street. They crowded around someone at the center that I could not see. My mother continued to push through, and all I saw were backs, arms, legs. As we struggled, people fell silent and still. Something in the air changed, like when a cloud covers the sun. My mother felt it too. She turned her head toward the car and a flash caught her eye.

I poked my head in between a monk and man with greasy hands, but all I saw was a trickle of water through sandaled feet. I smelled gasoline and heard a man with a deep voice chanting. I glimpsed an opening, so I released my mother's hand and stepped forward. Not far before me a monk sat. His robe was wet, his eyes were closed, and his lips curved into a little smile. He looked like the Buddha statue at the park near home—the same way of sitting, the same smooth face, the same smile. Then, his smile burst into bright flames. It was like that day at the park when I ran toward the Buddha and the doves flew away, their wings lit up by the sun.

My mother grabbed me, threw me over her shoulders and ran. She did not stop. She did not put me down until we were home. When she asked if I was alright, I nodded, but my right hand was clenched into a fist. She pried my fingers open and inside was the half-eaten *banh bao*. I had eaten the meat filling so only the bun remained, smashed and slick with sweat. She kneeled, took the bun, and placed it on the floor. She took a floral handkerchief from her purse and wiped my hand. Her gold cross moved up and down as she breathed. She put on a smile and hugged me. She said what I saw was just a bad dream and everything would be fine.

"But I wasn't sleeping," I said.

She did not reply. Instead, she noticed my sandals had gotten dirty, so she fussed over them and then combed her fingers through my hair. She said that my hair was getting long, perhaps she should cut it, and afterward we would go to the ice-cream parlor and get durian ice cream and paté sandwiches and have a long nap. As she said these things, I thought about the monk.

"Did he burn like the beetles?" I asked.

She looked at me, confused, so I told her about the game. My friend and I caught beetles. In the sunlight, we would hold a magnifying glass over them and watch as the beam of light ignited their little black bodies. Smoke burst from their crunchy shells as they wriggled and spun their legs faster and faster. She told me it wasn't a nice game, but I said that they weren't hurt. When we turned them right-side up, they flew away.

"I don't think the fire hurt the monk either," I said.

My mother did not reply. She ran her fingers through my hair and tucked it behind my ears. She wiped my forehead, my cheeks, my lips. She asked how could I know such a thing.

"The monk smiled at me," I said.

She held my shoulders and looked into my eyes. She searched and searched, her pupils dark like pools though inside them something shone and glimmered.

West

I HAD JUST FINISHED BREAKFAST with Professor Truong and we were strolling through downtown, discussing whether or not I should continue my studies in the United States.

"There is nothing for you here, boy," he said.

"I'm afraid my English isn't very good," I said.

"You can learn it in a few months. Besides, physics isn't in English. It's the universal language!"

I laughed at the idea of physics as the next Esperanto.

"And what would you do if you stayed here?" he added.

"I was thinking of our country, of the Viet Cong. Surely, it is my duty..."

"You are no fighter, my boy."

The professor and I continued talking until I noticed something was burning a few blocks away. When we arrived at the intersection, I saw that it was a person. His entire front side was gone. His empty face stared at me like a grotesque mendicant, asking for nothing. The wind shifted and the smell of his flesh overwhelmed us. Professor Truong covered his nose with a handkerchief as my stomach turned. I hunched over and threw up my breakfast. The half-digested noodles looked like worms on the ground and the sourness of them clung to my mouth.

I covered my nose and turned away. That's when I saw the young woman. She wore a short blue dress and stared at the fire as if entranced. She walked toward the flames, but her boyfriend pulled her away. Something bright fell from her. I wanted to tell her, but the couple disappeared into the crowd. I followed to where the object had fallen and found, wedged in the cracked asphalt, a crystal earring. The teardrop dangled and spun. When I held it up, each facet reflected the burning man behind me.

South

LAM KISSED ME, HIS HAND CRAWLING UP MY LEG. In the mirror, I saw the eyebrow of the taxi driver rising. I told Lam to stop, but he laughed, saying that he was willing to wait.

"Don't be so sure of yourself," I said and pushed him back to the other side of the taxi. I pulled down the hem of my dress, which was cut short according to the fashion of the time.

Traffic was unusually congested. I could feel the morning air beginning to warm, so I rolled down the window to let a breeze through. They were building a complex along the Saigon River for the Americans. The bones of it were up, pillars of steel and concrete. Workers hauled bags of cement and pushed carts filled with cinderblocks. In the background, bulldozers tilled the red earth.

"It will be the largest office complex in Vietnam," Lam said.

I nodded, continuing to look outside.

He kissed me on the cheek. I turned toward him, surprised by the sweetness of his gesture.

"I like your freckle here," he said, touching my right cheek. "You know what they say, red freckles bring good fortune."

"And what would I be lucky in?" I asked.

He looked at me solemnly. "Whatever you choose, my dragon lady."

"Has your mother bothered you anymore about your little fiancé?"

"My mother bothers me all the time."

He was evasive about the status of his engagement, arranged since he was a boy. Whenever I brought it up, he would deflect it in some way or we would joke about it, but I knew that, at thirty-four, he must marry soon. I chose again to make light of it, his poor mom, the waiting bride, the reluctant groom.

As we joked, the taxi slowed and I noticed orange after orange robe. When we stopped, monks stood on both sides. I stuck my head out the window. At the end of the next block, more monks were gathering. We sat waiting, hoping for traffic to clear. But it was useless, so Lam paid the driver and we got out. Lam was agitated—the protests in Hué last week had turned violent, and he wanted to leave the area as quickly as possible. But I was curious. I stopped a nun and asked her what the gathering was about. She bowed, but did not answer me. I asked another and she did the same. I was curious by their reticence, but another nun tapped me on the elbow and said, "If you want to know, you must go see for yourself." I followed her and Lam yelled at me, but I dodged into group of lay people. An eerie silence moved through the gathering. Then something ignited. A roar of flames shot into the air, and I smelled the flesh of an unknown animal. The hair on my neck and arms stood up. When we passed through the thicket of people, I saw in the clearing a monk engulfed in fire.

His eyes were closed, his skin lifted into the blaze. Fire ate where flesh was weakest: at the ears, the nose, the eyes. After a few minutes—he sat so still—his features burned away so that his face was but a horrible emptiness. The fire continued, consuming the robe, the body, his silhouette no longer orange, no longer covered in cloth. By degrees, he turned from ash-colored to black. His arms and legs melted into his torso, and the warmth of him, the warmth of him...

I wondered with which flame his spirit climbed and in what direction. I moved closer, wanting to know, but Lam pulled me away. We hurried to my flat on Madame Curie Street. We did not talk. The mid-morning sun bore down on us. In the sky, there was no hint of the afternoon rains, and my feet ached since the heels I wore were not made for the battered streets.

When we arrived at my building, I felt faint, so Lam carried me up the last two flights of stairs. On the divan, he removed my shoes and massaged my feet. He put the back of his hand on my forehead.

"I called your name several times, but you didn't hear me," he said.

How could I tell him that I saw something in the flames? That I wanted to catch it—angel or devil, saint or sinner, I wanted it. Instead, I traced Lam's face, the rise of his cheeks, the angle of his jaw, and rested my finger on the downward curve of his lower lip. He took my hand and kissed it.

When I woke, Lam was stroking my hair. It was dark outside and I heard sirens in the distance. I got up to find food in the fridge. By the time I came back with leftover noodles, he had turned on the lamp and was looking at the picture of my mother and me.

"You look so much like her," he said.

I sat down and picked it up. She was wearing First Wife's pearl neck-lace. The photographer had suggested it, to brighten her face, and in her smile I saw her shame. She wore that necklace as if every one of those pearls burned her.

"That was a long time ago," I said.

I gave him the noodles. I had never asked Lam for a commitment nor wanted one. He was a womanizer and I accepted this. In return, he treated me as an equal.

"Do you think we will go to war?" I asked.

"We are already in one now," he said.

"Can you do something for me? Can you tell me if you could ever love that girl?"

He said, "What a silly question."

For all his talk of democracy and progress, Lam was traditional. I knew he would never defy his parents' wishes, and I also knew that his fiancé was beautiful. Every night, her face filled the television screen, reading the news.

"I saw you with her outside the Continental. You two looked like you could almost be a real couple," I said.

"I only took her out for drinks."

"I could tell. She was so stiff and proper. I wouldn't be surprised if she shook your hand at the end of it."

We laughed, but he did not answer my question.

"Lam, I don't want to be like my mother. You have to choose," I said.

"Right now?" he asked.

"Right now," I said.

He looked away. Blood flushed through my cheeks, warm and red.

That night, I dreamt of the monk. Through the flames, he reached out to me. He gave me his hand and I took it. When I stepped into the fire, I couldn't feel heat or pain. Everything glowed around me, filling my heart with a tenderness that I had never known.

North

I SAW THE MONK BURN. I had just arrived in Saigon by bus from Trang
Bang, my legs numb, my back sore. The whole city felt like a giant open-
air market, but instead of women haggling over fish and produce, it was
people, cars, buses, schools of mopeds and bicycles, all haggling over space
and sound and air. I sat for a few minutes, adjusting my senses to the com-
motion. Then, I bought a *banh bao* from a street vendor who gave me directions to my uncle's house.

I decided to walk since I wanted to see the city. Halfway, I noticed a dis-
turbance to the south, a crowd gathering around a fire, and I noticed that
many were monks. Three policemen ran past me. They wore army fatigues
like the soldiers who patrolled our village.

Out of curiosity, I made my way toward the flames. At the intersection
I saw the most fantastical sight. A man sat burning. His body was completely charred. His face had disappeared, and I could tell by the way he
sat—in the lotus position—that he too must have been a monk. He looked
like wood without embers and the smell was indelible. Years later, I would
smell it again in the tunnels, with the flame-throwers and screams and
burning flesh.

But that day the monk was silent. People around him were distraught:
nuns cried, street urchins cursed, policemen stood stoically, and a few
Westerners with cameras were pale like ghosts.

My brother had told me about the unrest in Hué the previous week. He
said the government had killed nine monks. I said that he, a communist and
an atheist, could not possibly care. He replied that even though the monks
were selfish and misguided, being interested in only their own salvation
before that of the people, they were not materialists, not capitalists like the
Catholics. He said that I should learn these things, that I should see with
my own eyes.

I stood for a long time watching the monk's slow collapse. Afterward,

I continued walking toward my uncle's house. A woman let me in and I entered a courtyard garden with a pond, a red bridge, and ornate shrubbery. I saw fish glide in the water. Their coloring, silver and gold, spots of red and black, was unlike anything in the rivers at home.

"Do you like the koi?" a man asked.

I turned around and a stout man stood in the corridor. He wore a white suit and leaned on a walking cane. Even though he was portly, the way that he held himself reminded me of a rooster.

I bowed my head down to him. "Uncle," I said.

"No need for formalities," he said, walking toward me. His eyes judged my worn sandals, my wrinkled shirt, my overgrown hair.

"How old are you, boy?" he asked.

"I am nineteen," I said.

"You look like your father," he said with a hint of disdain.

"That's what Mother says."

"How is your mother?"

"She's not well, sir."

The woman brought a tray of tea, logan, and biscuits. My uncle told her to put it in his study.

"You should have told me you were coming. I could've had Le pick you up at the bus stop."

"You did not receive my letter, sir?" I asked.

"No. What letter?"

"I sent you a letter, informing you of my mother's condition."

"Hmm, hmm," he said. He steered me to his study, complaining that he was a busy man, that relatives should have the consideration to call before visiting. His study was filled with many books. Against the far wall, a globe and flagpole stood on either side of a large mahogany desk. Uncle sat behind the desk and poured tea as I ate the biscuits. He did not inquire further, so I asked him directly if he could help with my mother's medical care.

"Only my brother is working and the money he makes as a teacher is not enough," I said.

"Hmm, hmm," he said, stroking the ivory handle of his cane. "I told her to come to Saigon. I told her I could find her the best doctors, but that obstinate woman chose to stay in that backwater godforsaken town."

I remained silent.

"And now, how is she?" he asked.

"She can barely get out of bed, Uncle. The doctor says she doesn't have very long."

"You know they found the cure for tuberculosis years ago?"

"I had no idea, sir."

"Backward country, full of superstitious people," he muttered. He hit the tile floor with his walking stick. After a moment's hesitation, he opened his jacket and removed his wallet. He handed me several bills.

"Take it," he said. He then dismissed me, saying that he had an important meeting.

On the street, I counted the money—it was barely enough to pay for my bus fare home. Defeated, I walked back toward the bus stop. On Phan Dinh Phung Street, nothing remained of the monk except a black scar on the pavement.

Center

THAT DAY, I ONLY DRANK A CUP OF TEA. My attendant gave me chrysanthemum tea, knowing that it was my favorite. Then we drove from the temple to Saigon.

Since I had no hope when I sent my list of demands to President Diem, I had no regrets as we entered the city. As we passed people starting their day—a street vendor fanning her stove, a girl selling baguettes, a row of cyclos full of sleeping drivers, worn and brown like the earth—I breathed deeply, letting these images enter and pass through me.

Some of my brothers had questioned my decision. They said that my act would not lead to peace and nonviolence. I listened to them, feeling their concern, and I smiled gently. At that moment an ibis flew overhead, tracing the arc of the sky. I gestured toward the horizon and asked if they could see any remains of the bird's flight. Did the ibis fly completely, without fear or regret? When I asked them this, they fell silent. One by one, they bowed, leaving me to the quietude of my decision.

As the car meandered through Saigon's busy streets, I stopped looking outside and let go of the city. I remained calm, clearing my mind of all impressions, but without warning an image of my grandfather's midnight cactus flashed into my mind. I had not seen this flower since I was taken to the orphanage. Yet, there it was, as clear as the slant of sunlight through the car window. Its succulent leaves looked like praying mantises climbing on top of each other, branching outward and upward, and at the tip: the flower bud, with pink tendril-like petals about to bloom.

I observed the flower, the luminous branches that defied gravity and time. Within its leaves, I felt my grandfather's love. I remembered him drinking tea next to his flower, the sting of his bamboo rod, his thundering laugh as he chided me for my bad temper, the smell of durian lingering in his room, his serene face the morning he passed away. I breathed evenly, letting these childhood memories come and go, feeling old sorrows swirl within my heart, allowing them to rise and pass.

By the time we reached downtown, my mind was clear again. I chanted verses from the Lotus Sutra, keeping my attention on an open heart. When the car stopped, I felt the vibrancy of everything around me. With this awareness, I opened the door and walked through traffic, letting cars, cyclos, motorcycles weave through me.

I sat down on the warm asphalt and folded my legs into the lotus position. My brothers poured gasoline on me. When it soaked through my robe, I motioned for them to stop. The fumes rose, creating a halo around my body. I heard the chanting of my fellow monks. Brother Hanh handed me a matchbox, then stepped away. I felt his fear, so I offered him a smile. Then, I lit the match.

The fire roared and wrapped itself around me. I let it be. I kept my attention on an open heart, on the half-smile of my grandfather's serene face. Folding my hands into the cosmic mudra, I let the fire be. Heat was heat, pain was pain, and I continued breathing. I breathed until all the cells in my lungs burst.

Behind the inferno, I saw it was not me that was burning. It was the world. I saw bombs fall, presidents murdered, jungles stripped of trees, mouths wide open in hunger. I saw flags raised in victory, faces buried in defeat, and knew they were nothing but different aspects of the same phenomenon. My mind spun around these images, then came thunder and lightning, and wrathful emotions that shook the earth and Avalokiteshvara embracing all until I became a part of him.

After the flames died, I am. After the images have been caught and reflected, I am. After all wars have been won and lost, I am. My heart expands in all directions and becomes light, touching everything.

Sean Murphy

The Tale of
THE

HERE ONCE WAS A "THE" named *THE,* who was restless from birth. Composing with his kin one of the more populous clans of the page, he was raised, in the best tradition of his kind, to feel rather superior to his cousins, the indefinite articles—not to mention the other, less important parts of speech, such as prepositions, interjections, and conjunctions.

"After all," sniffed his mother, "language could function perfectly well without *them*, couldn't it? But what would even the grandest of proper nouns be without us? *The* Queen, *The* President, *The* Holy Spirit…the list is endless!"

His ancestors, his parents told him, had been chipped in stone, or hand-lettered upon papyrus—sometimes even written in blood. Later, their likenesses had been stamped onto pieces of metal and covered with ink, then transferred to page upon page—"And ever since," his parents said, "We've been *everywhere!*"

Still, as a child, *THE* dreamed of going beyond the limitations of his kind, of soaring aloft in realms of poetry and rhetoric. But he could never escape the creeping sensation that he was scarcely different from his fellow definite articles, all the other THEs.

"We're a bunch of clones," he thought to himself, "dressed in our identical spellings, merely pointing the way to more powerful parts of speech—why, we don't even really have a definition to call our own!"

And so, to the horror of those closest to him, as *THE* neared adolescence, he began to rebel. He grew his serifs long: **THE**; strutted about in boldface: **THE!**; mixed his upper and lower cases: tHe; boasted of his font size: THE.

"He's just trying to define himself," his mother said, as if to defend him.

"He's going through a transition," agreed his aunt.

"He's living on the margin!" grumbled his father.

"Why should I be definite?" became *THE*'s motto. He hung around with expletives, loitered with negations, ran with irregular verbs—and even caused a scandal in his sentence by consorting with a young and extremely curvaceous BUT.

"A THE just doesn't fit with a BUT," his grandmother told him. "It doesn't make sense. What you need to do is to find yourself a nice noun and settle down!"

But *THE* would hear none of it, and as he came of age he determined to go off and seek his fortune.

"No one who's left the paragraph has ever returned," cautioned his grandmother.

"There's nothing beyond the end of the page," asserted his mother.

"The text is flat," warned his father. "When you reach the edge, you'll fall off and drown!"

THE paid no heed to their warnings. Early one morning, before anyone else had awakened, he slipped away from his boyhood sentence, vaulted over the forbidden period at the end, and set off into the unknown. In the pale light of dawn he crept past tired, still-sleeping phrases, leapt over semicolons and dashes, sidestepped between parentheses, and hopscotched through the first ellipsis he'd ever seen. Soon *THE* came to the end of his paragraph, beyond which no one he knew had ever ventured.

Stepping gingerly across the opening indentation, *THE* passed into the next paragraph; and here he found himself in a new universe of freedom and wonder. Participles dangled about as they pleased, metaphors mixed freely and openly, infinitives split and rejoined without a second thought, sentences ran on as long as they liked and stopped when they were good and ready. *THE* strolled through vast, wide-open fields of inquiry, frolicked through looping, unpredictable turns of phrase, was lifted aloft by heroic and inspired rhetoric. He flirted with shapely figures of speech—he even took up, briefly, with a sweet young MINE, although he eventually found her too possessive for his taste. Throwing away all caution, abandoning every convention, *THE* pranced through it all like a dreamer awakened, swept away by the boundlessness of possibility. His only regret was for his loved ones, trapped in their prisons of grammatical conformity; and he vowed that someday he'd return home and show others the path to freedom.

YES, THIS NEW PARAGRAPH was a liberation—as was the next, and the one after that. But the text held many possibilities, and as *THE* pushed on, he found his surroundings growing ever wilder and more chaotic. He clomped through quagmires of unclear usage, hacked his way through thickets of untrimmed verbiage. He passed through realms of slang and sarcasm, universes of invective where subjects and verbs, no longer in agreement, struggled in open conflict, often doing violence to a tender turn of phrase.

With each subsequent page, *THE* found his situation becoming ever more challenging. He was beset by masculine pronouns, who found the lisping *th* of his opening phoneme effeminate, and accused him of being a homonym. He was set upon by brutal copyreaders, savaged by editors— even beaten by a group of burly interjections who thought his *h* was laughing at them. He crossed deserts of clichés and wastelands of insipid phrasing, camped amid the ruined remnants of weak constructions. He weathered storms of hyperbole and sank in the swamps of syntax, while terrifying pairs of dactyls swooped overhead. He entered lawless realms where definitions had been abandoned and the laws of usage were ignored, where spelling no longer functioned and even the proper use of the alphabet was unknown.

THE finally entered frontiers where he found no words at all, only wildernesses of pure punctuation:

                                                        #....?"':;;;;>>,,

                         ^^^+—_//!!~(**%!

!+^<)!!!!!!!
@@@@?./<;,>

                    """""""""[{[]{[}+—)))(
                              #####!!

                              ?/?

          ''''''

                              ....
                              <><><><.....,,<<{{&&

&&%$$ ——-
              ?????

Lastly, and most frighteningly of all, *THE* passed through a page of complete blankness, utterly void and empty of meaning:

Lost in uncertainty, unsure of his proper place or function, *THE* fell into confusion and thence into despair. As he re-entered the settled realms of verbiage, he found himself treated as an outcast, an object of derision, banished to the ends of unfamiliar phrases, scorned by the stately proper nouns and others of their ilk. Yes, he had achieved freedom of a sort, had broken boundaries, revealed new possibilities for oppressed parts of speech everywhere—but what, he asked himself, was his role in the new order he'd helped create? Was there no place that was truly his own? Was he doomed to merely repeat the function of his forbears, to point the way for other, more important elements of speech, like a servant who opened doors or delivered messages, but otherwise stood invisible? For a time, *THE* even contemplated deleting himself from the text altogether.

At last, trusting that there must be something beyond the tragic episode in which he now found himself enmeshed, *THE* turned to religion: and here he entered upon a new chapter. Setting off boldly once more, he sought out soothsayers, prophets, and those who spelled in tongues. For a time he followed a path which claimed there were thousands upon thousands of possible pages, all of them divine manifestations of the One Great Book that contained them all. He stumbled about for many paragraphs in a holy daze before discovering an alternate system which held that there were no pages whatsoever, nothing definite and no definitions, and that even the text itself was an illusion. He flirted for a time with a sect that preached that *each* word was the very word of God, and attributed all suffering to the condition of Original Syntax. He even became involved with the New Page movement, which posited that all words created their own usages, and that far from being confined to any single position or meaning, all were essentially free.

None of it brought him lasting peace.

"What do I *mean*?" *THE* cried out in despair.

But after many a dark page, his cries were answered by a seer who taught him to turn his attention inward, to accept what he was, and rather than asking what he meant, to discover his true function. "In the beginning was The Word," asserted this visionary. "And *you* are *it!*"

It was here that *THE* found what he'd been looking for. After many pages of self-contemplation, he came to realize that all his attempts to be less definite had been illusory, self-deceptive. Why, his very nature was to be a definite article, right down to the vowel at his end! He could be exactly what he was, and still know freedom.

At last, he'd achieved consonance.

After many chapters and many further adventures, *THE* finally made his way back to his home paragraph, as he had promised himself long ago. Here he spread tales of pages beyond pages, of infinite options for self-definition, and the hardships and possibilities of reaching them. He told of realms words would enter in the future, where they would not appear upon a page at all, but would come into being by unimaginable processes, manifesting instantly from a domain of pure light. Phantasms, shadowy bits of nothingness, such words could scarcely be thought to exist at all.

In time, in recognition of these efforts, and of his deep insight and serenity, *THE* became known among his people by the fond title of "The Genuine Article." But by now he'd grown old and his print was faded, and the denizens of his page were too frightened to set off and see for themselves, so that at last his tales came to be regarded as fables, mere fairy stories invented to amuse the lowercase letters.

Legend has it that in his final years *THE* vanished once again, having found a lasting partnership with the noun of his dreams—one who oddly enough reminded him, in a certain way, of that first fond conjunction of his youth, his beloved BUT. It is said that the pair traveled together through page upon page, chapter after chapter, until they reached the very limit of verbal experience, the edge of the text, and their own true position at the completion of the story:

THE END

Pico Iyer

Abandon

B Y THE TIME JOHN GOT BACK TO CALIFORNIA, he was feeling displaced somehow, as if the love song in the airport taxi in Damascus, slow and plangent, was still coursing through him in some way. Finding hidden manuscripts of Rumi was proving more difficult than getting fragrant reminders— echoes—of him in the mosque.

"So the prodigal returns," Alejandro said in his ironic way, outside the lecture hall, as they bumped into each other in the corridor, on their way to hear the visiting lecturer.

"And the fatted calf awaits him."

"How was Syria?"

"Amazing; really amazing. It sounds stupid, I know, but it really puts you in your place."

"I can imagine. Hafez Assad has that effect, I've heard."

Though Alejandro had been in California three years or more, he'd never lost the raised eyebrows of Buenos Aires. Hiding his light was an article of faith with him. John thought of his classmate whenever asked why he chose to study Rumi and Islam at the university and he'd respond, "I don't know. I suppose they're everything we didn't learn about in school."

"And you?" asked John. "What have I missed?"

"Everything. Nothing. I toil in the pastures of the heartbroken. Becoming a doctor who can't heal when I wish only to be a bachelor once more." He spoke a strange, overflowery English, fluent, but sounding, often, as if it had passed through Spanish first.

"And so our investigation into the death of God proceeds," his friend went on as they passed through the open doors and claimed some seats a few rows in from the back. "'Can you tell us where you were on the night of May 17? We have reason to believe that it was then that this person with whom you were involved—the "Higher Power," as he is sometimes called—first went missing. Unless you can shed some light on when you saw Him last, we will have to presume Him dead.'"

Around them the same faces as usual were taking the same seats as usual, some near the back, with a view to a rapid escape, others near the front, in the hopes of rapid ascent. Religious Studies was in permanent danger of following the gods it studied into oblivion; it presented itself now as a science, and offered classes on "Rage" and "Men's Wildness." A researcher from MIT—so the persistent rumor ran—had actually been called in to conduct experiments on how laboratory mice responded to an image of the Virgin Mary.

Professor Sefadhi still fought a rearguard action, however, and he was a seasoned and determined fighter, "from a culture where faith is not such a dirty word," as he was fond of saying, glossing over some of the finer points of Persian history. He'd made it his mission to bring in wandering speakers, like prophets from the desert, to remind the rabble of "primordial fire," as he called it. Now, standing at the podium, he shuffled through his notes and motioned for a lowering of the lights, a return to sacred silence.

"Fortune, the ancients held, favored those who paid homage to it in secret," he began, speaking with the forgotten courtesies of his native

Isfahan. "Much as a woman might drop a handkerchief to lure a passing knight's gaze towards her window. Just so, we in Religious Studies must have been burning offerings in private to merit the visit of one such as Ryan McCarthy."

There were a few uncertain snickers, the inevitable rolled eyes. The ornamental phrases rolled on and on—treasures scattered out of a jeweled box—and their object, a man with tufts of reddish hair around his ears, and an aging herringbone jacket with huge patches on its sleeves, stood up to take the stand.

"Many of you, I know, are familiar," Sefadhi continued, bald head glinting in the lights (and the visiting dignitary sitting down again), "with Professor McCarthy's ground-breaking work on scriptures in a secular world, *Sensuous Seducers*, with its elegant subtitle, *Lures and Gambits in the Bible*. All of you, I know, are acquainted with his exchange with Huston Smith in the *Journal of Religious Studies*. But none of that, I think, can prepare us for what he will be sharing with us tonight. It is with something more than honor, and with a feeling much deeper than pride, that I give you Professor Ryan McCarthy."

The applause was scattered, and then the promised savior got up again and trudged over to the podium, looking around all the while as if he'd blown his cue again. When he faced them, they could see, even if he could not, that his blue-striped shirt was misbuttoned and his shoelaces were loose. He looked like a passerby dragged by mistake into a frat-house party.

He cleared his throat, straightened the papers before him, and, looking down, began to flick, half-desperately, through them.

"Another step forward in the long march of the soul," muttered Alejandro, who had the schoolboy's way of defining himself by what he could see through.

"The subject of my address to you today," McCarthy began, speaking faster as he picked up the thread of his talk, "though hardly worthy of the praise that Professor Sefadhi has lavished on it, with such characteristic generosity" (he glowed down at the front row), "is what I have called the 'Higher Temptations.' The devices by which we are pulled toward the good. By this, of course, I refer not to those common wiles and stratagems that seem to take us farther from our destinies, but to those that return us to our original mission, if I may put it into those words."

Bodies slumped lower in their seats, and all around was a faint scattering of whispers exchanged, and notes passed back and forth.

"It is commonly supposed, even—I dare say, especially—by us Catholics" (there was a ripple of laughter, as if to acknowledge that he was trying to be human), "that the Devil has been given all the best lines. Iago is a wordsmith, Othello professes inarticulacy. Satan makes off with the poet's verses. Yet why, I wonder, should Satan's master and maker—his evident superior—not have as many words at His disposal? Are we to surmise that words themselves are a part of the fallen Creation? All life, after all, is a constant, agitated battle between those who see this world as the only one that matters—earthly patriots, as we might call them—and those who remain true to another order. Are words the instruments only of the mortal?"

Every now and then someone laughed, but it was in the nervous, uncertain fashion of someone laughing at a foreign film as if in happy surprise that these people were just like us.

"Scholars might assert, in fact, that Satan's greatest temptation to Jesus is to imagine himself beyond the temptation of a Satan. 'Tell us you're the son of God,' he says, like a master logician, 'tell us you can never die.' His offer, in effect, is to make Jesus a lord of infinite riches in a world that doesn't exist."

This was more, perhaps, than any of those in attendance had expected, and the audience had not yet given up on him entirely.

"Here, perhaps," he went on, putting down his typescript and picking up a large book, "I can give you an example of a higher calling.

"'Like an apple tree among the trees of the forest, so is my beloved among young men.'" His voice was high and shaky, and the words got lost or smothered, yet something of their tingle still came through. "'To sit in his shadow is my delight, and his fruit is sweet to my taste. He has taken me into the wine-garden and given me loving glances. Sustain me with raisins, revive me with apples; for I am faint with love. His left arm pillows my head, his right arm is around me.'"

He put the book down again, and faced his startled audience once more. "Thus we can see how some scholars maintain that 'Eve' comes not from the Hebrew for 'life,' but from the Aramaic for 'serpent.' Which of us, after all, would be proof against such lines?

"And yet, of course, to the believer this is as it should be. The sensuous words are a call not to pleasure but, if anything, its repudiation—or, at least, transcendence. They mark a summons to what we might call, without undue exaggeration, the highest and best in us." He beamed over at his listeners from his place onstage. "All religious verse, we may say—and here I refer not only to the poetry of our own tradition, but to the love songs of the Sixth Dalai Lama, the Zen verses of Ikkyu, the riddles of the Sufis—all religious verse is written in a kind of code. It is administering a test to us. That could, in fact, be adduced as one of the signs of religious verse: that it moves as if inside a veil."

Here, as he rose towards his climax, the papers on the podium began to form new patterns of disarray, and it seemed as if he would as easily move from omega to alpha as the other way around. He fumbled for a moment over a word he couldn't read, then realized he'd lost his place.

"The sensuous seducer claims another conquest," murmured Alejandro, sinking deeper into his seat.

"Thus," the visitor continued, trying to regain his momentum, "all religious verse speaks to us in a language we can understand. To those with eyes and ears the poems are a kind of holy come-on; to those without, they appear as love songs, emblems of profanity. These ceremonial seductions, if so I may denote them, are a way of defining our relations to the world around us. A good man sees a man in rags, sitting in the street, and recognizes him as an angel traveling incognito; another man sees the same creature, and writes him off as a homeless beggar. We are no greater than the height of our perceptions."

Again, he put down his text and broke into an antique, mock-poetic voice.

"'May I find your breasts like clusters of grapes on the vine, your breath sweet-scented like apples, you mouth like fragrant wine flowing smoothly to my caresses, gliding over my lips and teeth.'"

"Where is Joni Mitchell when we need her?" asked Alejandro from his place, slumped down towards the ground.

"Who you are, in short, what you believe, and where you stand on the cosmic battlefield—everything is in its way revealed, perhaps defined, by how you respond to these verses. Do you see a sensual incitation or an epithalamion in the realm of the invisible? All that separates one from another is a curtain of assumptions. And no argument or preaching or scholarly discourse can raise the curtain for those who see it, or lower the curtain for those who don't. The religious transaction is—it has to be—a love affair conducted in the inner chambers of the heart. Those not party to it"—he cleared his throat here, for his crescendo—"can do no more than turn away in embarrassed silence, or cling to their own quite different loves."

A round of surprisingly enthusiastic applause greeted the end of the talk, and not only because it was the end; if nothing else, the man himself had seemed a performative statement—his very being brought home the point of his lecture more forcibly than his words could. To those with the right kind of ears, he could seem a luminous messenger; to everyone else, just a vague figure staring over his stand at the scattering of claps, and squinting without much pleasure as someone said something about the Song of Songs as the only book in the Bible that failed to mention God and someone else said something about the second-century rabbi who, in spite of that (because of that?), had called it the "Holy of Holies."

Faced with their challenges, he peered over the lectern like an uncle who suddenly realized that he was supposed to bring the Christmas presents.

"Of course there is much virtue in what you say," the lecturer said, in answer to a question about the sovereignty of the subjective. "The death of the author is a way of talking about the death of God. The world itself becomes a poem whose author disappeared long ago. Like, in fact, the Song of Songs. Yet for me—born, perhaps, into a different world, and a different generation, from your own—every comma is, in a way, a fragment of God. I stand, so to speak, on the far side of the invisible veil."

He'd put himself out of harm's way, though for most of the beings in the room his admission merely underlined his irrelevance.

"What better note on which to end?" said Sefadhi, abruptly rising to his feet, and bringing the confrontation to a close. Averting bloodshed was his strength. "Or, should I say, on which to begin? For what Professor McCarthy has given us today is not just the fruit of decades of deep scholarship; it is, no less, the stimulus for decades of serious thought to come. Thank you, Professor McCarthy; and thank you, one and all."

A few bodies began to get up, and then Sefadhi went on. "I am reminded of the ancient Sufi tale in which a seeker, knocking at his master's door, hears the sheikh call out, 'Who is it?' 'It is I, sir, me,' he responds, and the teacher's voice calls back, 'Go away! Where there is an "I," there can be no true instruction. Come back when you are no one.'"

More bodies got up now, as if to force him to be quiet, and, with some claps of relieved applause, they all began making for the refreshments next door.

"So God, we learn, is an Irish mystic," said Alejandro, gathering his books and standing up.

"I liked it," replied John. "He didn't make distinctions between religions; only around them."

"He knows his audience," said Alejandro dryly, and led him into the room where plastic bottles of Diet Coke and 7-Up sat sentinel above paper plates filled with unpromising wedges of cheese. He cast a quick glance around the room to see who might be worthy of his attention and then said, "That girl over there? You know her?"

"She was at the back of the hall, I think. With someone else."

Not missing a moment, Alejandro began walking across the room to see where this new adventure might lead. As he and John went over, slipping between bodies, they heard someone say something about Eliade, and the "erasure of the Other"—"apocalyptic pressures" and the "abolition of Eternity"—and then they found themselves in front of the stranger, as she looked up in startled shyness.

"You are," said Alejandro, "a spy, perhaps, here to inspect us lesser mortals? Or eager to see what happens to those of us who make raids upon the unknowable?"

The woman looked up at him, bewildered by his extravagance. "I'm here with my friend," she said. "She's—somewhere over there." She pointed toward the crowds, and Alejandro turned around for no more than a second. "Are you from England?"

"Buenos Aires," he said, "but it comes to the same thing. I studied with the nuns in Hurlingham."

"Great," she said, uncertainly, going back to her cheese. "That sounds really exotic."

"And you," he continued, pantomiming some Latin charmer, "you are a supporter of Professor McCarthy? Or just a passing admirer?"

"It's my friend," she said, unhelpfully. "She's into this stuff—or at least her sister is. I just came to keep her company."

"A surrogate spy, then. You are forgiven."

She looked up at Alejandro with a smile that said she still didn't know what was going on, and he, with all the gallantry he could muster, looked around the room. "I'm sorry to say I must return to my labors," he said, "but I wish you sweet dreams, and good data to take back to the sister," and then walked towards the exit.

"The passage from the spirit to the senses," Alejandro called back to her over his shoulder, "may be less direct than the good professor would have us believe." Not realizing, perhaps, that a higher temptation might be standing in the corner.

Dan Zigmond

Humans

L ONG ARMS ARE NOT AN ADVANTAGE in sitting meditation. They don't fit on your lap. They pull your shoulders forward, force your spine out of alignment. They strain your lower back. They get in the way.

I knew Daidaiiro must hate sitting. His body was made for climbing trees, for navigating the tangled web of branches and vines that rose a hundred feet above the forest floor. But he followed me as I walked down the narrow path through the creaking bamboo, up to the hilltop where my predecessors had fought back the jungle to create our outdoor *zendo*. I had abandoned formal robes months ago, but I still wore my black *rakusu* to these sittings and it fluttered around my neck like a child's bib, slapping my stained T-shirt with every step. I carried a sutra book and a damp foam cushion from the supply tent. I still hadn't gotten used to sitting on the mossy ground, and I had heard that vipers hid in the fallen logs littering the earth.

You me sit, I signed to my hairy companion when we reached the clearing.

Want you peek-a-boo, Daidaiiro replied. *No sit.*

Sorry. I flashed an exaggerated clown frown. *Peek-a-boo later. Now sit.*

No sit. Please you peek-a-boo. Peek-a-boo now.

No peek-a-boo. Sorry. You me sit now.

Please chase. You me chase. Sit later. Now chase.

This was the conversation I was having one week before the first visit from Bishop Koyu Yoshida, Director of International Missions for the Zen Buddhist Sotoshu Shumucho. I sat down on my cushion, Daidaiiro signing furiously at my side.

MY MOTHER ALWAYS SAID THAT LIFE ISN'T FAIR. She believed she was sharing a profound insight, along the lines of "matter is composed of elementary particles" or "the way that can be spoken is not the true way." That her motto was so profoundly unsatisfying to a third-grade boy kept after school, or a teenager short-changed at the convenience store, only strengthened her conviction. These were her words to live by.

So I spent my youth looking for moral clarity, for cosmic justice. I studied philosophy in college, hoping to find the answer in the Western canon. After graduation, I fell in love. I got dumped. I spent the next month reading all the books my ex-girlfriend abandoned in our apartment, and among them I discovered Buddhism. With its karmic laws of moral cause and effect, the Dharma gave me an answer at last. In the long run, good deeds *were* rewarded, and evil *was* punished. If life looked unfair on the surface, it was only because we lacked perspective: justice would prevail in future lifetimes. The sadistic teacher, the ignorant shopkeeper, the two-timing lover would all get theirs in the end.

The Buddha taught that our actions on this earth earn us another place in one of the six realms of life. If we've been very good, we return as gods or demigods, blessed with a lifetime of power and pleasure. If we've been particularly bad, we are doomed to haunt the earth as hungry ghosts or live for an eon among the miserable inhabitants of hell.

It is the two middle fates that concern us here at the Mission: the realms of humans and animals. Buddhists have long believed that only humans can make the moral choices necessary to change their karma, that animals are condemned to live their lives in ignorance, slaves to primitive desire. The Buddha explained that humans alone can choose to follow the Buddha's Way, discover Nirvana, and depart the Wheel of Life forever.

Or did he? How well do we really understand the vocabulary of an Indian prince from twenty-five hundred years ago? The Malays call orangutans "wild men of the forest." Do we know for certain who the World-Honored One considered human?

IT WAS A LETDOWN TO BE ASSIGNED to the First Zen Mission to the Apes. After converting to the Buddha Dharma that summer twenty years ago, I had been a rising star. I drove my old Honda to southern California and ordained as a monk after four years of meditation in the San Jacinto Mountains. The abbot there sent me to Japan for two years at the great Eiheiji monastery, and then made me, as a freshly commissioned brown robe, head priest in his temple back in America. From there, the Sotoshu gave me plum assignments every few years. Establishing a new sitting group in Mendocino. Taking over a thriving temple in Eugene. Finally, a cushy office job at Zen Buddhist headquarters in L.A., dispensing cash from the old country to the struggling temples of the new. I was almost sorry our sect didn't require a vow of celibacy. I was ready to give everything to my newfound faith.

And so it seemed especially ironic when the letter came last year from the bigwigs in Kyoto. Everyone knew it was a lousy assignment, the shortest straw a Buddhist cleric could draw. No more plush office in Little Tokyo, no more hot tea and miso soup left on my desk by the shuffling old woman in a crisp kimono. I was ordered to fly out in ten days, stopping for two months of language training in Tokyo, then on to Jakarta. From there it was two short flights to Pangkalan Bun on the island of Borneo, and a five-hour boat ride up the tea-black Sekonyer River into Tanjung Puting Reserve, orangutan capital of the world, home to our modest tent temple in the bush.

The project was already more than thirty years old when I got here twelve months ago. In the early seventies, one of the bishops in the Soto hierarchy read an article about teaching sign language to captive chimpanzees in America. He was intrigued. Not only could the apes communicate with their human colleagues, but they showed an inkling of right and wrong, good and evil. They could lie, love, and make sacrifices. They could mourn.

If chimpanzees could do it, why not Asia's native apes? And if apes can make choices, doesn't the Bodhisattva Vow require us to teach them the Path? So the Office of International Missions quietly negotiated with the Indonesian government, and the project was born. The first step was establishing a means of communication, so my predecessors studied the American results and began teaching sign language to our orangutan neighbors. This went reasonably well, and their journals faithfully record many conversations with their students:

What want? signed Rev. Takahashi. He had been there for more than a dozen years, a real trooper.

Gimme banana, answered Daidaiiro, the current star pupil. I was the first non-Japanese missionary, so all the orangutans had Japanese names. Daidaiiro means "orange," the color of his short, furry beard.

What size want? Takahashi persisted.

Big banana, signed Daidaiiro.

And so forth.

They brought me in to take things to the next level. Enough about bananas. Let's talk about Buddha.

ORANGUTANS IN THE WILD ARE SOLITARY CREATURES, foraging alone for weeks up in the forest canopy, passing one another in the tall trees with barely a glance. But over time, a few of our orangutan friends have become more social. Depending on the day, I had as many as half a dozen in my would-be sitting group. We didn't force any of them to come—that was an important principle of the Mission. They could visit our encampment at will, and some stopped by for food and then vanished for weeks. Of the six thousand orangutans in the preserve, I had met perhaps twenty or thirty. But some stuck around, mostly adolescents, no longer clinging to their mothers but not yet ready to strike out on their own. The only problem was they wouldn't sit still. They insisted on running and climbing, wrestling me to the ground of the dried peat swamps or playing hide-and-seek behind a nipa palm in the jungle's perpetual shade.

They also wouldn't shut up. Every day I emerged from my hut and prepared breakfast of rice and fruit, making sure there was enough to share. This was the only way to guarantee their attention. I didn't sign at breakfast, continuing the monastic tradition of silence during meals. It drove my companions crazy.

Tea drink.

Eat orange.

Hurry eat now.

Afterwards, I would squat with them in a small clearing and begin the day's lesson. Daidaiiro was always there, and he usually did most of the talking.

No sit, he signed yesterday morning. *Enough sit. Please come tickle.*

Me sit, I explained. I didn't know what else to say.

To be honest, I don't know if there's much hope. Meditation requires reflection. We seek to live in the here and now, but to do this we first step away from the now, and sit still rather than involving ourselves in the everyday world. Yet, having taught the orangutans to speak their minds, it hardly seems fair to silence them. I fear our ape cousins may never master the Holy Eightfold Path.

THIS MORNING, I LIT A STICK OF INCENSE and sat on my small cushion in the jungle for forty minutes. My students knew not to touch the burning stick. That, at least, I had taught them in my year here, but it seemed unlikely to impress Bishop Yoshida.

Sitting here is nothing like sitting in an American or Japanese *zendo*. It is never truly quiet, and every meditation period risks interruption from fire ants or torrential rains. But I've always enjoyed sitting in groups, and I was glad to have company, no matter how restless. Only three of the apes stayed to the end, playing with each other and climbing on nearby trees. When I rose, Okii, the tallest, came over.

Good good sit, he signed.

Thank you, I told him.

They say the first Zen monk to live in America didn't speak of Buddhism for seventeen years after he arrived. With the orangutans, the head office decided to wait twice as long. But this was supposed to be the year.

You sit, I signed to Okii. *You me sit*.

Daidaiiro dropped from a high branch and joined us.

What you do? he asked.

Sit, signed Okii.

Hachi, the youngest of the group, remained in the trees. He vocalized loudly, and signed *Come*.

Yes again sit, signed Daidaiiro.

I got excited. This felt like it could be the breakthrough. It seemed wrong that a promising monk like me should be banished to this backwater mission, saddled with an impossible task. Perhaps if I could show a little progress, the bishop would grant my request for a transfer back to America, or to one of the nascent temples springing up in Germany or France.

I sat down again and crossed my legs. My students squatted low, the lotus position as unnatural for them as knuckle-walking would be for me. I let my eyelids drop, half-closed, and took a long, deep breath. I didn't look around to see if the others did the same, but for a moment there was calm. The squeaking and hooting, the beating of hands, the thrashing of trees, all stopped, leaving only the low hum of cicadas and our own rhythmic breathing to fill the humid air.

We must have lasted about thirty seconds. Then Hachi threw something from the tree, and Okii took off after him at phenomenal speed. A barrage of branches and leaves rained down on me as he climbed. By the time I looked up, only Daidaiiro was with me. He gave me a bashful look.

No more sit, he signed.

I smiled and scratched his hairy arm, something he always liked. Daidaiiro reached over and gave me a rough embrace. After so many years as a monk, I still flinched at being hugged. I thought I should say something, but I didn't know the signs for what I felt. The truth was, I didn't know much more sign language than he did.

I walked back to camp, Daidaiiro tagging along behind me, rummaging through the leaves as he went. The bishop would be arriving soon, and I had work to do to prepare. He would not transfer me, I was sure of that. The Buddha Way is a path of unending patience: if not this life, then perhaps the next. Giving up was not an option. I would sit again tomorrow. My karma was here now.

I looked at my friend and he looked back, the whites of his eyes eerily human in the early light. Did Daidaiiro understand the unfairness of this world? The Buddha showed us the way to know ourselves, but even he did not explain how to know others. Language is so inadequate to describe human experience. Whoever the humans are.

Daidaiiro and I didn't speak as we walked, and we remained silent as I cleaned the temple's open-air shrine and arranged flowers and fresh fruit on the makeshift altar inside. At last he tapped my leg with his huge hands to get my attention.

Can't, he signed. He pointed to himself. *Can't sit.*

I know, I answered. *I know.*

Michele Martin

The Later Years of Her Life

AT AGE EIGHTY-FIVE, Mother had come to visit me in Kathmandu where I awaited her with some trepidation. She liked far away locales, but she liked her comfort, too. This placed a burden on the people she visited, especially a daughter. Further, Nepal was not a developed country: the water had micro-organisms that could lay you low; the roads were a slow stream of old Toyota taxis, trucks spewing black smoke around their lopsided loads, flower-painted rickshaws, and worn bicycles, all weaving their way around the sacred cows, chewing their cud in the midst of the shifting lanes.

I found a hotel where the professors stayed. It doubled as a museum of Nepali wood carvings, harboring old window frames and graceful temple struts that lasted centuries, while the brick walls that supported them went up and down as the Himalayas grew their inch-plus a year and earthquakes made adjustments. In her woven bamboo rocking chair, Mother was at home here, taking breakfast in the garden and chatting with other visitors. I filled the bookshelves in her white-walled room with clean glasses, bottles of filtered water, and snacks of cheese and crackers imported from

New Zealand. A notice went up on the mirror: "Bottled water for brushing your teeth!"

Mother insisted on not missing a thing, so just a day after her twenty-hour flight, halfway around the globe, we headed up to the monastery of Nagi Gompa. On the north side of the valley, its buildings scattered themselves down the upper slopes of a foothill, visible in the evening as distant lights falling through the night space, so dense and dark that it held them suspended on their way down. During the day, the hill became an anchor for the horizon-wide spread of immense and brilliant white peaks that seemed from another realm, coalesced out of the azure sky they defined, hovering there, ragged and magnificent. We rented an old red taxi, owned by a Nepali who would be our driver for the duration of her visit. Battered by time and the elements, the car looked barely able to make the journey but somehow rumbled up the dirt switch-backs to the monastery's small landing. From there, it was a fifteen-minute trek up steps carved out of the mountain side. Nuns coming down the slope in their maroon robes carried bags for shopping and smiled as they passed. We paused so Mother could catch her breath and look out over the valley far below, now a miniature of tiny pink houses and emerald fields, splayed in uneven lines around the white dome of the Baudha stupa, its eyes, ever-open, gazing out in the four directions. We watched an airplane as it came in over the southern ring of mountains, circled, and swooped onto the landing strip.

"Remind me what a stupa is," Mother asked.

"It holds relics of a buddha or a realized master," I replied. "It also symbolizes the Buddha's mind."

"Oh, yes," she said. "His mind."

We continued our climb up to the residence of Tulku Urgyen, one of the great masters who had escaped Tibet when the Chinese invaded. He lived atop a traditional Tibetan temple with huge vermilion doors set into white walls, long windows framed in black, and a curved roof that looked poised for flight. Mother was breathing hard as we mounted the last turns of the stairs up to his room. I worried about altitude sickness, which could be fatal for someone her age. I asked how she was. A former Christian Scientist, she waved away my concern, and breathed softly, "I'm just fine."

I remember years ago my grandfather sitting in his armchair next to the fireplace, reading a book by the founder of Christian Science, Mary Baker Eddy. While the warmth of the flames reflected off his cheeks, he read with a slight smile and a focus that seemed to carry him into another world. Mother had taken this faith into college, but gradually let it go as philosophy and literature courses brought questions she could not answer. In her seventies, Mother became a Buddhist, a shift not so far away from the Christian Science she knew as a young girl. When I asked her about it, she replied, "I feel at home. I like that both talk about a science of the mind. That all is infinite mind and its infinite manifestations."

We had visited many lamas together, but this was the first time she would meet Tulku Urgyen. A nun brought us cups of steaming tea, and I was relieved to see that Mother's breathing had calmed down. Once our cups were empty, a nun lifted the door curtain, inviting us into Tulku Urgyen's room. We made three bows and sat in front of him on the floor. With thick glasses magnifying the kindness in his eyes, he spoke to Mother about the *bardo*, about what would happen when she died, how the elements would dissolve into each other and how a bright light would appear. "Recognize this as the indwelling nature of your own mind."

Mother—just five years short of ninety—leaned forward, not to miss a word, her head turned a little to the side. As I watched this timeless scene of teacher and student, I was proud of her still wanting to learn. Tulku Urgyen said, "Practice by calming your mind and learning to rest in unborn naturalness. Like a grandmother watching children at play, observe thoughts arising and ceasing by themselves."

Mother nodded laying in her mental notes.

"Do your thoughts come from outside?" he asked.

She straightened and thought for a moment. Late-afternoon light flowed into the room, illuminating the warm reds and yellows. "Well, no, I don't think they do."

Tulku Urgyen smiled. "Then look into your mind to find their source. With practice, you'll discover *rigpa*, pristine awareness."

BEYOND THE LAMAS AND HER DAUGHTER, whom she always wanted closer in the family circle, it was the mountains that drew Mother to Nepal. She never said why she liked them, only that she did, and I was left to speculate. Was it the contrast to the corn and wheat plains of her Midwestern youth where hedge rows and barns were all that broke the skyline? Or was it the affair she had at Oxford when she and her beau traveled to Switzerland for a winter vacation near the curving peak of the Matterhorn? Or was it what they do to your mind, the upward thrust carrying it beyond the ordinary into a world of white sculpture and infinite blues, beyond whatever held you down or back? If you looked long enough, you could drink space and feel your bones turn to lightning.

On the third day of Mother's visit, we took an eight-seater plane down the ribboning wall of the Himalayas. As we headed west to Pokhara, Mother sat next to a window where she remained silent, looking at the rivers branching brown and dark green through the undulating hills while the abrupt ivory of the Annapurnas soared into view behind them. Another old and dented Toyota, its navy blue baked opaque in the high-altitude sun and its chrome long gone, dropped us at the border of the lake. We carried our suitcases onto a small wooden platform that tilted back and forth in the shallow water. The raft, without a single stick of railing to grasp, was a rope-drawn pontoon that carried us to the lodge on the lake's far side. I worried that Mother might be afraid, but as we were pulled slowly across the spread of water, she only had eyes for the mountain and the colors of sunset spilling down its side. Our Fish Tail Lodge was named after Machhapuchare, the rough pyramid of a mountain that torques its stony weight upward from the surrounding range. Resembling the Matterhorn of her college years, it was doubled by reflection into the still, blue lake that held time immobile across its mirror surface.

That night in the lodge, we dined on fish from the lake, baked in lime and butter, while we watched a small group of English tourists, ready to trek the heights in their tennis shoes and flowered skirts. Mother laughed, "The Intrepid British!" Retiring early to do some meditation before turning in, we sat on pillows at the head of the twin beds and slipped under the covers when finished.

Early the next morning, Mother announced, "I'd like to go down to the lake for a last look." So we dressed with sweaters against the cold and descended the wooden steps set into the soft green hillside. The shore was damp in the early hours. As I had during the whole trip, I held Mother's arm to steady her gate and to catch her if she fell. "Just this once," she said, "I'd like to walk on my own," and she moved away towards the shore and its view of the mountain, which split open the morning sky as it lifted above the fog. I looked away for a moment and heard her give a little cry. When I turned back, I saw that she had slipped on the wet grass and lay on the ground, one leg folded beneath her. Fearing the worst, I ran to her. "It's nothing. I'm okay," she said, extending her arms for me to pull her up. But she winced when I lifted her body and was unable to bear any weight on her left leg. With my arm around her waist and hers around my shoulder, I half carried her up the stairs, thinking, *"Ice. Elevate leg. No hospital here. Flight leaves at two-thirty. One hour to Kathmandu. Clinic closes at four."*

After I eased her into a chair next to our bungalow's twin bed and raised her leg onto a pillow, I said, "Breathe deeply. I'll be back in a minute with ice."

She nodded and stared out the window. She was obviously in a great deal of pain. Her leg was swollen and red. But the only emotion she showed was disappointment, as if she had let the team down.

I hurried around to the back door of the kitchen. The cook first smiled and then, seeing my face, asked, "What's wrong?"

"I need ice for my mother's leg. She fell." He turned to the tall fridge and pulled out four metal trays, the old style with flexible fins down the middle, and broke them into a dish towel as easily as he had filleted our fish the day before. I thanked him and was out the door. Back in the bungalow, I poured the ice onto a pillow, gentled Mother's leg on top, and put my arm around her. She felt a little feverish and shrunken.

"I don't want to leave you now," I said, "but things have to be done before we go." She nodded, her blue eyes now softened and her jaw set firm against whatever might come. From the lobby, I called the clinic in Kathmandu and spoke with Peter, the doctor there I knew best. He assured me he would stay beyond the clinic's hours to treat her.

The hotel manager arranged for Mother to be carried by two sherpas, mountain dwellers renown for their strength on the long treks into the Himalayas. She was placed in an arm chair with turquoise blue upholstery and lifted from our room to the car. A small truck with her chair followed us to the airport. She was again carried into the small building and transported in mid-day pomp right onto the plane. Though she was in pain, I cannot say that she did not enjoy this royal treatment.

Our driver met us at the airport in Kathmandu and drove at top speed through the obstacle course of its streets to arrive at the clinic ten minutes past closing. Peter was waiting for us, framed in the dark wood of the front door. I could feel Mother relax as she saw a Westerner and the well-groomed compound, a world apart from the dusty, cacophonous streets.

Peter, we discovered, had trained with Mother's doctor in Chicago. She delighted in such connections—the high-wire act of her life flew over this safety net of relationships, and once more it had spread out, stretched half way around the world, and caught her. Peter confirmed that she had broken her fibula, the thin bone on the outside of her leg. He referred us to an orthopedic surgeon named Dr. Mandal, who had trained with the best in California and returned to Nepal to take care of his people. Peter gave Mother an old pair of wooden crutches, pills to relieve the swelling and pain, a prescription for her x-ray the next day, and his home phone number, just in case.

On the return trip to the hotel, our driver slowed down to a Nepali pace, waiting for the flow of sari-clad women to eddy across the street, steering around a bicycle laden with dangling chickens tied to the handlebars and a bagful of spinach greens lolling off the back. The hotel's entrance was now guarded by a short and stocky Gurkha, a mountain tribe known for being steadfast in battle. He stood proud in his scarlet jacket, its row of ten brass buttons glowing in the late-afternoon sun. I motioned him to the car and indicated that Mother needed to be carried to our room. Before I could finish, he gently lifted her from the car and pulled her over his back fireman style. As he held Mother's wrinkled arms crossed in front, he moved over the courtyard in the lilting, suspended trot the mountain porters assumed to enliven heavy loads. Mother's body seemed to glide over the flat stones and fresh green lawn before disappearing behind the white screen door of our room. For the remaining days in Kathmandu, this was how she came and went.

On Saturday we went for the x-ray. On Sunday the whole town shut down. Mother and I spent the day in the shelter of the hotel's garden, closed in on all four sides by stories of dusty rose bricks. Here, the nineteenth century resurfaced to populate the lawn with white chaise lounges coated in flowered cushions, round glass tables shimmering through the stretch of grass like miniature pools that floated on their surfaces, milk colored vases filled with orange and red poppies, cups of dark tea next to little pitchers of cream and bowls of sugar that a uniformed waiter had carried in high on his tray. Despite her injury, Mother seemed happy in this neo-colonial world and occasionally dozed in the afternoon sun. With her leg raised on cushions, we dined that evening on rice, curd, and *palak paneer*.

On Monday morning, we returned to the clinic to see Dr. Mandal. The Spartan waiting room was filled with Nepalis, men in dark pants and white shirts, women in saris so radiant they seemed to bring the light inside. I could feel their sympathy for Mother with her injured leg. Several minutes before our appointment, two nurses in light-blue uniforms came over with an armchair. Mother smiled as they gently lifted and carried her upstairs into a cement-floored room.

When the chair was settled in place, a young nurse gave Mother a shot to numb her pain. The room had two beds with white-metal frames and thin, cotton-filled mattresses. One was occupied by a Nepali woman whose skin was sallow, eyes sunken, and black hair spread across the pillow. On the floor next to the bed, a young woman, the tail of her sari tucked in her waist, squatted before the orange hexagon of a small electric stove, its coils circling through the dim light as she stirred a pot of potatoes and greens. Nepali hospitals do not provide meals, and so relatives and friends come to cook and take care of their sick, often spending the night.

I rose to meet Dr. Mandal, as he strode through the door. He wore a well-tailored suit and a movie-star smile. With a light handshake, he said, "I'll see your mother, now. How's she feeling?"

"She's still in pain, I think, but she refuses to complain. What does the x-ray show?"

"It looks like a clean break and should heal up well in a couple months. I wouldn't worry too much." He went over to Mother and took her hand. Her blue eyes came alive, and she smiled up at him with the trust of young girl. "We'll put a cast on your leg now and you'll be fine," he told her.

An hour later, they brought her back, her leg in a thick, white plaster cast that went in a right angle from her toes up to her knee. It looked like something a fifties football star might sport.

I kissed her cheek. "We'll need a crane to carry you around now."

Back in the hotel parking lot, the Gurkha guard appeared undaunted by the added plaster and carried Mother directly to her room without missing a step. After waking from a short nap, she asked, "Isn't Khenpo Tsultrim teaching tomorrow night?"

"Yes, he is. He'll be talking about the *Thirty-Seven Practices of a Bodhisattva*, one of his favorite texts."

"Oh, I don't want to miss that, dear. We must go. And the day after, we must see Bhaktapur as we had planned."

That evening we drove to the house where Khenpo Tsultrim was teaching, Mother positioned carefully in the front seat. The gathering was on the first floor, and when we went inside we saw that those in attendance had already set a chair for Mother near the front of the room. Cushions were spread across a rust-colored rug and a slightly larger, brocade-covered chair awaited Khenpo Tsultrim. As he entered, everyone stood. Stocky and powerful, he had a no-nonsense air about him. He was known as a loner and somewhat of an iconoclast. After three bows, everyone settled back on the cushions and his talk began. Mother took her usual extensive notes.

Afterwards, Khenpo Tsultrim invited us into his reception room, painted a golden yellow with deep maroon Tibetan rugs and a tall wooden shrine along one wall where a butter lamp flickered. Mother moved slowly through the door and sat in the one chair. A nun brought us the usual tea and biscuits, while Khenpo leaned forward to ask about Mother's leg and how the accident had happened. Sipping tea, he talked about pilgrimage sites in the valley and how all the great Tibetan masters had passed through Nepal on their way to India.

Then he paused and a light came into his eyes. He said to her, "It's a wonderful thing that you've broken your leg. You're very lucky. Going through pain is an excellent preparation for the bardo."

After a while, she nodded, "Yes, that's true. It has taught me."

The next day our guard carried Mother to a red station-wagon in the hotel's parking lot, and, slipping her legs in first, carefully lowered her into the front seat. Since the main Durbar square was closed to traffic, we saw Bhaktapur from inside the car. When we returned to the hotel, there was a message from my travel agent. He had found us two tickets home. That night I finished Mother's packing and then did my own. I was torn about leaving, as I would miss an important translators' conference for which I had prepared a text, but I also sensed that something deeper was at work.

On the last morning, our guard and the whole staff of the hotel came to say good-bye. We drove by the Buadha stupa to say farewell, and then to the airport where young boys swarming around the door were only too eager to carry our suitcases. Inside, Lufthansa had a wheelchair waiting and gave Mother the VIP treatment. As I took care of the tickets and luggage, I glanced over at her and saw that her eyes were closed and her head bent slightly forward. It was as if her spirit had carried her over the arc of these last days and now that she had accomplished her visit, she could let go.

And so it was. Her doctor in Chicago checked her leg and said the surgeon in Kathmandu had done a perfect job of setting the bone and that she would be healed in eight weeks. I stayed to take care of her, shopping and cooking, renting movies and answering more questions about Buddhism. After setting up care for her, I returned to Kathmandu in the early spring. The next time I came home for a visit, it was to move Mother into a retirement community. As we cleaned out the house, sold the furniture, sent paintings to museums, and opened boxes that had been closed for half a century, she talked about her life.

I did not know it at the time, but she had been having transient ischemic attacks, TIA's, which her doctor had not diagnosed. With each of these mini-seizures, her brain was being destroyed, cell by cell. She was radiant in telling how she had felt during one particular seizure, when the whole sky had opened up and was filled with luminous buddhas and deities in brilliant lights and myriad colors. She remembered her body shaking a bit and could not tell how long it had lasted. Her joy, she said, had felt timeless.

Within a few months of the move, she went into assisted living, and eventually to the nursing ward. Her decline was rapid and obvious. These days when I see Mother, she can no longer put a sentence together. Sometimes there are no words at all. Her face dims to a mask, her eyes watery, her hands immobile. Sometimes she doesn't recognize me and just wants to circle around the corridors in her wheelchair, pulling herself along the handrails on the walls, pausing only for a moment when they end and she has to cross an open space. At eighty-seven, her arms are as strong as mine. Sometimes she goes for the doors, sets off the buzzers, and a nurse's aide must come to pull her back.

During my last visit, I rolled her down the hall into the dining room for a lunch of puréed meat, puréed vegetables, and mashed potatoes. We sat alone at her table waiting for a plate to arrive. Suddenly, with a deliberate movement, she sat up straighter. I could tell that she was gathering all her energy. She turned her head toward me, arching one eyebrow and opening her eyes bigger. This used to be her way of stressing an important point. She said clearly, "Medicine." Paused, and then summoning herself again, "Dead." My bones heard it.

Seeing her motionless at the dining room table, waiting for yet another bland meal, her vision and hearing almost gone, her mind unable to make connections, I knew that her bright spirit would not want this existence and thought that if I were truly courageous, I would follow her wishes. I would plan an overdose or stage an accident. Find something that would ease her on. But as a Buddhist, I had taken a vow not to kill. When I had asked the lamas about her situation, they had spoken of karma. "You never know what is actually happening deep within," they had reminded me. "The processes shifting through her are hidden. Only the Buddha knows them completely." I believed this and yet my heart also felt her suffering and wanted it gone. In the end, I had to accept that there was no easy answer.

A nurse had said that Mother would often take off her string of lotus-seed beads, the one she had used for meditation, and clutch it in her hand so tightly the nurse could not pry it loose. This revived my old concern: Could Mother remember her practice at the moment of death and the following passage through the *bardo*? What happens during this period determines the form of birth she will take. Will she remember anything she has learned? I once asked a lama about this and he assured me,

"When the time comes, she'll remember. No need to worry. She's done enough practice and met many teachers. The link is in place."

The spring weather during that last visit was beautiful, filled with a light that softened colors as it tumbled from the sky. After our meal, taken in silence, I took Mother outside along the tilting sidewalk to a bench that faced the woods, locked up her wheels, and sat down beside her. She had gone distant again, but I continued with my plan to read poetry to her, which she once loved.

I pulled out a book of poems by Mary Oliver, bent toward her, and began to read with a full heart. Slowly, I could sense her shifting towards me, then leaning on my shoulder. When I looked around, her face had come alive with a light smile. As I continued, she participated with sounds of appreciation that came from some deep chamber inside. They followed the intonational patterns of what she used to say, "Oh, that's wonderful. Just marvelous!" I found a poem stating there was no need to fear death and giving it the image of a luminous bird taking flight. I went back to it several times, hoping the meaning would come across.

"Remember the phoenix?" I asked. "How it rises out of the flames?"

Mother was so close that I felt our minds blending. I talked as if she were her old self. "When you die," I told her, "you'll rise like that bird, full of light. Your body will stay behind, but your mind will be radiant and beautiful." I could feel the intensity of her listening. "The clear mind that is you will go on and take another body. You'll have a new life."

Her face filled with that familiar, child-like joy, and she said, "I'll be a baby.... It's fascinating."

Sean Hoade

Samsara Suite

AOLO, MARIA, AND ESTEBAN WALK UP THE STREET, toward the discount tobacco store. They have been friends for five years, since sixth grade in Catholic school. When Paolo was born, he cried nonstop for a week. His parents didn't know what to do with him. The doctors didn't know either, so they said he had colic. He was fed intravenously and fell asleep each night with his mouth wrenched open, ready for his renewed cries once he awoke.

Creatures in the hell realms live for ten thousand years before finally succumbing to their agony. Immediately before he was born, Paolo endured a long and horrible existence in such a realm, paying for some crime he now cannot remember committing. The flames and terror have stayed with him in this life, however, even as a teenager.

When Paolo dies from lung cancer in his forties, he will return to the hell realm for another ten thousand years for having murdered his best friend in a jealous rage. When Paolo is newly born into this plane of ceaseless suffering, he will laugh and smile for seven days, remembering impossibly the pleasure of human life.

Maria is the rebirth of her father's younger brother, who died as a teenager. When Maria's father beats her, he doesn't realize that he is hurting the person who was once his beloved sibling. Maria will die young again as well, this time as a high school student, next time as a dog, the time after that as a fighter pilot. Her lives will all be short until she is born a minor god, and she will live blissfully for an eon before returning to earth as a blind baby.

Esteban earned a human life this rebirth by saving a foal when he was a farmer's horse, running into a burning barn and nudging the reluctant colt to safety. The barn collapsed and, just under ten months later, Esteban was born.

The three friends have orbited one another for eons, life after life after life. In this round, Esteban will be murdered tomorrow by Paolo, when Paolo discovers that Maria is sleeping with him. Maria, who is in love with Esteban, will throw herself from a bridge. In nine weeks she will be reborn as a mongrel dog in an animal shelter, and will be adopted by a wandering monk for companionship when he goes into the wilds of Canada for a year-long retreat.

The wandering monk will very nearly reach full enlightenment and escape the endless cycle of rebirths, having worked life after life, stretching back to beginningless time, to see the truth of existence. He knows this truth from books, believes in it fully, but has never seen it himself, never experienced it. That is why he gives in to desire and makes love to a female visitor three hundred and forty-five days into his retreat. Because of this, when he dies thirty years later, he will be reborn as a wandering ascetic, a woman this time, to try again. He will keep trying for a thousand years.

When Paolo, Maria, and Esteban arrive at the tobacco shop, they buy cigarettes from Mr. Duri. He always sells them cigarettes, even though the teens are underage, because he refuses to turn down business. The kids are going to smoke anyway, he says. Mr. Duri is Hindu, and makes merit through his generous donations to the temple. When he dies, he will be reborn as the son of middle-aged parents who had all but given up on ever conceiving a child. They will love him and give him everything he wants and will both die shortly after his seventh birthday.

Mr. Duri is married to a former actress he met when they were both still living in India. She was popular on daytime dramas and commercials, but she gave up the celebrity's life to marry this humble shopkeeper, to her the very image of a king in full command of his realm. She now runs a nail salon a few blocks from her husband's tobacco shop, quite fat and very happy. When she dies, she will be reborn as a man and fall in love with Mr. Duri's rebirth, the orphaned boy. They will romance one another surreptitiously, over three decades, never telling their respective wives. Mr. Duri's rebirth will nurse Mrs. Duri's rebirth while he is dying, and pass on shortly after him. They will fall in love as a Muslim man and woman in their next life, then as elderly people in a rest home, then as an arranged marriage in Indonesia, then as two cats who mate and are both killed in a barn fire. In one life, many rebirths from the one in which they are Mr. and Mrs. Duri, they will fail to meet, and it is in this life that Mrs. Duri's rebirth will attach to a new soul mate, leaving Mr. Duri's rebirth to drift alone once more through the cycle of samsara.

Mr. and Mrs. Duri's daughter, Amala, is a heroin addict. She steals from her mother's purse or sleeps with her dealer for her daily fix. Amala weighs ninety-nine pounds and looks like one already dead. Her parents have noticed, and pray at the temple for her health, but never talk to her directly about her addiction. In one month, after her wasted body can take no more, Amala will die and be reborn as a hungry ghost, between hell and the animal realm. Her belly will swell as big as an elephant's skull, constantly aching and growling for sustenance. But hungry ghosts have mouths as tiny as the eye of a needle, and can never eat enough to satisfy their craving. If they kill in a desperate attempt to procure food to eat, they descend in their next lives to hell. But Amala will endure her lifetime as a hungry ghost with generosity, and after a thousand years will be reborn as one of the earth's few remaining eagles, tasting freedom for the first time in many lives.

Amala's dealer is a man named Whitney. He is handsome and rich and likes sleeping with Indian girls. He doesn't sell drugs for the money. He does it for the sex. In the life prior to this one, Whitney was father to the previous incarnation of Amala—a girl named Patrice—loving her as he felt no father ever could, giving her everything she wanted, making her feel treasured and special, giving her a home on a farm, where the whole family felt safe and warm together. He swore that no one would ever hurt his little girl, that he would protect her until the end of time. He died rushing into their barn to save Patrice from a fire she had caused by accidently kicking over a kerosene heater while playing hide-and-seek. When he found his daughter, dead from smoke inhalation, his love for her was such that he refused to leave the burning barn, and stayed with her as the flames closed in, clutching her tiny body in his arms.

Whitney the drug dealer will never go to jail, and he will live a long, long life. But he will be reborn as a worm, time and time again, for the next thousand years, each birth a different species: nematode, leech, earthworm, tapeworm, roundworm, woodworm. Three hundred and ninety-eight generations from now, he will finally be reborn as a gopher snake, and down from the sky will swoop one of the last eagles on earth, who will crush his body with her beak and carry it back to feed her babies.

An old monk, near death and wandering through the nature preserve, will watch this eagle plunge down. And at the precise moment of her kill, he finally will see and experience the selfless, unsatisfactory, and impermanent nature of existence, as taught by his masters again and again and again over untold millennia. The old monk will collapse under a willow tree moments later, dry-eyed, his weathered lips crinkled into a gentle smile. He will not return.

Jeff Davis

Swallow Koans

Barn Swallow. *Hirundo Americana. Male. 1. Female. 2.*
No. 35. Plate CLXXIII. Drawn from Nature by J. J. Audubon,
ERS, E. L. S. Engraved, Printed, & Colored by R. Havell. 1836.

rawn from Nature? How many birds had Audubon killed for that drawing, Arthur wondered as he stood, sketch-pad in hand, in Nebraska's Sagataw Museum of Art. How does it feel to ensnare a bird, hold its tiny body with one hand, and with the other snap its neck? Arthur scratched the tufts of his wavy black hair.

He was obsessed, no doubt about it. Since a pair of swallows began nesting in the barn on the farm he'd rented alone for the past year, Arthur couldn't close his eyes without swallows circling his skull. The obsession was a welcomed diversion though—twelve months ago his wife had left him. Cloistered in the farmhouse, Arthur feared he'd become a topic of conversation among the gossipers at Garland's Depot. The hot-shot native son. The successful painter. The Zen Buddhist, whatever *that* might mean. He hoped they still thought of him as one of their own. But, since last winter, his only excursions beyond his house had been the weekly, ninety-minute drive to the museum, where he would stare for hours at the canvases the way he gazed as a boy at the stained-glass windows of the First Nebraska Baptist Church.

Arthur's worn, nimble hands tried, unsuccessfully, to capture in charcoal and corrugated paper the swallow's unsettled peace. Her nest was gray and daubed with hints of cedar brown. Straw-like lines straggled from the nest's bottom, as if the bird's mud house had grown whiskers, the raggedy kind he'd sported the summer he met Andi. The nest reminded Arthur of the open-roofed eco-home they'd dreamed of building into the side of the hill where for six years they'd lived together. That particular dream lasted only a few months before Andi let her desires light on something else.

Andi. A woman whose high spiritual aspirations could throw any man off-balance. "Hi, I'm Andi. I'm a shaman," she announced when Arthur first met her while hiking alone on the High Plains Trail. She was on her knees, digging up burdock root with a trowel. "Burdock's great for soul-retrieval rituals," she told him, a little out of breath. Arthur smiled, he hoped not patronizingly; it's not every day you find a fresh-eyed woman in Eastern Nebraska calling herself a shaman and wearing a trowel holster. And she was beautiful. Twenty-eight years young, she told him, with enormous blue eyes, an unbridled spirit, and what he knew within minutes was an innocent but profound drive to be extraordinary. Forty years old then, Arthur found her irresistible. By the end of the next autumn they were married.

When Arthur's pencil began to move again, his breathing relaxed. The swallow peeked over the nest's edge, her rust-colored head with its iridescent blue mask peering back to admire the sleek, midnight-blue strokes composing her smooth body and elegantly forked tail. She appeared at home, completely at ease. Another swallow was visible below her, his blue-black head pointing in the opposite direction. *Fool*, Arthur wanted to say. *Watch out*.

"WELL, SOME MALE BARN SWALLOWS at least *try* to help hatch the eggs." Rosemary Briar stood center stage in the Clarkson Community Center with the ease of an aunt talking to her nephews and nieces instead of as the expert ornithologist that she was. "So, either this behavior is a sign of an advanced male," she continued, "or a sign of an ancient phenomenon: the female *hu*moring the male." A few snickers from the twelve or thirteen members of the Clarkson Audubon Society, four college students, and two dozen curious locals, including Arthur.

Most people from Clarkson knew Rosemary. The Clarkson Audubon Society had invited her to give an update on the cliff swallows she'd been studying for the past nineteen summers, ever since several thousand of them gathered at Mead's Farm on the edge of Culsax County, some thirty miles of country roads east of Arthur's two swallows. Arthur had always admired Rosemary, her modesty and gentle charm; few other people could've lured him from his canvases on a Wednesday night. You had to corner her in Scheiner's Pub with a Harp lager before she'd say too much about herself, her PhD from Princeton, her seventy-eight published studies. Before Arthur met Andi, with nary an interest in swallows, he'd sometimes sit with Rosemary at the Depot over breakfast, teasing her about the silliness of science, the battiness of birds.

As Rosemary's lecture continued, Arthur scribbled in his notebook like an enthralled grad student, a copy of her acclaimed *Sixteen Summers with Swallows* secured in his lap. Rosemary's long auburn hair swayed as her arms danced to illustrate the male swallow's courting flight. "A male's long tail maneuvers the air and attracts potential female mates," he heard her say, not glancing up from his sketch, "but its length requires extra energy and thus makes it vulnerable to predators..." Arthur's pencil moved almost of its own volition, from the strong line of Rosemary's jaw, to her hair, lips, and thickly lashed eyes whose outer edges lifted and fanned out like those of an appealingly matured barn owl.

Seated next to Arthur in the audience, Becky Lamm leaned over to peek at the notebook. She caressed her short blonde hair, adjusted her black rectangular glasses, smacked her lavender-hued lips. Since first meeting Becky at Mac's Animal Clinic, where she worked, Arthur had watched with interest as his neighbor's life unfolded. Whenever he brought by Dutch, his German shepherd, Becky's freckled face shot them both a crooked smile. Married. Divorced. Currently plowing her way through the University of Nebraska's veterinary school. She seemed obsessively determined, and now lived alone in an apartment up the road from the animal clinic.

"Nice notes, Arthur," she said.

Arthur glanced up at the stage.

"I didn't know you were a birder," Becky said, her crooked smile suddenly flattening into a straight line. "A new interest? New models maybe?"

"It's not what you think," he said. "These birds. Now that they've made themselves at home in my barn, they keep creeping into my canvases." He chuckled. "I'm just curious."

"You *are* curious, Arthur. That's for sure. Any word from Andi?"

"Yeah, I get an email every once in a while. She's still in Japan. Working things out." It had actually been four months since he'd last heard from her. A cryptic message, in typical Andi fashion. Always on the verge of making a breakthrough, having epiphanies.

"I'm so sorry, Arthur," Becky said, "but, you know, maybe it was for the best."

On stage, Rosemary was wrapping things up. "...At first the birds perch separately," she told the audience. "Then, as they begin courtship, they gradually start to perch in pairs. A swallow can forage all day long by himself before congregating in the huge flocks that roost together at night."

Before the applause concluded, Arthur had closed his notebook and was heading down the aisle towards the podium.

WHILE ONE SWALLOW LIT OFF through the barn's westward window, the other waited patiently in the nest on a ceiling beam, its chestnut throat peeking over the cup-shaped edge. Arthur watched, holding a blanket and a dusty zafu cushion. Within minutes, the first swallow glided back inside the barn, bits of twig in tow, as the second immediately took off, a constant, if not enviable, trade-off of duties.

Three days since Rosemary's lecture, a week since Arthur's visit to the museum. He'd awakened this June morning intending to practice zazen in his barn while the swallows carried out their building rituals. He thought it would be an appropriate way to reclaim the practice he had relinquished nearly a year ago when Andi had flown off to Japan with his Dharma brother Nyogen. A way to bless this winged pair's home, Arthur had said to himself. With the barn broom, he cleared a small spot on the floor, laid out a wool blanket for the *zabuton*, stacked the *zafu* on top, and sat. His eyes remained half open, gazing softly at a fallen white feather resting a few feet before him. He began counting his breaths, trying to reach ten without his thoughts flying away.

The sitting, he quickly suspected, was less for the birds and more for himself. Yesterday, she finally sent word again. The postcard was a photograph of a monkey perched in a tree. Andi's loopy scrawl on the back read, "Everybody's got something to hide 'cept for me and my monkey! Loving Japan. Nyogen promises long Dharma letter soon. Miss you. Love, Lightning Bug." The nickname came from a moonlit night during their first year together. They had just made love in the grass. She rested on her stomach, sighing dreamily, as he told her his plans to someday paint the world's small creatures. As his fingers ran down her spine, he'd whispered, "The moon's light transforms your behind into a lightning bug's tail."

A breeze zipped just above Arthur's head. A whistling vibration near his left ear. Then again. His eyes focused and glanced up to see a swallow hovering near the barn ceiling's highest beam. The bird swooped down aggressively, coming just inches from Arthur's head. *Out, out,* the swallow gestured.

The bird was right. The cushions tucked beneath his arm, Arthur shuffled out the doorway.

THE BARN WAS EMPTY THE NEXT DAY, at least of swallows. No movement except for the occasional breeze that blew in the west-facing window. Perhaps he had observed the birds too closely, but how do you keep a respectful distance when you're so blasted curious and hopeful to learn something new?

Arthur stepped through the barn's back door and scanned the pale blue sky. Nothing. Not a bird in sight. He thought for a moment of Andi's postcard. Above all, she had always desired her freedom—freedom to wander, to get lost and find herself again, to venture. Still, he had always believed in his heart that his love for her and their marriage could help her attain her grandest aspirations.

One June evening, when he was a boy, toting one of his mother's Mason jars, Arthur had dashed across their back field in pursuit of fireflies. Beside his bed that night he'd placed the filled, oddly illuminated jar, its lid punctured with steak-knife holes, and fell asleep imagining the fireflies as his personal nightlight, his trusting friends who would light a path whenever he played in the woods. In the morning, however, he woke to discover all of the bugs dead or close to it, their mysterious fuzzy light-bulb tails all but burnt.

Hands fidgeting in his khakis, Arthur shook his head at the memory as he walked across his property, the dry grass cracking beneath his boots, and headed into the fifty-eight acres of woods that lined his farm. Eventually he found himself standing beneath a shagbark hickory tree. He reached toward a thick, angular branch, its limbs springy yet sturdy enough to weather a hurricane, and picked some of the nuts Indians had once fermented into a soup they called *powcohiccora*. As he sat against the dark, loose-plated bark, his Roper boot heels dug into the leaf-covered ground. Nothing, for once, was on his mind. For a moment relieved, he found himself, unexpectedly and without any apparent reason, weeping.

AN UNEASY TICKLING CRAWLED UP Arthur's right leg into his belly as Rosemary continued to glide about his studio. The swallow canvases were stacked in a far corner. Beneath the window stood a wooden table covered with a green velvet drape, in the middle of which sat a three-foot bronze Buddha head. A small vase to the left of the Buddha held two stems of dried wild rose berries. As Arthur watched Rosemary's august eyes slowly, repeatedly blink, a pair of monarchs' wings opening for the sun, he reminded himself to stop clenching his gut. Sweat was dampening his brow; the more attention he paid to it, the wetter his forehead became. He knew Rosemary's lovely nose could sniff out an amateur a country mile away, and he so desperately wanted her to approve of him and his work. Simple conversation, that's all he needed to muster. Just show her the paintings and get on with it.

Rosemary admired the Buddha from a distance. "Do you meditate before you paint?"

"Mmm...I used to." Arthur had anticipated the question but not his answer. "Not so much lately. Are you interested in Buddhism?"

"Used to be." She laughed faintly. Arthur knew that during her first two summers in Nebraska she had visited the Heartland Zen Monastery and tried practicing zazen. "That was a long time ago. I'm too restless to sit still. I like the *energy* and momentum of thinking, you know? My adrenals rise and I'm off gathering data." She laughed again. "Actually, Pamela Krauss and I used to sneak onto the monastery grounds in the evening when everyone was meditating, and we'd crawl up to the wall of the zendo and listen beneath the windows."

"You'd listen to people meditating? Are you setting me up to ask, 'What's the sound of one man napping?'"

She laughed again, heartily this time. "No, no," she said, recollecting herself. "Let's just say it was the scientist in me."

Outside the window a misty rain fell across the field, the first rain all spring. For a moment, the woods were cast in a pale green light. Even the maple and hickory trees shone with shimmering hues of green.

"So," she said, glancing around the studio as if to recall the door's location, "you promised paintings of swallows."

"Right," he said. One by one, in chronological order, he presented his six most recent canvases, all completed this spring, all depicting swallows or variations of swallows. "Swallow koans, I call them." As he showed her each painting in turn, her eyes fingered the canvas from top to bottom.

"These are quite moving, Arthur," she said, her voice almost hushed. Her eyes fixed on the final work, *Swallow Koan #6.* "This particular painting, though, seems so...still." Simple curved lines of purple and brown suggested a nest, and atop the nest, two symmetric green-black lines, crowned with lavender dots, hinted at the shapes of two nesting birds. A small pasted clipping of text on the canvas read, "To be enlightened by the whole phenomenal world is to cast off body and mind of self and other."

"This one's based on an Audubon painting," he told her. "Did you know he killed birds and mounted them on board platforms, striking them in poses?"

Rosemary read another clipping glued to the canvas's lower right-hand corner, "Spring enlightens the painter, the painter enlightens spring. Self is forgotten. Spring is forgotten." Both clippings were based on commentaries by the thirteenth-century Japanese Zen master Dogen.

"Yes," she responded dispassionately, her eyes set on the canvas. "Later in his life, though, I think he preferred to paint *live* birds."

Arthur gathered the canvases and returned them to a corner; he suddenly feared he had exposed too much of himself. The rain ceased, though mist persisted from the clouds hovering just above the pines. Five white-tailed deer had wandered out to feed in the field. No sign of the two swallows.

"You think what Audubon did was wrong?" she asked.

"Do I think killing birds for art is wrong? Yeah. Don't you?"

"Well, here's what I think, Arthur, take it or toss it: his art helped document this country's vast bird species and inspired scientists to understand more systematically fundamental matters such as bird migration."

Arthur watched the deer until they disappeared into the trees. He could feel Rosemary's gaze on his back and turned around. "Fine, but we don't have to kill something to know it."

For several moments they stared at one another, eyes wide. They were both enjoying this, immensely.

"Birds enlighten humans, humans enlighten birds," Rosemary concluded.

Arthur smiled and nodded.

"Hmm...I don't know," Rosemary said, staring at the canvas. It was her third visit to his studio in two weeks. Arthur had promised to show her his self-portraits, all of which were at least three or four years old. This particular work, admittedly glum-toned, was based on a wedding photograph taken of Arthur while Andi had been dancing with Neil, a former boyfriend. Rosemary seemed stuck on the white streak sweeping diagonally from the canvas's upper-left corner. The stroke, an addition made the night of Rosemary's swallow lecture, was part of Arthur's occasional practice of *zuihitsu*, "follow the brush," a way of painting he had incorporated more fully with his bird series. The Zen technique asks the artist to let go of anticipating the future and to focus instead on the truthful charge of the lines at hand.

Arthur blushed at Rosemary's attention and sat cross-legged on the floor near the canvas. He told her about the portrait's setting, the Le Buisson Hotel reception room, the wedding scene, the ambience and expectations, the dance, his fear that night, his sense of doom, his sadness about Andi and their failed marriage. A few lines of modest gray streaked Rosemary's long auburn hair. Her teal cotton dress smelled of earth and lavender. Her soft eyes and softer questions kept him moving deeper into a subject he hadn't touched out loud in nearly a year. Why he had loved Andi. Nyogen and Andi meeting at the monastery. The fool he was not to have seen their growing attraction. His abandoned practice. His loneliness.

Rosemary looked at him. "Have you thought of painting more self-portraits?"

"I'm beginning to think that's all I'm doing now."

THE SIGHT OF THE MONASTERY'S FARM TRACTOR that Sunday morning, alone beneath a tall hickory tree, triggered in Arthur a trickle of sadness that fell down his neck and back, a soft and comforting ache. He couldn't distinguish the source of his peace, whether it was from his progress with a new swallow painting or from sitting beside Rosemary beneath the zendo's opened window. The two of them had awakened early, drove to the grounds of the Heartland Zen Monastery, and crept to this spot between the stone garden and the rows of orange day lilies.

"I still can't believe you brought me here," Arthur whispered.

A series of hollow wooden clacks echoed from inside the zendo. Arthur and Rosemary froze. The meditators inside stilled themselves. Conditioned by the summons, Arthur's hips pressed into the grass, his spine lengthened, his breath deepened. Rosemary stayed reclined, right leg extended, her left knee bent, her left hand smoothing out her floral broomstick skirt. She grinned at Arthur's upright posture.

A red-winged blackbird croaked from the top of an evergreen near the tractor. Arthur leaned in toward Rosemary, and whispered, "Now what?"

"We listen."

An orange-and-black-striped milkweed bug crawled along the grass near Arthur's foot. The farm tractor's red paint had rusted in the three years since Arthur had last been here. Andi had started coming with him, ostensibly to learn about Zen. It took only a month for her to find in Nyogen, Arthur's friend and Dharma brother, a new teacher and, eventually, a new lover.

The milkweed bug crawled up Arthur's leg. A faint cough came from inside the zendo. Arthur glanced at Rosemary who grinned and nodded. Then someone, a man he inferred, sniffed. A throat cleared. A sniff again, though from someone else. A woman coughed, twice, her restless thoughts, Arthur imagined, dropping into one of three baskets: sex, anger, or fear. A groan from someone else, perhaps a young man worried about his ailing father, or a mother realizing she'd forgotten to pack the kids' lunches. Over the next hour assorted murmurings floated like dirges through the window above Arthur's head and on across the meadow.

Three measured gongs ended the meditation. A collective sigh followed by a clatter of popping knee joints, ruffled robes, more cleared throats.

"We should be going," Rosemary whispered, as she crouched below the window.

Arthur wiped his eyes and returned the milkweed bug to the ground. As they walked away from the building, he was tempted to take Rosemary's hand. Over the white poplars three black crows chased off a hawk. A ray of sunlight lit up part of the tractor's red body, revealing that in fact the old machine had recently been repainted.

Jake Lorfing

Distant
Mountains

T
HE BRIGHTNESS OF THE SUN'S RISE over the African plain
was dampened by the dew haze rising off the earth. The
grasses were high, beginning to seed—it had been a good
year, elements of earth, wind, water, and heat aligned. The
zebra herd ran southeast, toward the lake and perhaps because of the
angled sun, the haze, the grasses rippling in the gentle breeze, they did not
see the solitary hunter until he arose, almost in their midst.

The lion, no longer young and driven from his pride, was still capable
of immense speed and agility for short distances. He embodied discipline,
mouth open to focus the approaching smells, imperceptibly tensing forward so that his spring would align with the herd's direction, a taut cata-
pult hidden in the grass.

The zebra was an easy kill, legs weakened by age and arthritis. The
casual observer would not have noticed the slightly limping gait, but the
lion was no casual observer, his attention captured by weakness. The zebra
was stretching out of an evasive turn when the claws of the lion pierced her
flank, stalling her momentum. They somersaulted as one, and then the lion,

almost magically, seemed to glide up her body toward her neck. Her world was fear, pain, shock, black on white, opening and closing, wild mind grasping at a fading swirl of colors, smells, and sounds. Death came quickly, though it was not merciful, mercy having no home in the language of the hunt.

Minutes passed and the zebra, looking down in confusion, could see the herd, now reorganized, approaching the shallow lake. In the western distance were mountains, which made her curious. Directly below, her gaze was drawn to the edge of a shallow depression, where lay a body she knew to be her own, still, lifeless, neck akimbo and belly torn wide from which the bloodied lion's head now withdrew.

Recognition of death arrived like a fresh wind foretelling a needed rain. Watching the lion, now on its haunches in the shade of a small tree across the depression from her body, she fully relaxed into her own life, and death, as one does when exhaling a breath held too long. She let go of holding and breathed in the vast sweep of the African world.

The lion, its hunger sated, looked up at the immense umbrella of sky, the plain extending to meet it, and he sensed the zebra spirit, watching. And in that recognition was no lion, no zebra, no sky, no plain, no pain, no breath, no death. The lion yawned deeply, and with his resounding outbreath, the zebra began the short journey to the distant mountains.

Geshe Michael Roach

Meditation

T HE WORDS OF THE MASTER, Tsong Khapa, and I think now the death of my mother, affected me greatly. It was not that I was despondent, or thrown into despair; outwardly I was living a normal life, I continued with studies and writing, making a modest but comfortable living. The walk and the death, though, became constant companions in my mind; each one gave reason for the other.

It was true that my mother had lived a good and fruitful life; raised her children, contributed to her world, provided always and without hesitation for the needs of strangers that we brought home. But what was the meaning, if regardless of how she lived she grew old and died so horribly of cancer, and if all that she lived for—her sons, her home, her work—was already crumbling into dust, all to be forgotten, so soon after she herself was forgotten? She was proof of the truth of the words spoken to me by Tsong Khapa in the Garden, that even things which seemed beautiful and good were not so, if death and pain were how they always ended. And in my mind Tsong Khapa existed because of her: he had come to the Garden knowing my needs, and bringing some answers to my questions.

The death and the walk worked on my thoughts over the months, and so finally I was compelled to seek out a small hermitage some distance from our desert town. There I found a kindly, holy, and learned abbot, who gladly took me in, gave me a small, quiet room in which to stay, and secured me work as the assistant to the keeper of a rich collection of books in the manor of a nearby nobleman. I spent much time in the study of sacred texts, and in the thoughts that grew from the walk and the death, and came to feel that there was some path I could learn to solve my questions. I yearned for this path deeply. And so I was drawn back to the Garden, and entered just after dusk one year as the desert was entering its subtle springtime, a slight sweetening of the air, and greening of the spare but lovely grass and rosebushes, within the stone walls of that beloved place. I waited for the Golden One there again.

This time it was no long wait, but as disappointing as it was quick, for I sensed approaching, in the darkness from the gate, a wholly different step from Hers; this one was measured rather than skipping, sprightly but almost businesslike, and above all heavy. I turned and saw the Great Meditator—Kamala Shila.

He was nothing like I would have expected, for I had in mind a severe and austere presence, a face and body that had seen the rigors of deep meditation, hour after hour, on the side of a stone Himalayan cliff, eleven centuries earlier. But here was the real thing, and nothing of the sort. He was of medium height, and chubby, with his robes hitched up too high, nearly to his knees, giving him a sort of playful appearance—like a young boy. His face matched the rest: round, happy cheeks, a full nose, dark Indian complexion, little patches of ill-shaven white hair around the top of his head, and above all laughing, sparkling little eyes, in a constant state of giggling, as was he.

"Want to know the Path!" said he.

"Yes, of course," I replied, for it is a very serious thing to know the true suffering of the world, and to await anxiously for the way of escape.

"*Why not!*" he laughed, "and—why *not!*"

"I want to know why my mother died," I replied somberly, "and I want to know if there was anything I could have done, or if there is anything still I can do for her—and I want to know if it must always be this way."

"Yes! Yes!" he boomed back. "Can do! *Why not?* Got to learn to meditate!" and he plopped down on that patch of grass beside the carob tree, blessed to me because of the tender nights passed there with Her.

He motioned for me to sit beside him; I had done a little meditation with friends at the Academy, and had read some about it, and so I sat up straight, closed my eyes and tried not to think about anything.

He giggled and slapped me on the back. *"What are you doing?"* he demanded merrily.

"Meditating," I said.

"Would you run a footrace without warming up first?" he asked happily.

"Well, no."

"Got to do the *warm-up!*" he laughed, and jumped up again.

"What's the *warm-up?*" I said, getting to my feet grumpily, with thoughts of leg stretches and other unpleasant exercise.

For the first time, Kamala Shila looked at me a little sternly. "Everybody wants to meditate! Nobody knows how! *Got to do the warm-up right!*" he said.

"So what's the warm-up?"

"First *clean up!*" he yelled, and began running around the little patch of grass stooping over his little belly, picking up stray leaves and twigs, until the surface of the grass was smooth and clean in the moonlight, inviting to the eyes, a pleasant place to meditate. "Do this in your room, right?"

"Right," I replied, and started to sit down.

"Don't forget the *gifts!*" he squealed.

"What gifts?" I said.

"Important people are coming!" he giggled. "Need some nice gifts for when they get here!"

I glanced dubiously at the gate of the Garden, apprehensive at the thought of a crowd of merry meditators like himself. "Who's coming?" I asked.

"Nobody *you* could see!" he replied, and went over to the wooden bench, and from under the top vest of his robes pulled a bag of tiny little clay cups, which he began arranging in a row. Three he filled with a little water from the fountain, and then went and plucked a small red bloom from atop a thornbush (after what seemed a short prayer, as though he were asking the bush for permission) and placed it in the fourth cup.

From a sage bush and juniper lining the spring that led from the fountain he took a few sprigs, placed them in a fifth cup, and collected a bit of dry grass into the sixth. From the tangerine tree on the near side of the gate he took a fruit, peeled it, placed a few pieces in the seventh cup, and with relish ate the rest, talking as he moved and chewed, pushing a little slice into my hand as well.

"Suppose," he said between bites, "that some very important person were to show up in this Garden tonight, during our meditation. Maybe even a great Queen, with golden hair and a golden crown..." And he winked at me slyly, as if he knew why my heart kept me coming to this place. "You'd want to greet them properly, as you desert folks always do for your guests."

"But who are you expecting, really?" I asked.

"*Must* invite the Enlightened Ones!" he giggled. "How can you meditate, if they are not with you? How can you meditate too, unless you bring here, if only in your mind, your Heart Teacher?"

These last words, Heart Teacher, struck me deeply, with some pang in my breast, because the only thing I could imagine when I imagined "Heart Teacher" was my golden Lady.

"Here," he continued, leaning heavily over the little cups, "put them in order, like this. One cup of the water, it's a crystal cup of some wonderful beverage, nice to greet a guest that way."

"Next is another cup of water." He shuffled the little cups around, as if playing a shell game. "That's a warm little bowl of water from one of those mineral springs, nice to wash the guest's feet, tired from their journey."

"Third is the flower. *Everybody* likes flowers!" He took a deep sniff of the fragrance of the bloom. "Next is incense!" and he lit the fragrant leaves in the next cup with a spark from a flint, pulled from the bottomless folds of his vestments.

"Do you always carry these things around?" I asked dryly.

He turned slowly and looked in my face, dead serious. "Want the Path? Got to meditate. Want to meditate? Got to *warm—up!* Of course, I carry them everywhere, and I meditate...everywhere!"

He lit the dry grass in the next cup from the glowing fragrant embers. "Nice to light a lamp when a visitor comes. Here now, move that little cup of water next in the row; that's a fragrant ointment that you spread upon the guest—use your imagination now, enjoy it, I'm sure there's some guest you can imagine to whom you would like to offer this scented cream," and he glanced at me from the side, in a strange way, reminding me of someone.

"Now, last in the row, put here the slice of fruit, nice to feed an honored guest." I was wondering when, or even if, we would ever get to the meditation; he sensed, or knew, my thought, and said with a twinge of exasperation, "Must take time. Must put these gifts out right."

"What, do they actually use them?" I asked curtly.

"Of course not, "he said. "You think they, you think Enlightened Ones, need food to eat, or water to drink?"

"Well, if not," I responded, "why put these things out? I thought we were going to meditate."

"Want to run? Got to *warm up!* Can't meditate without them here, can't meditate without your Heart Teacher here, with you, helping, blessing, giving strength. Putting out gifts, it proves—you want them here, please ...come here, be with me awhile, as I meditate." And then, all of a sudden, Kamala Shila broke into a sweet little song, a prayer song, his face cherubic, uplifted, eyes closed but seeing, as if there were someone there, in the star-filled sky above us, to whom he was making an offering.

He stopped and lowered his face, and looked at me merrily. "That's the last gift, my favorite one to give—always give them some little music, before you sit to meditate."

"And so we can finally sit?" I asked, but tenderly, for no one could deny the beauty, and the feeling, of the place of meditation that Kamala Shila had just created; surely, the Garden, and my own heart, had indeed been *warmed up*, and it felt good, and right, to begin our meditation this way.

"Yes, *why not?* Time to sit!" he exclaimed. I stooped and began to sit, and felt his arm pulling me back up.

"What now!"

"You forgot to bow!" he said, as if surprised that I didn't know better. He put his palms flat against each other at his breast, and bowed with great grace and respect, as if some great being stood before him, and then slowly took his seat upon the grass.

I followed suit and then settled myself upon the grass, but like a little rubber ball he bounced back up again. I was really getting irritated, wondering how late it was getting, and sat grumpily staring ahead. He was flitting all around me, like a bee on a flower.

"Where's your seat? No meditation seat? Must get the back up higher than the front! And he grabbed my shoulder, pushed me forward, and shoved a wad of cloth (which had appeared mysteriously from beneath his vest) under my tailbone.

Next his hand was on the ankle of my left foot; "Get that up on your right thigh! Sit up straight!" slapping my back straight, "Get that right shoulder down even with the other!" pushing them down level, "Fix the head! Didn't they teach you anything?" I felt ready to strangle the jolly master.

"Don't point it down, don't point it up, just straight ahead, and stop leaning to the left!" His two hands were on the temples of my head, like a vise. "How's the tongue?"

"In my mouth, as usual," I retorted. He didn't seem to hear.

"Touch it there slightly, behind the front teeth, keep the mouth loose, everything just natural, like usual," he enthused. "Can't meditate if we're slobbering or swallowing all night, can we? *Stop breathing through your mouth!* You'll dry out!" And he had me completely straightened out, and I had to admit it felt quite good.

"Shouldn't I cross both my legs up on my thighs, like they do in the pictures?" I asked.

"A full lotus? Sure if you can, but you can't, till you practice more. The main thing is to be completely comfortable, so you can concentrate the mind, without worrying how much your knees hurt. If you want, you can even sit on the bench over there," he explained, and slid down next to me immediately in full lotus.

I closed my eyes, and went into a state of peace, here in the peaceful Garden, the Garden of my Golden One—and he was in my face once more.

"What, you going to bed?" he demanded.

I opened my eyes, and fixed them straight ahead, on a design carved into the side of the wall opposite us.

"You people around here meditate with your mind, or with your eyes?" he demanded again.

I looked at him angrily. "Well, if I'm not supposed to close my eyes, or open them either, then what do you want?"

"Watch," he said, and he sat with his head erect and straight, but the eyes half open, gazing slightly downward, and without focusing on anything in particular, as if he were in some deep reverie, which I realized was the whole point. "If it gets too distracting, you can close them, but your mind is too used to going to sleep when you do, so it might be hard. Make sure though not to open them too wide, or you will start to look around; and see to it as well that the background in front of you is plain, like a cloth or wall of a single color, with nothing moving to catch your eye and distract the mind."

I did as he said, and felt my mind immediately go into a clear state of focus. I prepared to empty my mind...

He was up again, running to and fro, and I despaired of ever actually meditating with this, the greatest master of meditation. "What now?"

"Do you hear something?" he asked anxiously.

I let my eyes back down, and concentrated. All I could hear was the familiar tinkle of the fountain.

"Just the fountain, over there against the wall," I replied.

"Got to *go*!" he exclaimed, and headed over to the bench, and made to collect the little cups together.

"What?" I jumped up. "All this work, and now you must go? Can't you stay for just a few minutes, and let me meditate near you?"

"Impossible," he announced. "Noisy, noisy. No good for meditation. Should have noticed it before. Impossible to meditate with noise around," and he pointed to the offending fountain.

"It's not so loud," I said. "Come, try."

Kamala Shila looked at me gravely. "You asked me to show you the Path. I told you there is no Path without meditation. You have to make choices. Your pretty fountain, or your meditation. Your life as it is—and as your mother's life was—or Freedom. Freedom or your fountain. Your life now will always be such choices. I'm going."

Desperately I looked around, and my eyes caught on the bricks stacked in a circle around the trunk of the carob. I caught one up and placed it on the opening of the fountain, and the water stopped. "Please now, can we meditate together?" I asked quietly.

"*Why not!*" he giggled, and we sat together on the grass, at peace, and ready to find peace.

The jolly little man transformed then before my eyes. The left hand went down upon his lap, palm up, and then the right one upon the left one, also palm up. The two thumbs touched slightly, a little off the palms. His sparkling face changed instantly, into the very visage of serenity, totally relaxed, totally quiet, a quiet that was so strong that it seemed to suck the entire Garden into it, a realm of total silence. It was a quiet that I hungered for, a quiet that my life had never allowed me, and I sat down eagerly beside him.

For the first time, thankfully, Kamala Shila was quiet, for a few moments at least. And then he whispered, "Did we talk about the *warm-up* yet?"

"Yes, yes," I whispered back urgently, hoping he would settle down. "Remember, we did that already."

"Not *that* warm-up," he whispered back; "the *other* warm-up."

"What are you talking about?" I said apprehensively, waiting for him to bound back to his feet. But he stayed serene, and led me with his words.

"If you will come with me, into real meditation, you must prepare your thoughts. Otherwise you will be left behind."

"Teach me, please."

"Now first watch your breath, the breathing in and out. See if you can count ten breaths without your mind wandering away. Start with the out-breath, and then the in-breath; this is one breath. See if you can count ten of these; at first, if you are honest, you will not be able to get to ten before your mind wanders off to something else."

I tried, and saw he was right. I never got past four before my thoughts went off, to the Garden itself, and to Her.

"It's enough," he whispered after some minutes. "The point of watching the breath is only to bring your mind to neutral, to pull it slowly away from the whirl of your worldly thoughts, and begin to focus it within. It's not as if watching the breath is itself a goal which would free us."

"Now think for a moment why you are here: you seek the Path, you seek I know to find the answers about the death of a good woman, and about the wisdom you have found from another. Decide now, here, that these questions cannot be answered elsewhere, and in fact are not even asked elsewhere. Children ask why good people must suffer and die, and adults teach their children not to ask anymore, and these children become the adults who tell their children, 'These questions have no answers.' Decide here why you will meditate with me. Decide here, and now, that you will meditate for a real goal, for an ultimate goal, and that you seek these answers in the Path. Do not waste your life, do not waste even the few moments we will spend here together, on any lesser goal."

I reflected on his words, and felt their truth, and felt a joy and rightness in meditating for this one reason.

"Next, before we start to meditate, ask the Enlightened Ones to come; ask your Heart Teacher to come, bring them here, to guide and help us. You cannot see them now, but you will; if they exist at all, if they are who they are supposed to be, they will hear your mind, and they *will* come. Ask them, sincerely, with deep reverence, now, to come, and they *will* come."

I did as he said, and thought I felt Her presence, close to me. My heart leapt with joy and devotion.

"We have bowed to them before we sat; bow again to them now, in your mind's eye, for I tell you, on the day that you *do* see them yourself, you will in one natural motion throw yourself upon the floor, at their feet, in happiness and awe."

Again I did as he said, and it felt good and right.

"Good, good, continue as I say. Sincere people around the world seek to meditate, but find they are unable to reach the depths and heights of meditation, because they have not found how to enter the door of the meditation, which I teach you now. Imagine next then the entire sky."

I did, in my mind imagined the entire expanse of the azure sky of my desert home.

"And fill it entirely with sweet crimson and ivory roses, and offer it to your Heart Teacher, and the Enlightened Ones, and ask them sweetly for their help."

I did, and again, it felt good and right, and my mind felt even closer to deep meditation, even before we meditated.

"Still we have a few steps to go. Clean now your conscience, for no person can meditate unless their conscience is clear. This again is why so many find it difficult to meditate, why so few ever see the miracles of the depths of meditation. Your heart must be clean, your life must be clean. Think now of anything you have done, or anything you have said, anything you have even thought that might have harmed another; admit it to yourself, be totally honest with yourself, decide that you did it, decide that it was not a goodness, and decide that you will try not to do it again. This one cleaning, for your conscience and your heart, will open to your mind doors of meditation that you never dreamed were possible."

I sat quietly, and reflected, not finding any great evils, but many small and daily harms to others, and cleaned them from my heart.

"Good, good, this is *real fun!*" he whispered happily. "Few more steps; now do the opposite, think of all the good things you do, all the good things you've said to others, all the good and pure thoughts you've had and have—oh, and by the way, think of all the goodness of anyone else at all, from your Heart Teacher on down, and just...*be glad, be happy, take joy,* in everything that is good."

I did, and it felt a good and proper balance to cleaning my conscience. My mind felt fairly bursting with good energy, and thirsting for meditation, like a warmed horse, about to race.

"Now ask them for guidance—your Heart Teacher and the Enlightened Ones. And ask that they continue to appear to you, in all the many ways that an Enlightened Being can appear (and you can hardly guess all the ways, and all the places, that they appear to you). Ask them to come to you as your teachers, both teachers who seem like teachers, and in the world and the people around you, teaching you, always teaching you, and guiding you along the Path."

With a deep sense of reverence, which drew me already into meditation, I followed.

"And now finally beseech them, from your heart, always to stay near you, seen or unseen, keeping you, and bringing you to them."

This I did, and from the goodness of these thoughts fell into a deep state of meditation, a total quiet. Which, of course, the great Kamala Shila could never seem to tolerate.

"Isn't the peace so nice?" he whispered.

"Oh... yes..." I could hardly make words.

"And what are you meditating upon?" he whispered back.

"I have emptied my mind, and I am trying not to think, and the thoughts I do have I am simply watching, as they pass by."

Somehow his heavy little body traveled the space between us in a flash, and he was in my face again, this time really angry. "Fools! The fools still live! Fools that I thought I finished off in the great debates, over a thousand years ago! I'm leaving!" and again he headed toward the bench and his little holy cups.

"Wait!" I started up. "What have I done wrong? Teach me what I have done wrong."

He sat before me, legs crossed on the grass, breathing heavy and intense, and leaning close, his face before my own. Then his look softened, and he asked gently, "Do you want me to help your mother?"

"Of course," I said. "You know my quest."

"Then think—what possible good would it be, simply to sit and empty your mind for an hour? Do not animals, like the rabbit, do the same? Are not the drunkards, who pass out after tankards of their mead, just the same? Are their minds not emptied and quieted, for a time? Come, think about it, tell me, why do you think we meditate?"

"Because we seek the truth; and the truth is in the silence of meditation."

"Only half true. Meditation is but a tool, not goal itself. It is an axe, a sharp axe, with which we cut a tree. Cutting the tree is wisdom, ultimate wisdom, and this is the heart of the Path. Meditating for the sake of meditation would be like burning an axe for firewood, rather than using it to cut firewood. What is the goal of the Path?"

"I hope to find some answer to the question, Why did my good mother die so painfully, why did she die at all, why must we all—good or bad—suffer and die; why does all life, and all the work of life and all the fruits of the work of life, turn to destruction and pain? This is the goal of the Path, for me."

"Good, and so it should be. So now, if you could sit for hours or days or months and empty your mind, would you find the answers—would you be freed from sickness, and the loss of the things and people you hold dear; would you be freed from aging itself, would the energy of your body and mind stop leaking away from day to day—would you not, in a word, die?"

"I suppose I would; I suppose that, even if I could sit here and empty my mind, and be quiet and peaceful and serene even for very long periods of time, and sit even through hot and cold, and rain or the heat of the sun, I suppose you are right, nonetheless one day I would fall sick, and eventually get older and become unable to sit here, and then die."

"So then please," he whispered to me urgently, "*please*...follow me now, and learn true meditation, and learn to use it for our real goals." He settled back near me, and this time settled with a finality that I sensed meant he would not rise again.

"There are three ways of meditation," he began, not moving from his own meditation posture. "For the first, I ask you to put before your mind a picture of your Heart Teacher."

This I did easily, and waited easily, for seeing Her, if only in my mind's eye, had always been for me a comfort and consolation.

"The first enemy of meditation," he whispered again, "is a kind of laziness; it is simply not to feel like meditating. And so it is good as we have done to remember the urgent and sacred necessity of our meditation. It is good as well," he giggled, "to choose an object of meditation which is both important, and which we enjoy. I don't think you will have laziness tonight.

"Now I will snap my fingers," he continued, "from time to time. I want you to mark your mind carefully, and tell me where your mind is at the very moment I snap my fingers. This way I can show you the other enemies of meditation, and how to battle with them."

I returned in my mind to my sweet image, and it brought me to thoughts of this Garden, which brought me to thoughts of the hour, which must be late, and I wonder if I will be in any condition in the morning to do my work at the library...*snap*.

"Where was your mind?" Kamala Shila asked.

"I lost the picture, I began thinking about my work," I said sheepishly.

"This is the second enemy," he said, "losing the picture. You fix this by becoming so familiar with the picture, by keeping it in mind so often, and on a steady basis from meditation to meditation, in meditations done steadily, during brief but frequent sessions through the day, that you always remember the object, that it is always close to mind. Now go back to the picture."

I did, and was able to hold Her lovely form somewhat better. My body was still, and the Garden still. The meditation felt good. I was beginning to feel comfortable, and more confident. My breath was slow, my body still, and She was always there, a kind of fuzzy golden light...*snap*.

"How is the picture?" he whispered.

"Good, good," I replied. "I am still, my body is comfortable."

"No, no," he said sternly, "the *picture*."

"Oh," I said, "it was fine, steady, a little fuzzy..."

"Typical," he said, a bit harshly. "Your meditation had slipped into dullness, a great enemy because he is an almost invisible enemy. In the extreme form he is more obvious: you feel drowsy, the head starts to nod. In his subtle form he is pure poison; he lies to you, and tells you your meditation is good, when really you are only in a kind of stupor—many meditators have wasted away a good part of their lives this way."

"So what shall I do?" I asked.

"Reserve a little corner of your mind; we call it watchfulness. Set it aside. Teach him what this enemy looks like; let him know the signs of his coming, and above all instruct him to raise the alarm, to alert you when mental dullness has come to drug your meditation. Now go back to Her."

I was a bit startled to realize he knew the object of my meditation, but settled quickly back. I held Her picture in my mind, and began to reflect on Her beauty, and the many spiritual lessons She had taught me here in this place. I remembered especially the night She had so innocently walked to the water leading away from the fountain, and stepped in without hesitation, clothed in Her golden hair, not crude or unclean, but with a total lack of desire and malice both; simply at oneness with...*snap*.

"Where was your mind?" Kamala Shila demanded.

"In good thoughts, holy thoughts," I replied tentatively.

"Good thoughts perhaps, but bad if they disturb your meditation. You wandered from the picture, to some other thought, and some other time or place, something that you like to think about, correct?"

I admitted it was so.

"This is the enemy of mental agitation; this is the one who comes most often, and he is mighty. I need not tell you more. Use your watchfulness, detect his arrival. And I warn you now of his companion, and the companion of dullness. This is inaction: failing to raise your sword when either of these enemies has crossed the threshold of your meditation.

"For dullness, inspire yourself back to fixation upon the picture, and clarity, working first on the outline of the picture, and then the details of the face, the hand, and so on. If dullness continues, put your mind upon a deep blue sky, a very bright and blue sky, let your mind become this sun-washed sky—it will refresh you—and then return. In an extreme case rise, splash your face with cold water, or lie and take some rest, if you must.

"For the agitation, gather your thoughts back to your heart, gently, softly, seek a deeper silence, stay still in mind and body. Slow your breath, count your breaths again if you must, and bring yourself back. Meditation is like the flight of great birds through the sky; as they hover through the wind at a distance, it seems to those of us standing upon the ground that they glide effortlessly. But in fact they are in a state of constant correction, tilting one way as the wind changes, tilting another as the wind changes again.

"Your meditation is similar, and you must continually watch and adjust, keeping it tuned like the string of a lute: not too tight, not too loose. Then finally there comes a time when, with much practice, the meditation is flowing smoothly. This is a time when you must watch for the final enemy, which is adjusting when no adjustment is necessary. Now follow what I have said, and watch the picture again."

I did, and brought Her image back, the true image. I held it clearly and silently, if only for a few minutes, and heard Kamala Shila say, "It is good. Now the second type of meditation, which we call problem-solving. I will give you a problem, and you focus your mind single-pointedly on this problem, and try to solve it. This is an important kind of meditation, and one which will serve you well later."

"I will do as you say."

"Focus now on some small event in your life, something perhaps accidental, but which changed your life, for the better."

I tried, and immediately thought of the pot, the pot that had been left behind at my mother's house on the feast day of Thanksgiving, the pot that had led me to Her door.

"Now consider, whether it was really an accident or not; do we know it was an accident; can we be sure it was an accident; could it have been arranged by someone; what would make someone arrange it; what are the possible motives, common or sacred. Think, consider, analyze, and conclude if you can."

I thought deeply. Considering its eventual effect upon my life, the accident of the pot was certainly very important to me. I had always assumed it was an accident. Even if it were not an accident, it would seem more likely that someone had simply wanted me to meet the girl, and less likely that someone could have known that this meeting would become the door to my entering the path of the spirit; and yet, if Enlightened Ones did exist, and if they truly did see the future, as clearly as we see now the present, then I suppose...

Kamala Shila interrupted me here. "It is late; you can consider that matter further on your own, and you must. Learn now the third type of meditation. I want you to review, one by one, the steps I have taught you tonight, beginning from the moment I began to clean the grass of leaves. Go mentally though the whole warm-up, of preparing the place and your own heart, for meditation; and then go through the kinds of meditation, and review the enemies I warned you of, and the ways of defeating them.

"Think lastly of the proper way to end a meditation: imagine a stone, thrown in the center of a pond, and see the ripples, going slowly out. The night we have spent together here, and each one of your meditations, is the same. It is an event, a sacred event, that has repercussions beyond what you can imagine; try to be aware of these ripples, think of them, and pray that they swiftly become waves of help and happiness that touch every living thing around you."

And I began the review, as he had instructed. He sat silently next to me, deep in some meditation of his own. And afterward the final question came to my mind, "But what is it, Master Kamala Shila, that I should meditate upon? What picture or problem or review in my mind can answer the questions we have spoken of?"

"Begin where we must always begin," he answered. "Picture your Heart Teacher before you, and let the picture become perfect to the point of real. Ask Her then for Her help, have faith, and perhaps," he said, with a twinkle in his eye, "She will come to guide you."

Anne Carolyn Klein

Dream of a Former Life

THIS IS MY DREAM, THIS IS MY LIFE.

Like everyone, I was born first in one place, then another. This time, out of long habit, I again took shape among our high snow mountains, glad as always to breathe the radiant air and scan the turquoise lakes. I had been honored there for many generations, and looked forward now to being welcomed for the first time as a woman. The traditions honoring religious masters and yogis saw no real differences between women and men. Though I was not naive about cultural conformity to this principle, I expected no difficulty. I was, after all, in a special position. Lengthy training had prepared me. I was a woman by choice.

I had selected this region of my country because of its relatively high regard for women, but soon found that this regard did not extend to my desire for religious training. My parents, despite my urgings, did not send me to the high order for study and practice. My family kept me at home, though I longed for my lineage and told them so. I remembered clearly how it had been before, when, recognized as a pathfinder from previous times,

I was sent at a young age to a renowned center of study and was soon granted close training and deep initiation by the Great Teacher. Once, after ritually blessing my forehead, throat, and chest with his golden scepter, he leaned down from his brocaded throne and stroked my cheek.

In this life, however, I grew up without any formal training. I struggled in lonely secrecy, lest I be overcome by the disparity between my present and my past. I recalled my former teachings as best I could, rotating in my mind the visions, words, and gestures by which I would eventually be recognized. The opportunity might come at any moment, and I must be prepared.

When I was fourteen, active with my memories and helping my mother make the family's cheese and yogurt and with the occasional trading of our animals, a group of three men came to our house on horseback, trailing a fourth horse piled high with goods. The oldest rider was familiar to me. Though I had not seen his face for over fifteen years, I recognized him as the brother of my earlier preceptor. I ran toward him as he dismounted and greeted him politely by name, at the same time taking care to avoid an overly familiar manner. There would be time enough to express myself, and to inquire after mutual past acquaintances. All my life I had been waiting for this ripe moment, the familiar examination, when a leather pouch or a cotton sack would be spilled open in front of me, revealing numerous anonymous items that included the beads, the bowl, perhaps a favorite book, from among my old possessions. Until then, I believed, I must not make a show of my clear recall of the past; indeed, this requisite modesty had precluded my declaring myself too adroitly even to my own parents. But once I identified my things, I knew, questions about my current aspirations would open the way for me to express my purpose in this life.

Initially, the elder ignored me. He bowed to my parents and motioned the others to bring forward a neatly folded bolt of silk brocade. My father declined this offering, which the man then placed on a shelf beside our shrine. He set his own leather bundle, bursting at the seams, by his feet, its bulk partly resting on the leg of our low table. No further word was spoken as all were seated. My mother motioned me to prepare tea. The silence in the room surrounded me as I churned the buttery tea in its long wooden tube. I was afraid the loud swooshing would prevent me from hearing important words about my future, so I paused to listen between pulls, but it always seemed that the murmuring stopped when I did.

I served the tea and was offered a space to sit. This was exceptional. My mother, working the fire, remained in the background as usual, but her face confirmed my father's gesture. Stay put.

The elder spoke. "We greet you respectfully," he said to my father," and respectfully we inquire about your health."

"I am well," my father answered. "And how are you, my gentlemen? Are you tired from your journey here?"

"No, no," said the elder, nodding to the two young men with him, "we are very well."

"But take some rest," said my father, passing an absent glance at his visitor's wooden bowl. I rose immediately to replenish our guest's tea, and his. Then I resumed my seat on the rug by the fire, resting my hand on the warm sculpted wool. I held my breath, wondering at their silence. Usually searchers were so eager to accomplish their task that they immediately pulled out the carefully chosen objects, mixing amulets and beads together, all the while making small talk, engaging the child in a dozen different ways so that they could observe his character, test his memory, question his intentions. Oddly, however, these guests barely cast their eyes in my direction. Indeed, the young men in particular were extraordinarily circumspect. Perhaps they were wondering how to adjust custom under the unusual circumstance of their candidate being a young girl. Or perhaps, I thought, they meant only to be decorous, to show that though they came from far away they could match the refined ways of our city. The smooth manners of our region were well known, though not universally admired. The outer regions, where I had often taken rebirth in male bodies, mocked the fawning language we used. My family was not of noble rank, but gentile by our country's standards. Perhaps the visitors were simply being cautious in an unfamiliar setting. If they could bide their time, so could I.

My mother came to the center of the room, holding a wooden platter piled high with golden twists of bread, fresh and warm. She gestured for me to remain seated as she offered the platter. "Oh no, we are not hungry," chorused our guests, though they had been riding all day in open country.

"Please, I am offering these to you. Eat."

"No, no, we do not need anything."

Their requisite protest accomplished, the bread was handed around and eaten without further demur.

During this long half hour I remained still, watching and recalling myself. I knew I must not disappoint their expectations, for they might easily dismiss my candidacy, which sometimes happened—in a false moment or temporary distraction, recognition could be thwarted. I prayed then, as I had all my life, that this would not occur. I did not care for the honor itself; I would have been content simply to take my place among other young acolytes of my tradition. But I understood that recognition would be my only chance to escape the fate of ordinary women, my only chance to devote myself, as I always had, to my study, my practice, my teaching. My longing was intense, but I made no sign of urgency as I poured tea, distributed bread, ignored the bulging pouch-bag at the elder's side, and waited for the steamed dumplings to be cooked.

The table talk continued, always directed at my father, a conversation burgeoning with polite comments on the good status of our family, toasts by our guests to the success of our new cloth shop at the temple circuit. For his part, my father offered to introduce our guests to the temple abbot and to personally show them the rooms filled with gold and silver images where pilgrims had been bowing down and offering butter lamps for over a thousand years. I took this turn in the conversation to be a good sign, though still their glances did not include me.

My mother tested the air above the steamer, holding her thumb a half inch from the stream of heat and then rubbing it against her forefinger. When, on the third pass, she flicked her fingers apart again with an air of conviction, I rose to help. I brought to the table a variety of pickled relishes, and then, as my mother set the platters of dumplings on the low table before us, I replaced the milk-butter beverage with freshly brewed clear tea.

I waited for the food to be passed around, staying calm yet keenly alert. I knew that a flurry of protests followed by a stream of compliments must be given full expression before we could move to the real reason behind our guests' appearance.

By then the sun had slid behind the western peak and the room had darkened. I took candles to the fire, lit them there, and placed them on the table. Their glow gave each participant a bright complexion and hid a section of their faces in shadow. The atmosphere grew denser as I filled our guests' tea bowls with the translucent liquid. I took my seat once again. I was ready.

It was not the elder but my father who then turned to me. And he gestured, not to the bag of my memorabilia the elder was surely about to bring forward, but to our younger guests. "Daughter," he said in a voice full of ceremony, "these brothers wish to marry you."

I swooned internally at his words. My life dipped and took an irrevocable turn. Even now, I cannot think of those moments without tremor.

I recalled that when the leader of our lineage first met his own teacher, he found his arrival already augured. "I dreamt last night," this great teacher told him softly, "of a wonderful bird, a divine bird. Together with a flock of a thousand birds they carried my words in all directions. This is a sign that my teaching will spread widely through you." In my own early years at the monastery, a long time ago, the preceptor and I discovered by chance that we had each had the same dream the night before. A small magic bird, yellow with an orange glisten to its wings and head, flew out of a clear blue sky and landed on my shoulder. We both understood it to be a messenger from that ancient flock. I was much encouraged. But that was long ago.

Despite myself, I could not fathom my father's words. Perhaps he too was part of my examination? I must not be so easily distracted, I chided myself, and sighed with relief. I allowed myself, for the briefest moment, to delight in thinking that soon I would be able to share with my beloved preceptor how I was almost taken in by his clever ruse.

I opened my mouth, prepared to express my devotion to my lineage and to my new mission of bringing women into it. This was the moment for me to express to my family and their guests the depths of my longing. I was prepared to divulge completely my fourteen years of yearning to take up again the drum and bell, to rejoin the singing circles of cemetery practitioners, to stride the land on lifelong pilgrimage. I would marry no one. I was ready to prove who I am by naming the secret caves, far from this place and unknown to my family, that I previously sought out for solitary vision. Now that my moment had come at last, I was upright with the urgency of communication.

My father gestured for me to remain silent as the elder turned to his leather pouch. When I saw the shadow of his hand touch its large bulk, I held my breath. I brought two additional candles to see more clearly. Hope leaped from my heart like a rainbow. And then, one by one, the elder placed on our table the contents of his bag: Newly finished bolts of brocade. Tins of rarified butter. And an exquisite piece of turquoise jewelry for my mother, honoring her, as is our custom, for having nursed a now marriageable daughter.

Dean Sluyter

Nothing

THROUGH HIS CLOTHES, the red vinyl banquette seat was starting to feel sticky. The soft clatter of dishes, the drift of cigarette smoke from the couple of old-timers having pie and coffee at the counter, the occasional sweep of headlights through the picture window as a car turned off Route 22 into the parking lot, even the bouncing of the light and the repetition of empty tables in the mirrors that covered the diner's interior—it all seemed slower, more tired, at this late hour. Half a dozen booths away, four young guys, probably seniors from the local high school, had reached the point in their beery Friday night where boisterous joshing had given way to occasional subdued quips. They were sharing a platter of disco fries: huge, starchy French fries smothered in brown meat gravy and melted Velveeta. Only in New Jersey, he thought.

Across the table, she leaned the left side of her head in her open hand, her elbow on the table. Her eyes were downcast—gazing, as far as he could tell, into her once again empty coffee cup, surrounded by torn and empty blue Equal packets. At that angle, her thick brown hair hid most of her face. Much earlier, when their long conversation hit a lull, he had flipped absently through the pages of song titles on the little wall-mounted jukebox over the table. It offered a generous collection of hits from previous decades, but he had not played any. Now someone in another booth had fed the machine some quarters, and it was playing Tommy James and the Shondells. Crimson and clover, over and over. What did that mean? he remembered wondering years ago, and wondered again.

"So that's it," she said, not looking up. "That's what it comes down to: nothing makes me happy."

He looked at her for another moment, then looked past her, over her shoulder at the big window, into the parking lot, into the headlights on Route 22, and into the hills beyond the highway, which in the dark he could not see. Crimson and clover, over and over.

"Yeah," he said. "It makes me happy too."

Mark Salzman

The Laughing Sutra

N THE SEVENTH YEAR OF THE PEOPLE'S REPUBLIC OF CHINA (1956), in a remote village of Yunnan province, Kuo Hsiao-mei gave birth to a son with extraordinarily well-developed earlobes. In many parts of Asia, long earlobes are considered a sign of great wisdom; Buddhist and Taoist deities are usually depicted as having earlobes that hang down practically to their shoulders. So Kuo named her son Sheng-hui, meaning "Flourishing Knowledge," and believed that the boy would grow up to be a famous scholar. Kuo took her son to the village fortune-teller, expecting him to confirm her belief, but after determining the exact hour of the boy's birth, throwing yarrow sticks, and consulting the *I Ching*, the fortune-teller came to a different conclusion.

"The boy," he said, shaking his head gravely, "will leave home when he is very young. He will encounter sorrow and loss as he grows up. Then he will wander all over the world."

This was hardly what Kuo wished to hear, so she cursed the old man and reminded him that he had once predicted she would marry a northerner and move to Peking, but in fact she was an unwed mother and still stuck in Yunnan.

Kuo decided that if Sheng-hui was going to become a scholar, he would have to learn early how to read and write. One day, while picking tea leaves, she had an idea; she took some of the leaves home and wrote a single Chinese character on the back of each. She showed the characters to Sheng-hui one at a time, at the same time loudly pronouncing them, in the hope that he would imitate her and eventually connect the characters to the sounds. Sheng-hui was only a few weeks old, however, and did not appear to be aware of the leaves dangling in front of him, nor did he seem capable of producing the appropriate sounds. But Kuo did not give up. Each night, after returning from the fields, she lit a candle in the reed hut and flashed the leaves in front of Sheng-hui as he suckled at her breast.

After a year of this, he showed little progress toward recognizing the characters written on the leaves, but one day he reached out and grabbed the leaf in his mother's hand and swallowed it. That leaf happened to have the character *yu*, meaning travel, written on it. This alarmed Kuo, because it reminded her of the old man's prediction. After trying unsuccessfully to get Sheng-hui to cough up "travel," she wrote *liu tsai chia*—"stay at home"— three times on another leaf and forced him to swallow it. So ended Sheng-hui's early education.

In 1960 a famine struck most of China, partially due to a series of natural disasters but mainly thanks to the economic policy known as "the Great Leap Forward." Part of the Great Leap Forward involved destroying vegetable and fruit crops and replacing them with rice fields, because Chairman Mao thought that fruits and vegetables hinted of bourgeois decadence. Kuo's village had cultivated mango, banana, and citrus fruits for centuries, but visiting political cadres forced the villagers to chop down all the trees and plant rice. That spring there was a drought, so the rice crop was spoiled as well. At the end of that summer, with nothing to harvest,

Kuo and many of her fellow villagers had to forage for dry brushwood, which they gathered into huge bundles, carried on their backs to the village, and sold in the outdoor market. In no time at all, brushwood became scarce around the village, forcing Kuo to wander farther and farther out into the hills to gather it.

On one of these exhausting journeys, with Sheng-hui marching beside her, dutifully holding some twigs, Kuo came upon an unfamiliar valley thick with black bamboo, a rare variety whose graceful stalks and branches look as if they are carved of ebony. They found a path that led them through the bamboo grove down to a river, where they heard a steady roar coming from somewhere downstream. Deciding to put their work aside for a while, they dropped their loads and walked along the riverbank in the direction of the roaring sound. It got louder and louder, and the bamboo forest got thicker and thicker, until all of a sudden the river and forest simply ended at a sheer cliff and opened up into a blue sky. Surprised, Kuo and Sheng-hui nearly tumbled over the edge of the waterfall.

Catching their breath, they made their way as close to the edge as they could safely get, but even then they could not see the bottom of the waterfall for all the mist kicked up by the crashing water. As they stared down in wonder, they heard a sound behind them, and turned around in time to see a deer crashing through the bamboo forest, leaping away frantically. Kuo could hardly conceal her delight.

"This is a special place!" she exclaimed. "A deer is a sign that an immortal lives somewhere nearby!"

Sheng-hui looked back at the falls and asked, "What is an immortal?"

"It's a magical being," his mother answered, "a person who never dies."

"Why don't they die?" Sheng-hui wanted to know.

"Because they are living Buddhas," said Kuo, clasping her hands together in prayer.

"What do they look like?" Sheng-hui asked.

"They have long white beards and bald heads because they're so old.

And they have long earlobes like you, that's why you'll be so smart. And they collect rare herbs in valleys that are hidden by mist, so no one will see them. There's plenty of mist at the bottom of the falls, so maybe an immortal lives down there! We should say a prayer now." Kuo bowed her head and began chanting, but Sheng-hui tugged at her ragged skirt.

"Why does a deer mean an immortal lives here?"

Kuo frowned for a moment, then answered patiently, "Because deer are afraid of ordinary men, but they aren't afraid of immortals. Immortals are so gentle they can ride deer like horses!"

"So why did the deer run away?" Sheng-hui asked.

"Because it saw *us!*" Kuo snapped. "Now keep quiet while I pray to Buddha for good luck."

When she had finished her prayers, Kuo suggested that they take a refreshing bath in one of the shallow pools along the riverbank. Just as they got up to their knees in the clear, chilly water, Kuo sensed someone behind them. She turned and saw a man, ragged and desperate-looking, stumbling out from the bamboo grove. He walked toward them uncertainly, and Kuo pulled Sheng-hui toward her. As the man closed on them, she picked her son up and thought of trying to run across the river, but she quickly realized that the current would pull them over the waterfall. She screamed for help as loudly as she could, but no one answered.

The man grabbed them and dragged them both ashore. He shoved the boy aside and wrestled Kuo to the ground, but she clawed at his eyes and throat. He bellowed in pain, yet he managed to grab both her wrists with one hand. But when he drew his other hand back to strike her, Sheng-hui seized it with both hands and bit down with all his might, holding on like a wild animal. Cursing, the man dragged Sheng-hui toward the water, pried the boy loose, and threw him into the deep part of the river.

Kuo struggled to her feet and charged desperately toward the river, but the man grabbed her and held on while the boy thrashed and coughed in the rushing current, heading straight for the falls. Just as he went over the edge, he let out a piercing shriek. When Kuo saw that, the world became dark for her, and she felt no more pain.

The man shook her as hard as he could. He wanted her to be alert so that she would be afraid of him. She did not wake up, though, so he dragged her to the river as well, threw her in, and let the current pull her toward her son.

"IT MAY SEEM CONFUSING," the old monk pointed out, "that Buddhist literature often reminds us that true knowledge cannot be found in books. If that is so, why is there any Buddhist literature at all?"

After a pause, he continued:

"When asked this question, an enlightened master once said, 'If I see the moon, but you do not, I will point at it. First you will watch my finger to see where it goes. Eventually, however, you must take your eyes off my finger and find the moon yourself.' So it is with the sutras. They point you toward the truth, but must not be confused with truth itself.

"You might ask yourself then, 'Why should I read the sutras at all, if they do not contain the truth, if they cannot tell me the true nature of reality? Why waste time on them?' But then you would be making a grievous mistake. How would you know where to look for truth if the sutras did not point you in the right direction? Would you look under your bed? In the woods, perhaps?"

After another pause, the monk shook his head wistfully, then said, "No, one wouldn't know where to look, of course. That is why one must keep reading."

His lecture ended, the monk Wei-ching took off his glasses, wiped them clean with a piece of cloth, then dabbed at his forehead. A white cat, his only audience, yawned, licked a paw, then slipped out of the tiny hut to chase rats on the grounds of the ruined temple. It had been a dreadful summer, and even at night it was still sweltering. Wei-ching sighed, then opened one of the drawers of a large wooden cabinet behind him and removed a scroll from it. He carefully unrolled the sutra, placed a few smooth river stones on the corners as paperweights, put his glasses back on, and began reading.

Wei-ching had been living alone here for nearly twenty years. The temple had once sheltered more than a dozen monks, but during the war with Japan it had been almost completely demolished by an unfortunate accident. A group of Chinese soldiers marching toward Kun-ming to bring supplies to a besieged airstrip camped near the temple one night. Just before daybreak, a soldier on guard duty, trying desperately to stay awake, smoked a cigarette as he paced back and forth in the woods. When he heard the signal announcing that his company was breaking camp, he flicked the cigarette aside and joined his comrades. By the time the brushfire began, the soldiers were already on their way.

When the fire reached the temple, the other monks fled to safety, but Wei-ching stayed behind. Fearless for his own life, he carried bundle after bundle of the scrolls from the temple library to the river, and tossed them in where the fire could not reach them. Only when he was sure he had removed all of the scrolls did he jump into the river himself and swim to safety.

When the fire died down, Wei-ching returned and dragged the scrolls out of the river. Then he carefully unrolled them and hung them to dry on charred tree branches. Realizing that soon the water-damaged scrolls would crumble and fall apart, he built himself a little hut in the ruins of the temple and spent the rest of the war years transcribing the sutras onto fresh rolls of cloth.

Before that time, he had felt indifferent toward the scriptures, believing that meditation alone led to enlightenment. But the pious act of copying them out, character by character, page by page, chapter by chapter, gradually changed his mind. He came to believe that the fire was not an accident at all but a sign indicating that he must devote himself to the study and preservation of sacred literature. He gave himself the religious name Wei-ching, which means "Guardian of Scriptures," and after the war made a pilgrimage each year to a different part of China to visit other temple libraries. Whenever he found a sutra not in his own collection, he copied it out and brought it back with him. His goal was to assemble a complete library of the major Buddhist scriptures in his lifetime, and by the age of sixty-four he had located and painstakingly copied out all of them except one—a sutra so rare Wei-ching could not even be sure that it still existed.

Just after the Communist revolution, Wei-ching traveled northwest to visit the Tun-huang Buddhist caves in the Kansu Province. Tun-huang used to be an important oasis along the old Silk Road, the last truly Chinese city before one ventured west into the murderous Takla Makan Desert on the way to India and beyond. Traders who stopped there paid handsomely to maintain and improve the religious paintings, statues, and libraries in the caves, hoping that such pious donations would build up enough good karma to get them through the deserts and back to China alive. When the ocean routes made the treacherous overland journey unnecessary, the caves were abandoned to the desert and forgotten for nearly a thousand years.

In 1906 a lone monk was living there when an explorer under commission from the British Museum, Sir Aurel Stein, stumbled on the caves and brought many of their treasures back with him to England. After that, a large number of foreign archeologists and collectors flocked to the caves, taking most of the best artwork and scrolls out of China. Around 1920 the Chinese government somewhat belatedly forbade any further looting from the caves and made Tun-huang a museum.

When Wei-ching got there in 1952, the old monk who had been living at Tun-huang was still alive. He confided that in 1948 another rich foreigner, an American named Fo-lan, had visited the caves. He was another museum collector, and made it clear he wanted to buy some religious artifacts in spite of the government ban. At that time, China was devastated from the war with Japan and then the fighting between the Nationalists and Communists, so a corrupt local official made a deal with the American and sold him a few statues and a trunkful of scrolls. According to the old monk, that trunk contained the last extant copy of the Laughing Sutra, a scroll so precious that whoever understood its message would instantly perceive his Buddha-nature, and—this was the remarkable part—achieve physical immortality as well.

At first Wei-ching was skeptical; if this sutra was genuine, how could it be that he had never heard of it? The Buddhist canon had been copied and spread over libraries in China for nearly two thousand years. It seemed hard to believe that a sutra that offered both enlightenment and immortality could have disappeared so completely. But the monk from the caves insisted it was genuine. The reason the Laughing Sutra had been ignored, he said, was that few could recognize its true value.

The sutra was based on a private sermon Gautama Buddha gave to one of his most talented disciples. In that sermon, Buddha described the formless, chaotic nature of existence. He insisted that the human situation is utterly hopeless, the universe unknowable, and our individual souls mere illusions. When the disciple heard this, he tumbled into fathomless despair. In that moment of total surrender, he directly perceived that he had been enlightened and immortal from the very beginning, and dissolved into laughter so profound and free from delusion that even the stones around him shook in sympathy.

Unfortunately, the monk said, most people who read the Laughing Sutra misinterpret the disciple's response as derisive laughter and assume that he took Buddha for a fool. That is why the sutra never became popular, and why that particular disciple had long since fallen into obscurity. After hearing this testimony, Wei-ching vowed to travel to America to recover the Laughing Sutra, both to attain immortality for himself and to make the sutra available to others.

IT WAS GETTING DARK OUT, so Wei-ching put away the book he was reading and called the cat in for the evening. He lit a gas lamp, washed his hands and face in a bucket of cold river water, ate some warm rice gruel, then sat down on the little rug in front of his cot and chanted his evening prayers. Lately, he had been praying to Kuan-yin, the Goddess of Mercy, asking her to look out for him now that he was about to embark on his pilgrimage to America.

Toward the end of his prayers, he felt an odd tingling sensation in his chest. He paid little attention to it, since he noticed as he got older that he had new aches and pains all the time, and kept on chanting. Then he heard a knock at the flimsy door to his room. Unused to visitors in the remote temple, he hesitated before answering. The knocking ceased, and Wei-ching peered out of a crack in the wall to see if he could catch a glimpse of his visitor. He looked around but saw nothing except for the fleeting image of a fingerprint just before it poked him gingerly in the eye. Wei-ching fell back onto his mat, rubbing his eye, and heard a voice say in a strangely archaic dialect, "Open the door or I will remove it." Wei-ching, now trembling with fear, opened the door expecting to see a soldier or bandit, but instead saw a man unlike any he had ever seen before.

The visitor wore a ragged suit of leather armor of a sort that Wei-ching had only seen in ancient woodblock prints. He was of average height but powerfully built, and fearsome to look at. His arms and chest were covered in dark hair, and his facial hair grew out under his cheekbones almost all the way to his nose. He had thick eyebrows that swept up toward his temples, and a pair of burning yellow eyes that did not blink or even seem to move. He carried a rusted iron pole that glistened dark and wet on one end. Lichen and moss covered his armor, as if he had lain outdoors for years without moving. Wei-ching thought he looked like a bronze statue come to life.

"You live alone here, isn't that true?" the visitor asked. Wei-ching managed to nod, but for some reason he could not bring himself to speak. He noticed that the tingling sensation in his chest had become more pronounced.

"You have a guest," the visitor said, and pointed to a shivering, naked boy with long earlobes standing nearby.

"Someone tried to kill this boy today," the strange man continued. "I happened to be nearby, so I was able to save him. Unfortunately, I was not able to save his mother." The visitor frowned and looked at the boy. "He needs dry clothes and some food. After that, you can find out where he lives and return him to his village."

Wei-ching made a great effort to regain the use of his tongue and finally blurted out, "But you should take him to the police! I am just a monk; I wouldn't know how to take care of him! And I am about to begin a long journey, so I won't have time to—

The visitor's eyes narrowed and seemed to burn more fiercely. Wei-ching felt the tingling in his chest even more strongly, as if an electric current were passing through his body, making his arms and legs feel heavy. The strange man raised his right hand and pointed at Wei-ching. "You are a monk, and you have vowed to alleviate suffering. This boy is suffering, so it is your duty to assist him. You will postpone your journey and care for this boy!"

"B-but what about the murderer?" Wei-ching asked. "What if he comes here? Shouldn't you—

The stranger's upper lip twitched with anger. Wei-ching noticed that he had long eyeteeth, like a wild animal's. "The murderer will not come here," the stranger said. "He has been punished in a manner suiting his crime." Then he came so close to Wei-ching that their noses almost touched. Wei-ching was terrified, but found he could not budge.

"If anyone asks," the stranger hissed, looking hard at Wei-ching with his unblinking eyes, "the boy wandered here on his own. You never saw me. If you say otherwise, you will regret it." With that, the stranger left, carrying his rusted pole, and Wei-ching led the shaking boy into the temple.

AT AROUND MIDNIGHT, Sheng-hui began shivering so hard that his chattering woke the old monk. Wei-ching laid his own blanket and his extra clothing over the boy and gave him some herb tea, but the chills turned to fever and Sheng-hui fell into delirium. Wei-ching sat up all night with him. The next morning he hurried to the nearest village to find a doctor. Unfortunately, the only doctor in the vicinity was a poorly trained "barefoot doctor" who could only recommend that Wei-ching keep the boy warm and quiet.

The boy dropped in and out of consciousness for four days, during which Wei-ching hardly slept or ate for worry. During the worst spells of fever, Sheng-hui cried out for his mother and mumbled in a dialect Wei-ching couldn't understand. When at last the fever broke, Sheng-hui seemed shrunk to half his original size, and his eyes looked like those of an old man. Most worrisome, though, was that he seemed to have lost the ability to speak. His mouth would open purposefully, but no sound would come out, and he would sit there frozen, like a picture of someone caught in mid-sentence. Eventually, the boy would panic and tears would fill his eyes, but even his crying was soundless.

When the boy was strong enough to walk, Wei-ching led him around to all the nearest villages to find out what he could about the foundling's background. No one recognized the child or had any clues as to where he might have come from. If Sheng-hui could have spoken, someone might have recognized his village dialect, but whenever anyone asked him a question, the poor child only stared back anxiously. Finally, Wei-ching and Sheng-hui made the long day's journey to Ling-feng, the closest town large enough to have a police station, but the police had no information about a missing woman or child. Since Kuo had no living relatives in the village, her starving neighbors there assumed she had decided to take her son to a place less stricken by the famine.

Days, and then weeks, passed, but the boy's identity remained a mystery. Wei-ching hoped that some kind village couple with no children or only daughters would offer to adopt him, but perhaps because of the famine or the little boy's muteness, no one did. Wei-ching had lived alone most of his life, away from the cares of the material world, and feared that raising a boy would distract him from his pursuit of enlightenment, not to mention his search for the Laughing Sutra. Still, he couldn't bear to think of leaving the child at an orphanage. "Perhaps," Wei-ching began to say to himself, "it is Buddha's will that I care for this child."

When a month went by and Sheng-hui still could not speak, Wei-ching began to fear that perhaps the boy had been permanently damaged by the fever. The old monk despaired to think that he, who had such a passion for learning, might spend the rest of his life caring for a moron. To try to prevent this, Wei-ching began reading sutras aloud to the boy at night, hoping that it might nudge his brain awake.

Actually, Sheng-hui's brain worked just fine, but whenever he tried to speak, it felt as if a pair of invisible hands clutched his throat and squeezed it shut. The harder he struggled to force the words through, the tighter the hands squeezed, until he could hardly breathe. As the weeks passed, though, he came to understand the old monk's dialect, and gained strength from the chores Wei-ching gave him around the temple.

Wei-ching, in the meantime, both pleased and disappointed himself by growing fond of the boy. He knew that to attain the spiritual goal of enlightenment one had to cast off all attachments to the world, especially emotional ones. On the other hand, by showing the boy mercy, he was almost certainly acquiring good karma for himself, so even if he failed to attain enlightenment in this life, he would definitely have a better chance in the next one. Also, small things like watching how much the boy enjoyed eating or playing with the cat brought Wei-ching unexpected pleasure. His only regret was that, considering how arthritic he was already and how many years it would be before the child could take care of himself, Wei-ching would probably never be able to make the long pilgrimage that he had planned for so many years.

IN TIME, THOUGH, Wei-ching began to entertain the dim hope that one day the orphan would make the journey for him. With that in mind, he named the boy Hsun-ching, which means "Seeker of Sutras." But even with such a fortuitous name, Wei-ching thought, how would the child become interested enough in sutras to want to travel to the other side of the earth in search of one? Most people didn't appreciate that sort of religious literature until well into middle age. Wei-ching realized that his only hope was to appeal to something in the boy more universal than a desire for spiritual advancement: a love of adventure. Toward this end, Wei-ching stopped reading sutras to the boy at night and instead began reading him *Journey to the West*, a famous novel about a T'ang dynasty monk and his magical companion, who walked all the way from China to India to find Buddhist texts.

One rainy evening Wei-ching was reading a particularly exciting chapter in which the priest's magical companion, known as the Monkey King, had to use his prowess in the martial arts to subdue a formidable pig-demon. Just at the climax of their battle, a strong gust of wind flung the temple door open and extinguished the lamp.

"I guess the fight will have to wait until tomorrow," said Wei-ching, getting up to close the door. Suddenly, out of the blackness, a small voice pleaded, "But does the Monkey win?"

Wei-ching turned around and stared in the direction of the boy. "You spoke!" he nearly shouted. Hsun-ching was even more shocked than the old man; the words had just fallen out of him. He opened his mouth to say more, but the words became like a crowd of men trying to crawl out of a single window in a burning building, crushing against each other in a panic. He felt the invisible hand bear down on his throat once again, and he was unable to say anything more that night.

Over the next few weeks, though, the invisible hands loosened their hold, and perhaps because he had been mute for so long, Hsun-ching became obsessed with language. He talked incessantly, mostly in the form of questions about the Monkey King, and when Wei-ching begged for some peace and quiet, the boy simply talked to himself. It was a remarkable recovery, but not a complete one. Whenever Hsun-ching got overexcited, he began to stutter and had to wait until he calmed down before he could speak fluently again.

Now that the young Hsun-ching could talk, Wei-ching tried once again to find out where he was from, how he had become separated from his family, and the identity of the strange-looking man who had brought him to the temple. As much as he wanted to, though, Hsun-ching couldn't answer any of those questions; he could see his mother clearly in his mind, their house and their village, but he remembered nothing about the day they wandered out to the waterfall.

Wei-ching, in the meantime, took it as a good omen that the boy had taken such an interest in *Journey to the West*. He began to read from the novel in the morning as well as in the evening. Even that wasn't enough for Hsun-ching, though; he wanted to hear about Monkey all day long. Finally, he begged Wei-ching to teach him to read so he could devour the novel on his own. This request delighted the pious scholar, and he turned back to the beginning right away, so that Hsun-ching could learn the characters as they went.

Hsun-ching's obsession with speaking quickly shifted toward reading about Monkey and his adventures. It turned out that he was gifted with a nearly photographic memory, so that within only a few months he knew enough characters to read more than a page a day. By the end of the year, he was able to read all by himself, using a dictionary to look up the unfamiliar words and only occasionally having to ask Wei-ching for help.

One autumn day Wei-ching returned from his herb garden to find Hsun-ching lying facedown on his cot, crying. He asked the boy what was wrong, but Hsun-ching was so upset he could only stutter. Wei-ching made him some chrysanthemum tea, which soothes the nerves. When Hsun-ching had settled down enough to explain the cause of his unhappiness, he pointed to the foot of his bed, where the tattered, yellowed novel lay, and blurted out, "I f-f-finished it!"

Wei-ching thought this should be cause for celebration, but Hsun-ching felt as if the world had ended. No more adventures for Monkey, no more demons to vanquish, no more corrupt bureaucrats to tweak, no more savage deserts to cross. What was left?

Wei-ching realized that what the boy needed was a sense of accomplishment to make up for his sense of loss. He patted him on the shoulder. "You have finished your first book. It is a very important moment. But to show that you are ready now to move on to other books, you must do what all great scholars do when they finish their first books."

"Wh-what do they d-d-do?" Hsun-ching asked.

Wei-ching straightened himself up to look more formal and said gravely, "You must show your understanding of what you read. You must tell me the story in your own words. Are you prepared to do that?"

"B-b-but...you already know the story," Hsun-ching protested.

"That doesn't matter! I want to know if *you* know the story!" Wei-ching countered. "Your report should be complete, and you may take as long as you like. Are you ready?"

Hsun-ching sat up and dried his face on his sleeve. The old white cat jumped on his lap and purred loudly, which helped cheer him up, and he began to think back to the first chapter of the novel, which he had started reading almost two years before. He felt a thrill of pleasure as he recalled the story of Monkey's birth.

"Th-the name of the book is *Journey into the West*," he began. "It's about Sun Wu-k'ung, the Monkey King, who—"

"No, no—it's about the Buddhist monk Hsuan-tsang!" Wei-ching interrupted. "He is really the main character!"

"It's m-m-my rep-p-port," Hsun-ching said, lowering his head and beginning to stutter. Wei-ching apologized, told the boy to relax, and let him continue.

"Th-th-the Monkey King hatched out of a stone egg more than two thousand years ago. He was a stone monkey, but he was as smart as a man, and he could talk. Also, h-he was very strong and brave. He became king of a band of regular monkeys, and led them to a magical place known as Flowers and Fruit Mountain, where they lived and played for years and years.

"After a while, though, Monkey got bored with swinging around and eating fruit day after day, so he left the mountain to find a famous Taoist master who could teach him magic secrets. Monkey found this man and became his best student. H-he learned how to somersault over clouds, change himself into any animal or object he wanted, and make an army of spirit monkeys by pulling some of his hairs out, chewing them up, then blowing the pieces into the air! Each piece became a tiny soldier.

"When Monkey finished his training, he traveled under the oceans to the palace of a D-D-Dragon King, who had a great collection of magic weapons. Monkey went there and found a giant staff called the Compliant Golden Rod, which weighed thirteen thousand, five hundred pounds. He picked it up easily. Then he found out why it was named the 'compliant' rod—when he mentioned that it was too long to be carried around, it changed just like that to the size of a sewing needle! Monkey slipped it behind his ear and announced to the Dragon King that he wanted to keep it. When the Dragon King said no, Monkey h-h-hit him over the head with the staff and told him not to be so stingy toward his guests!

"Then he made his way up to heaven, where he just walked in to the palace of the Jade Emperor, ate all the Peaches of Immortality, and ruined an important party for high-ranking immortals! H-he wasn't afraid of any of them! After that, he called himself 'Great Sage Equal to Heaven.' This made the Jade Emperor very mad—he called Monkey a conceited ape! So he sent a whole army of heavenly warriors down to earth to punish Monkey. B-b-but Monkey was such a good fighter he sent them all back to heaven beat up and crying!

"At last Buddha invited Monkey up to heaven, where he challenged Monkey to a test. He said to Monkey, 'I hear that you can somersault over the clouds for great distances. But I don't think you can even jump out of the palm of my hand! If you can, we will give you the Jade Emperor's palace. But if you fail, you will be a p-p-prisoner!' Monkey said, 'I can do that easily!' Buddha stretched out his hand and told Monkey to prove it. Monkey hopped onto his hand, then did one of his somersaults, and he jumped more that thirty-six thousand miles. When he landed, he was at the base of a great mountain range that had five pink mountains. To prove he had been there, he p-p-pissed on one of the mountains, then somersaulted back thirty-six thousand miles and landed right on the Buddha's palm!

"But then the Buddha got mad and yelled, 'Foolish ape! You jumped nowhere! You never got out of my hand.' He pointed to the base of one of his fingers, where Monkey saw a tiny puddle of piss! Before Monkey could say anything else, Buddha's hand grew huge and closed on Monkey, then he threw Monkey into a m-m-mountain p-p-prison!

"Monkey stayed there for over five hundred years, and all he had to eat was iron pellets! At last, Buddha said he would let Monkey go, but only if Monkey would do a good deed."

"And what was that deed?" Wei-ching asked, thankful that at last they had reached the relevant part of the story.

"M-M-Monkey had to protect Hsuan-tsang on his trip to India."

"And who was Hsuan-tsang? Where did he come from?" Wei-ching asked.

"He was a famous monk. Before he was born, a bad man killed his father and married his mother. When Hsuan-tsang was born, the bad man wanted to kill him, because he said it wasn't his baby. So the mother put the baby on a little boat and put him on a river, hoping that somebody would find him and take care of him. He floated down the river, and a monk found him, so he grew up in a temple. Kind of like me now."

"Yes." Wei-ching smiled. "Kind of like you. Then what happened?"

"Th-then he grew up and became a famous monk and decided to go to India with Monkey," Hsun-ching answered, rushing through what he felt was the most boring part of the story. "The problem was, Hsuan-tsang was a c-c-crybaby! They had to go through all sorts of dangerous places, in deserts and mountains, where there were lots of demons. Whenever the monsters attacked, though, he just started crying and gave up, so Monkey had to save him all the time. The first monster he fought was—

"That's all right," Wei-ching interrupted again, "you don't have to tell me about all of the monsters. What about their pilgrimage to India—what did they do when they got there?"

Hsun-ching pouted. "The m-m-monsters are the best part."

"Yes, of course," Wei-ching sighed, "but you can tell me about them another time. Today I would like to know how the story ended."

"W-w-well," the boy continued, "they finally got to India where Buddha gave all the sutras to Hsuan-tsang. Then they went back to China, and Monkey went back up to heaven. B-B-Buddha forgave him, and now Monkey lives there with the other immortals, and he can do wh-wh-whatever he wants for the rest of eternity!"

Wei-ching was disappointed that Hsun-ching seemed so much more interested in the fairy-tale character of the Monkey King than in the historical character Hsuan-tsang and his holy mission. Still, he nodded his approval, then asked expectantly, "And what do you feel after reading this book? Would you want to be like Hsuan-tsang someday and make a great journey like that?"

Flushed with excitement, Hsun-ching answered breathlessly, "N-n-no! Hsuan-tsang was a w-w-weakling! I want to be like M-Monkey and kill m-m-monsters!"

AFTER THAT DAY, Wei-ching began teaching Hsun-ching classical Chinese. That way, he reasoned, the boy's desire to kill monsters would be gradually replaced by a desire to read old books. Hsun-ching did not show much enthusiasm for this austere language, but nevertheless learned it at an astonishing rate.

By the time Hsun-ching was nine, he read samples of poetry, history, and even some of *The Analects of Confucius*. Wei-ching also tried to lead him through some of the more important sutras, but Hsun-ching found these hopelessly boring. Wei-ching eventually had to admit that the Buddhist canon was hardly designed to appeal to little boys, so he postponed that part of Hsun-ching's education until later. Instead, he dug out of his book collection an old English-language primer he had bought for himself years ago in Nanking, and told the boy to teach himself English. He felt convinced now that karma had pointed to Hsun-ching as the one to make the pilgrimage: He had been miraculously saved from certain death and then raised by a Buddhist monk, just like Hsuan-tsang more than a thousand years before, and he had been moved to speak again by the novel about Hsuan-tsang's journey to India. Also, according to his official biography, Hsuan-tsang had long earlobes, and Hsun-ching shared this physical trait. It would be an unpardonable sin if Wei-ching did not do everything he could to prepare Hsun-ching to follow the T'ang monk's example. And since Hsun-ching's modern pilgrimage would take him to America, it made sense to encourage him to learn English.

When Hsun-ching reached the end of the primer, Wei-ching decided to take him to Kun-ming, the capital city of Yunnan Province, where they could find more advanced English books. Also, it would be a good chance for Hsun-ching to get out of the forest and see the world. In their five years together they had taken plenty of trips to nearby villages to buy supplies, but Hsun-ching had never seen more than a few dozen people at once.

Wearing their best saffron-dyed robes, they packed some food and started walking toward the closest town with a bus station, about twenty miles west from their temple following the river upstream.

After several hours they rounded a bend and saw a waterfall. Wei-ching smiled. "This is called the Dragon's Breath Waterfall, because the mist

kicked up by the falls looks like steam puffing out of a dragon's mouth."
Wei-ching imagined how spectacular the sight must look to someone who
had never seen it, but the boy looked pale and sullen.

"What's the matter?" Wei-ching asked. Hsun-ching only shrugged his
shoulders, so they got back on the path and resumed their walk.

To get to the top of the falls, they had to climb a precarious stairway
carved right into the side of the cliff. When they at last reached the top,
Wei-ching suggested they have a little rest near the edge to enjoy the view.
Hsun-ching seemed willing, but as soon as he got near the edge, he felt ill,
so they ended up having their rest in the bamboo grove nearby.

That night they camped out under the stars in a grass clearing. After a
good meal of rice gruel steamed in plantain leaves, they lay on their backs
and talked about what they would do and see in Kun-ming. Long after Wei-
ching had fallen asleep, Hsun-ching was still awake. He was thinking about
that waterfall; something about it was familiar, but he couldn't quite
remember what it was.

Hal Hallstein

In Search of the Rainbow Body

O
m *Mani Padme Hung.*

I can taste the trail heading west out of the village of Pisang. My shoes are coming apart at the toes, and with each step the rubber flips a little cloudburst of dust into the air in front of me. It makes perfect sense, my shoes being this way, in the rain shadow of the Annapurna Range. The realities of impermanence are more directly visible here than in the lowlands. Everything around me is eroding and wasting, from the decaying drip-castle hills, to the sun-bleached and wind-worn faces of the people who call this valley home.

Sabin, my traveling companion, walks in front of me down a line of rattling prayer wheels, mindfully turning each one. *Om Mani Padme Hung.* I follow after him, turning each wheel as it slows. Sabin stops and unloads the basket he carries from his forehead onto the front step of a building that houses a gigantic, colorfully painted prayer wheel. As he enters and turns the heavy drum three times, I wait outside on the step. I sit next to an elderly man who considers our whiteness with curiosity. I choose not to speak to him until after I have turned the huge wheel myself.

Returning to the old man's side, I introduce myself in Nepali. I tell him that we are on our way to see the footprints of Padmasambhava, and ask him what he knows about the route. He says that he has visited the place a number of times, but he prefers to talk about a different pilgrimage. He is disappointed that he has never been able to go to Bodh Gaya, the place of Guatama's enlightenment, and worries that his age may prevent him from ever getting there. I ask him why he wants to go to India so badly. He thinks for a moment, and then explains to me that visiting the site of the Bodhi Tree is the highest merit that a layperson like him can earn in a single lifetime.

As he finishes his thought, an elderly woman appears around the corner of the wheelhouse. She carries her own personal prayer wheel mounted on a handle that she twirls as she walks. Without a word she hands the spinning wheel to the old man in a perfectly fluid motion and enters the building. *Om Mani Padme Hung.* As I listen to the big wheel churn and rattle inside, I watch the old man as he spins the small wheel, waiting patiently for the woman to come back outside. A few moments later, without a word spoken nor a prayer lost, she retrieves the little wheel and disappears around the building.

I ask the old man about the merit he would make by going to Bodh Gaya, what it might do for his future. He explains that the karma he incurred as a yak herder would be overridden and that he would be reborn as a monk, better able to continue his practice. The man's confidence makes me smile. After a moment of reflection, he stands and enters the wheel house. Three slow rotations and then he turns, wishes me a good journey, and walks across the trail to the tiny stone houses perched on a neighboring hill. *Om Mani Padme Hung.* Sabin and I sit quietly for a good while as the momentum of the Great Wheel carries blessings up the trail behind him.

As I listen to the low grinding of the wheel's axis, I think back on our trip to the boulder-strewn banks of the Modi Khola River below the village of Siklis. After living there for two weeks with Gurung families, our Nepali mothers presented us with garlands of bright yellow flowers and bid us farewell. Sabin and I happily wore the beautiful necklaces as we wandered down the long hillside, through the rice fields, toward the river where our pilgrimage began. Once we reached the river, we rested on a huge boulder beside a rickety bamboo bridge. We took off our garlands, tossing the flowers one by one, as an offering, into a swirling eddy. The petals circled slowly in the flotsam until a bright yellow spiral formed. We sat and watched the flowers spin together, and smiled as each blossom was pulled under by the small whirlpool. *Om Mani Padme Hung.*

As Sabin and I crossed the bridge to begin our pilgrimage in earnest, leaving the whirling flower-pool to the eyes of the forest, neither of us had much to say. But now, in the mountains, with all the prayer wheels noisily spinning around us, the yellow blossoms in the eddy take on new meaning. As the giant wheel turns and clatters behind us, I feel for the first time fully present within the Mahayana.

Within the Great Vehicle we practice to be aware of the community of beings who ride alongside us on the Wheel of Samsara. It does not much matter if one thinks of the Six Realms as physical places where beings are reborn, or as psychological states we revolve through. Either way, no matter where we think we are headed, within the Mahayana the understanding that we are *all* going is what is key.

Sabin and I rise from the steps of the wheelhouse and begin the day's hike to the elusive footprints of Padmasambhava, our shoes kicking up red dust. With the flavor of the path in my mouth, I give quiet thanks to all those who provide company on the Great Wheel. In the mandala of our minds, all the spinning wheels we have turned, all the worn faces we have met, all the tattered prayer flags we have seen—all of these spiral together in the flowered pool.

As Sabin squints his eyes toward the snowy peaks ahead of us, I make a silent dedication of the empty space in our tracks.

Om Mani Padme Hung.

About the Contributors

Andrew Foster Altschul is a Lecturer in Creative Writing at Stanford University and also teaches in the MFA program at the University of San Francisco. His work has appeared in *Fence*, *Swink*, *One Story*, *Story Quarterly*, and *Pleiades*, as well as the anthologies *Stumbling and Raging: More Politically Inspired Fiction* and *Best New American Voices 2006*. He lives in San Francisco and, occasionally, in Cuzco, Peru.

Robert Olen Butler is author of ten novels and three collections of stories. In addition to a Pulitzer Prize in 1993 and a National Book Award in 2001 (both for fiction), he has received a Guggenheim Fellowship in fiction and a NEA grant, as well as the Richard and Hinda Rosenthal Award from the American Academy of Arts and Letters. He teaches creative writing at Florida State University.

Lama Surya Das is an American-born lama trained in the Tibetan Buddhist tradition. He has completed two three-year cloistered meditation retreats and spent over 35 years studying and practicing with the great teachers of the major Tibetan schools. He is an author, poet, and translator; his most recent books include *Awakening the Buddhist Heart*; *Awakening to the Sacred, Creating a Daily Spiritual Life from Scratch*; and *Awakening the Buddha Within, Tibetan Wisdom for the Western World*. The founder of the Dzogchen Center and the retreat center Dzogchen Osel Ling outside Austin, Texas, he lives in Cambridge, Massachusetts.

Jeff Davis was born in Texas, taught at Southern Methodist University and at the University of New Mexico's Taos Summer Writers' Conference, and now lives in upstate New York, where he teaches at Bliss Yoga Center and practices zazen at Zen Mountain Monastery. He is author of a poetry collection and *The Journey from the Center to the Page: Yoga Philosophies and Practices as Muse for Authentic Writing*.

Anne Donovan has written for radio and stage and is author of the novel *Buddha Da* and the short story collection *Hieroglyphics*, both published by Canongate. *Buddha Da* was short-listed for the 2003 Orange Prize, the Whitbread First Novel Award, and the 2004 Scottish Book of the Year Award, and was nominated for this year's International IMPAC Dublin Literary Award. She lives in Glasgow.

Hal Hallstein is a recent graduate of Colby College. He has studied with a number of Dharma teachers from different traditions and also abroad in Nepal. This is his first published story.

Sean Hoade is author of the novel *Ain't That America*. A graduate of the University of Alabama's MFA program in fiction, as well as a longtime Buddhist and Vipassana meditator, he is currently at work on a novel about Buddhist monks acting as ambassadors during a holy war between Islam and Christianity.

Pico Iyer has been traveling in the Himalayas since 1974 and living in Japan since 1987. He is author of eight books exploring cultural convergence, including *The Lady and the Monk,* (about wandering around Buddhist Kyoto), *Abandon* (a novel about mysticism), and, most recently, *Sun After Dark* (a journey into impermanence and uncertainty, beginning with long chapters on Leonard Cohen and the XIVth Dalai Lama). Author of the text to *Buddha: The Living Way*, he writes often for both *Shambhala Sun* and *Tricycle*.

Keith Kachtick received an MFA from the Iowa Writers' Workshop and has taught literature and creative writing courses for almost twenty years. He has written for, among other publications, *Newsweek, Esquire, Texas Monthly,* and *The New York Times Magazine*. His first novel, *Hungry Ghost,* was a 2003 New York Times Notable Book of the Year. A long-time teacher of awareness-based practices, he is the founder and director of Dharma Yoga, a Buddhist yoga and meditation center in Austin, Texas.

Anne Carolyn Klein (Rigzin Drolma), a professor of religious studies at Rice University in Houston, Texas, has written four scholarly books on Buddhism, including *Meeting the Great Bliss Queen*. Since 1970 she has studied and practiced with leading lamas from several Tibetan traditions and was given rein to teach in 1995. She is a translator and the founding director of Dawn Mountain, a Tibetan temple, community center, and research institute in Houston.

Jake Lorfing lives in Austin, Texas. Recently retired from the directorship of the Austin Shambhala Meditation Center, and mostly retired from a career in psychiatric nursing, he is pleasantly adjusting to a new sense of space and time. For the past several years he has actively explored issues of the holocaust, through the Bearing Witness activities of Peacemaker Circle in Poland, and is working through writing, workshops, and videography to share this view.

Michele Martin has been practicing Buddhism for over thirty years, with seventeen based in Japan, Nepal, and India and twenty spent as a translator for oral and written Tibetan. Her most recent book is *Music in the Sky: The Life, Art, and Teachings of the 17th Karmapa Ogyen Trinley Dorje*, which was included in *The Best of Buddhist Writing 2004*. Forthcoming is a translation from Jamgon Kongtrul Lodro Thaye's *Treasury of Knowledge*. She lives in the Catskill Mountains of upstate New York.

Sean Murphy has been a Zen practitioner for nearly twenty years. He is author of three darkly comic novels that delve into the realms of the spiritual, the political, and the creative. *The Hope Valley Hubcap King* won the Hemingway Award for a First Novel, and was a Book Sense 76 recommended title. *The Finished Man* was nominated for the 2004 Pulitzer Prize. His latest, *The Time of New Weather*, imagines what might follow if the American government were acquired in a corporate buyout, and thereafter run as a profit-making entity. His nonfiction book *One Bird, One Stone* is a chronicle of Zen practice in America, as well as a collection of contemporary Zen teaching stories. He leads writing workshops based on meditation and mindfulness principles for a variety of regional and national organizations, including his own Big Sky Workshops.

Anh Chi Pham was born in Vietnam and grew up in California. She received an MFA from Antioch University in Los Angeles and is a former resident at the Ragdale Foundation. Her stories have been published in *Hunger Mountain, Nimrod International, Santa Monica Review,* and *The Baltimore Review.*

Geshe Michael Roach is a fully ordained Buddhist monk and is the first American to receive the title of *Geshe* (a degree from a Buddhist monastery roughly equivalent to a Doctor of Divinity). He is also a scholar of Sanskrit, Tibetan, and Russian. He founded the Asian Classics Institute and the Asian Classics Input Project and has been active in the restoration of the Sera Mey Tibetan Monastery, where he received his training. His books include *The Garden* and *The Tibetan Book of Yoga*. He lives in New York and Arizona.

Jess Row taught English at the Chinese University of Hong Kong from 1997 to 1999, the two years immediately following the handover of Hong Kong to China. His short story collection, *The Train to Lo Wu*, was published in 2005. His stories have appeared in *The Best American Short Stories 2001* and *2003* and *The Pushcart Prize XXVI*, and he has received a Whiting Writers' Award and a fellowship in fiction from the National Endowment for the Arts. He is on the faculty of Montclair State University, and since 2004 has been a Dharma teacher in the Kwan Um School of Zen. He lives in New York City.

Mark Salzman is author of *Iron & Silk*, an account of his two years in China; the memoirs *Lost in Place* and *True Notebooks*; and the novels *The Laughing Sutra*, *The Soloist*, and *Lying Awake*. He lives in Los Angeles with his wife, the filmmaker Jessica Yu, and their two children.

Samantha Schoech lives in San Francisco and spent many of her formative years at Karme Choling, a Tibetan meditation center in northern Vermont. She has written for the *Gettysburg Review, The Sun, Seventeen, Glimmer Train*, and other publications.

Dean Sluyter is practice leader of the Dzogchen Center's New Jersey sangha, chief meditation instructor of Aikido Schools of New Jersey, and a visiting Buddhist chaplain at Northern State Prison, Newark. He is on the faculty of the New York Open Center and of The Pingry School. His books include *The Zen Commandments* and *Cinema Nirvana: Enlightenment Lessons from the Movies*.

Mary Yukari Waters is half Japanese and half Irish-American. The recipient of an O. Henry award, a Pushcart Prize, and a grant from the National Endowment of the Arts, she has been published in *The Best American Short Stories 2002, 2003,* and *2004*. She earned her MFA from the University of California, Irvine, and lives in Los Angeles. Her first book, *The Laws of Evening*, was published in 2003.

Kate Wheeler grew up in South America and has traveled all over the world. Her stories have won both the Pushcart Prize and the O. Henry Award and have been anthologized in *The Best American Short Stories* and elsewhere. Her books include *Not Where I Started From* and *When Mountains Walked*, and she edited *Nixon Under the Bodhi Tree and Other Works of Buddhist Fiction*. Ordained a Buddhist nun in Burma, she now lives in Somerville, Massachusetts.

Dan Zigmond is a Zen priest, ordained by the late Kobun Chino Roshi, and currently lives in Germany. He received an MFA from the Bennington Writing Seminars and has published in *Shambhala Sun,* the *San Francisco Chronicle*, and *Tricycle*, where he is a contributing editor and frequent book reviewer.

First Appearances

About
Wisdom Publications

WISDOM PUBLICATIONS, a nonprofit publisher, is dedicated to making available authentic Buddhist works for the benefit of all. We publish our titles with the appreciation of Buddhism as a living philosophy and with the special commitment to preserve and transmit important works from all the major Buddhist traditions.

To learn more about Wisdom, or to browse books online, visit our website at wisdompubs.org. You may request a copy of our mail-order catalog online or by writing to the following address:

Wisdom Publications
199 Elm Street • Somerville, Massachusetts 02144 USA
Telephone: (617) 776-7416 • Fax: (617) 776-7841
Email: info@wisdompubs.org • www.wisdompubs.org

The Wisdom Trust

As a nonprofit publisher, Wisdom is dedicated to the publication of fine Dharma books for the benefit of all beings and dependent upon the kindness and generosity of sponsors in order to do so. If you would like to make a donation to Wisdom, please do so through our Somerville office. If you would like to sponsor the publication of a book, please write or email us at the address above.

Thank you.

Wisdom is a nonprofit, charitable 501(c)(3) organization affiliated with the Foundation for the Preservation of the Mahayana Tradition (FPMT).

Wisdom's Next Anthology of Short Fiction

If you'd like to be notified if Wisdom is soliciting contributions for our next anthology of Buddhist Fiction, go to the following web address and join our listserv: http://groups.google.com/group/WisdomBuddhistFiction